THE WAR STAGE

BOOK 2 IN THE WAR PLANNERS SERIES

ANDREW WATTS

Severn River
PUBLISHING

Severn River Publishing

This is a work of fiction. Names, characters, businesses, places, events and incidents are either the products of the author's imagination or used in a fictitious manner. Any resemblance to actual persons, living or dead, or actual events is purely coincidental.

ISBN: 978-1-951249-35-9 (Paperback)

ALSO BY ANDREW WATTS

The War Planners Series

The War Planners

The War Stage

Pawns of the Pacific

The Elephant Game

Overwhelming Force

Global Strike

Max Fend Series

Glidepath

The Oshkosh Connection

Books available for Kindle, print, and audiobook. To find out more about the books or Andrew Watts, visit

AndrewWattsAuthor.com.

Give me control of a nation's money, and I care not who makes its laws.

   —Mayer Amschel Bauer Rothschild

PROLOGUE

Osaka, Japan, 2011

"How much do you know about how money really works?"

She shrugged. "I'm sure very little, compared to you."

He nodded. "You are not alone. Most people don't know very much about what happens to their money after they place it in the bank. Or how it is valued. Many people today who live in first world countries—especially you Americans—have never even experienced the terror of rapid inflation."

She placed a recording device on the table and pressed the button with a red circle. She asked, "Do you mind if I begin?"

"Do we need to record this?" He squirmed in his chair.

The reporter looked at him. She sat in a small wooden chair across from him at the room's only table. Her legs were crossed and her skirt parted just above her knee. She was pretty. Long black hair. Big, beautiful eyes. The kind you saw on billboards, staring back at you when you crossed the street.

"It would help me to make sure I don't misquote you." A polite smile. Her voice melodic.

He shook his head. "And here I was, thinking that no one would ever find me. Perhaps I was being naïve."

"So what is it that you were just saying? You believe that most people are ignorant of how the global monetary system works? Is this a source of frustration for you?"

He looked out the window. The clean oceanside city of Osaka, with its majestic mountain views, had been his home for the past thirty years. He wondered if he would be able to remain here, now that his identity would be revealed.

He said, "No. I do not take issue with someone not understanding the complexity of money. Nor do I expect the common person to understand the complexity of physics. All people are bound by the rules of physics, yet most don't truly understand it. But the laws of physics were not created by man. There are, however, men that created monetary policy. There are today men who are in control of monetary policy."

"And you don't like that?"

He watched her. She didn't take notes. Just looked at him as she spoke. She didn't strike him as a reporter. Her expressions, her tone, the look in her eyes. There was something there that he would not have expected in a reporter, but he couldn't identify what it was.

He replied, "I take issue with the idea that some men have the right to create a system of rules that all others must abide by, whether they agree with them or not." He smiled. "You are an American. Surely you can agree with that concept? The idea that all people have inalienable rights—to life, liberty, and the pursuit of happiness."

She smiled. "I'm interested in what you think."

"I think that people should be free. I think that the proliferation of the Internet is much like the proliferation of the printing press. The spread of information is changing our world. I believe that the Internet has helped advance the rights of the common man. But their wallets are still bound by regulations that they do not understand. And these regulations are not always in their favor. Their wallets need freedom, too." He smiled back at her, wrinkles forming on his forehead.

"And bitcoin will provide them that?"

He slapped his knee and shot her a wide grin. "I can only dream."

"How would you describe it?"

"Describe what? Bitcoin?"

She nodded. "Yes."

He frowned and looked at the floor. "One of the benefits of my seclusion and anonymity has been that I have not had to explain it to people that were not fluent in the languages of money and cryptology." He let out a heavy sigh and then looked back at her. "Let me ask you for your help. How would you describe it, knowing what you do?"

She said, "I would call it the world's first widely adopted digital currency."

"Widely adopted? I think that you are being generous."

She shook her head. "They say that by 2014, over one million people will possess bitcoin currency. It's hard to get that many people to agree to anything. And now they are all agreeing to use a new form of money."

He cocked his head. "Your accent, where is it from? Where did you learn Japanese?"

The reporter said, "America."

"Of course. You speak Japanese very well. But were you born there? In America?"

She said, "No, I wasn't." She shifted in her chair and leaned forward to adjust the recording device on the table. "Now it's your turn to answer. What is bitcoin? Your words."

He looked back out at the city. On the busy streets below,

crowds of men and women in suits walked on crosswalks. "It's a means to an end."

"And what end is that?"

He motioned out the window, toward the skyscrapers of Osaka. "Three years ago, the world's financial system almost collapsed. All those people in suits were ready to jump out of windows. Then the men in control realized that they had become too greedy, and began to make changes. It got better for a few years, but the markets will collapse again. This cycle happens over and over. History is repeated by those that do not learn from it. And the young generations rarely remember their forefathers' lessons well. You can argue over the reasons why each financial crash occurs. But the world's financial system is still regulated by national governments and global entities supported by those governments. A very powerful few, with mixed motives."

The reporter asked, "What does that have to do with bitcoin?"

He said, "I was born in Japan. But I ask you, what if I don't agree with everything that my government says? I can tell you right now that I don't. What if the global economic and currency regulators make decisions that I disagree with? Once, there was nothing that one could do. But we have reached a turning point in technology. A turning point in the rise of peer-to-peer networking. Today, the individual has the freedom to use a currency that is unregulated by any government. Prior to this technology, that was not possible."

The reporter looked skeptical. "So you are saying that bitcoin will free people from the bonds of government?"

The man laughed. "No. But it is a start. Let me ask you one question. What is the global reserve currency?"

"The US dollar."

"Correct. The US dollar. Do you know what it means for a country to wield such a power? It means that the United States holds an economic advantage over every other nation in the world."

"Are you anti-American?"

"Not at all. I have been to America. A wonderful country. But the system is not fair. If one nation can control the global reserve currency, it can raise the largest, most powerful military. That same nation can create wealth beyond the wildest dreams of all other nations. The United States is a leader in technology, in industry, sports, and media. Its culture is dominant. People from all over the world envy America, whether they admit it or not."

She smiled. "Is that really all due to the dollar being the global reserve currency?"

"Oh, yes. Look at the history books. The Roman Empire, the British Empire...all empires rule in part by establishing a dominant currency. Americans don't have to worry about real inflation. Bread might cost a few percent more next year, but not twenty percent more. Not fifty percent more. Not so much that children can no longer eat three meals each day. Or that parents must sell their home or pick up another job."

"The United States has battled inflation before, hasn't it?" She looked uncertain.

He raised his chin. "Yes. But overall, its status has been significantly better than that of the rest of the world. Other countries bow down to the United States. Perhaps not publicly. Not in their words. But in their policy, and in their action, countries around the world behave as if they are subservient to America. For instance, could you imagine what the US president would say if South Korea or Germany or Spain or Brazil wanted to place a military base in California? They would laugh. And yet the United States has military bases in many countries around the world. The American Empire."

"But that's due to the history of wars, right? That is why the US has military bases in some countries around the world."

"In part. But also because those countries don't want to anger the most powerful nation on earth."

He could see her thinking. She narrowed her eyebrows and said, "So how will bitcoin change the status quo? Do you hope that the widespread adoption of bitcoin will crash America's economy?"

"Not at all. I love America. I hope that it continues to flourish. But I hope that the adoption of bitcoin, if it indeed continues, will eventually create a balance of power that can't exist today. As long as people must rely on governments to print money and influence the value of global currency, there will not be balance."

"I see."

He smiled. "It is complicated. But there is another important reason why something like bitcoin is so helpful to the common person. Our world is racing into a digital future. How often do you pay for things in cash today?"

"Not very often. I usually use a credit card or a debit card."

"In first world countries, that is becoming the normal way to buy things. Let me ask you another question. Every time you make an online transaction, where does that money go?"

She said, "You mean if I buy an article of clothing or something like that online?"

"Yes. Where does your money go when you click purchase?"

She made a face like the answer was obvious. "To the clothing store."

"Some of that money, yes. But some of that money will go to the credit card company. Some of that money will go to the bank that issued you the credit card. Some will go to the acquirers—the middlemen that pass batch information along so that merchants can complete transactions. And some of your money will go to the account providers—more middlemen. These middlemen manage the processing of the credit card. Your money will be sliced up and every one of these people will get a cut. That doesn't even include the payment gateway—the online portal that facilitates your website's shopping cart."

She looked surprised. "I didn't realize there were so many hands involved."

He nodded. "Instead of just paying one or two parties to facilitate your transaction, you are paying many. So everything costs you more. It leaves you with less money. A lot less, if you pay like this all the time. But bitcoin eliminates much of this. The software makes it possible to send cash payments without all the middlemen."

"But if merchants want to use it, won't they need a third party to facilitate the transaction?"

"Yes. But at a fraction of the cost. So the consumer and the merchant can both keep more of their money. And you know what the best part is?"

"What?"

"It's anonymous. Bitcoin transactions do not require any personal information. And what does that mean?"

She nodded. "No taxes. This was going to be my next question. How would a government tax or regulate it?"

He shook his head. "They will have a very hard time doing so. The system is designed so that all transactions are anonymous. No taxes. It truly levels the playing field. There are countless other great potential uses for bitcoin, such as microlending, but I could go on talking about it all day. I will let you ask your questions."

The reporter opened up her notebook and read. She said, "In 2008, someone wrote a paper describing how bitcoin worked. They published under the name Satoshi Nakamoto. No one knows whether Nakamoto was really one person or many. He began to collaborate remotely with software developers for the next two years."

He said nothing.

She continued reading, "Recently, he has indicated that he

intends to hand over control of the source code and other important information to several prominent members of a now-loyal bitcoin community."

The man smiled and placed the tips of his fingers together.

She read on. "Satoshi Nakamoto created the world's first widely used digital currency. Over the past few years, dozens of potential Satoshi Nakamotos have been 'outed' by the press. One was a legal scholar and cryptographer from the United States. Another was a Japanese-American physicist and systems engineer. One news source claimed that Satoshi was actually a group of prodigious computer programmers from several different nations."

The man smiled.

She said, "Could you please state the name that you use on the bitcoin message boards, for the record?"

The man crossed his legs and sat back in his chair. "Satoshi Nakamoto."

"Is that your real name?"

"No. But that is the name that the world has come to know me by."

The woman pressed the red button. "Thank you, Satoshi. Let's take a quick break." She reached inside her purse and pulled out a mobile phone.

"Of course," he said. "Do you mind if I ask where you were born, if not in the United States?"

"China."

"Oh, where?"

She said, "The south. Guangdong Province. But I haven't been there in many years." She was typing something into her phone. Then she placed it back into her purse.

Her demeanor had changed. The bright, friendly look of a reporter was gone. He had been at ease with her tone and her charming smile. She leaned a bit farther forward in her seat. Now she seemed to be dissecting him with her eyes.

"A few more questions. Off the record."

He eyed her. "Go ahead."

"Tell me, what would happen if a single nation were able to control the supply of bitcoins?"

He frowned. "That is impossible. First of all, that would negate any incentive to use bitcoins. If a country could control it, why would anyone use it?"

"What if the people didn't know?"

"No. That is not how bitcoin works." He sighed. Hadn't she been listening?

"Why not?"

"There are already many systems for digital transactions. PayPal. Countless others. Bitcoin is not just about convenience. It is a means for the common person—for every person—to cast off the bonds of the banks and the regulators. Think of it like this. A Greek baker could accept payment in bitcoins. Or he could simply place all of his holdings in bitcoins. If his national economy was destroyed by inflation, he would not feel the pain."

"Sure, alright. But hypothetically, let's pretend that the value of bitcoin is controlled by a single regulator, yet the users are not aware. Would that be possible? Would one entity be able to regulate supply?"

"No. Every member of the bitcoin community can see all transactional data."

"And that can't be reprogrammed? Hacked? Surely a man of your talent could make it look like there was a certain supply and artificially change the value. Or perhaps someone could skim tiny bits of each person's holdings and eliminate any trace of that occurring?"

He shook his head furiously. "*No.* That is not possible. I have the code written in a way that—"

"But what if we changed the code?"

He was exasperated. Some people just didn't understand, or weren't capable. He said, "I'm sorry, I am so forgetful. Could you please tell me your name again?"

"My name is Lena Chou."

"Lena, I can assure you that the way this code is written, those things could not occur. And soon I will be sending out the source code to trusted programmers around the globe. Just as you said, I am ready to be finished with this stage. Bitcoin is ready to be released to the world. There will be many eyes on the gears of this machine. It will not be possible to tamper with, I promise you."

She had a funny look. Like she was weighing what to say. "Satoshi, you believe in balance. You believe in equality. But do you really think that people are capable of creating that balance and equality themselves?"

He was taken aback. "What are you really asking? You are asking me if I believe in the goodness of mankind?"

"More or less."

"Then my answer is yes, I do. I believe that those who have the power grow corrupt from it. So my life's work, my gift to the world, is to give them a monetary system that gives power to the people, and removes it from the powerful few."

That look in her eyes again. Cold. Calculating. She said, "I disagree. I believe that the world has been shaped by a few great people. It is these people who can truly create change for the better. Behind those great leaders, that balance and equality that you talk about can persevere. But left to their own free will, the masses make disastrous choices. This is what history has taught us."

This was such an odd interview. Not at all what he expected. She still had the recording device off. He frowned, "Lena, how long have you worked for your news magazine?"

A knock at the door.

"I'm afraid I don't work for a news magazine."

He blinked. "Excuse me?"

Another knock at the door. Harder this time. He glanced over towards the entrance and began to get up. Lena placed her hand on his shoulder and pressed him back into his seat. Their eyes were locked.

She said, "Please remain seated." She walked to the door and opened it. Two rough-looking men came in. They watched Satoshi as they walked to the center of the room. Their hands hung loose by their sides, like attack dogs waiting for an order from their master.

Lena sat back down across from him and said, "Now, where were we? You were telling me about the innate goodness of mankind?"

He began to feel the nervous shiver of a man trapped. "Who are they?"

She didn't look at them. "My colleagues. And just so you know, I would not characterize them as two fine examples of mankind's good nature. They can be violent. But only if I require it."

Satoshi's hands began shaking under the table. "Who are you?"

"My name is Lena, just as I have told you."

"And why have you come to see me? Why have you really come, if you are not a reporter?"

"Because the man I work for is forging a great future for our world, and he hopes that your work will be a part of it."

"You want to use bitcoin?"

She nodded.

He began to think about her questions. "You want to control bitcoin?"

She said, "It will be the world's first truly global currency. Think of the power one would wield if they could manipulate its value. You created bitcoin transactions to be anonymous. That works out perfectly for us. It helps us to retain anonymous control. A world that thinks it is free is a happy world. Ignorance is strength."

His eyes showed anger and fear. "You can't do that. I won't allow it. Besides, that's not possible, I've designed—"

She shook her head, clicking her tongue. "You will make it possible. And we will give you great support and incentive."

He crossed his arms. "What? You'll physically hurt me if I don't help?"

She leaned forward. "Oh, yes."

The way she said it sent another shiver through him. The two men standing behind her didn't blink.

Lena said, "You will come with us now, and disappear from the life you know. If you do this, we will not hurt you. You will also provide us your very best effort to assist us in completing our goals."

"What if I do not—"

She didn't wait for him to finish his sentence. "If you do not comply, we will still not hurt you."

He was confused.

Lena said, "We will hurt the ones that you care most about. Great change requires great sacrifice."

His mouth was open. His shaking hands were clenched into fists under the table, but he had no will to raise them. "Look at you. How could a woman like you say such things? How can you be so...evil?"

Lena stood and looked down on him. "Mr. Satoshi, there is much evil in this world, but I am not it. I am but an instrument, a tool. I have a duty to create change. Some of it may be ugly, violent, and despicable to you. But mine is an honorable duty with a noble cause. You can now be a part of this great cause. One day I hope that you will see this as a gift."

She held out her hand to help him up. Her face transformed into a brilliant smile. "Come help us create a better world."

He didn't take her hand.

She stayed there for a moment, holding out her hand and waiting for him. Seeing that he made no move to get up, she raised her hand into the air and snapped her fingers.

The two men stepped forward. Satoshi noticed that one of them held a syringe.

1

The Persian Gulf
15 Nautical Miles South of Abu Musa Island
Present Day

Hamid rubbed his eyes with the back of a greasy glove. He then looked at the analog clock positioned next to his boat's magnetic compass. Almost time. He peered out into the sea. He could hear nothing but the drone of the loud diesel motors.

This was madness, he thought to himself.

The sailors under his command didn't know any better. They would follow orders, just as the Iranian Revolutionary Guard Corps Navy (IRGCN) had trained them to do. But as the boat rocked in the blackness of the sea, Hamid knew just how unusually dangerous their task was.

He called out, "Cut the engines."

One of his sailors pulled back a lever and the noise of the engines dropped to nothing. Then he looked at Hamid with curious, expectant eyes. The dim yellow light hanging from the pilothouse ceiling illuminated his face. They stood quiet, looking at each other for a moment. Nothing but the sound of the small waves of the Persian Gulf tumbling into the hull.

Hamid said, "You have a question for me?"

The second sailor climbed up the ladder to the pilothouse. He too looked curious. The first sailor said, "No, Chief."

"Good. As I told both of you before we left Abu Musa, it's best not to ask questions about what we are doing tonight. Whatever you see out here, you are never to speak of it. Never. To anyone. Just remember to do as you're told tonight, and don't ask any questions."

The sailors nodded. They were good men. Not men. Boys. The older of the two couldn't have been more than twenty years old. Hamid had picked them because they were hardworking and trustworthy. And also because they had no families on the island. He hated himself for it, but that had been a consideration.

"The stores are laid out on the main deck as you asked, Chief."

"Thank you."

"It's enough supplies to feed a company of soldiers for a month. I'm not sure who would need that out here..." The sailor seemed to realize that he was asking a question and stopped. He said, "Is there anything else we need to do before the rendezvous? I checked the charts, and this is the right location."

Hamid had triple-checked the time and location himself. He didn't want to upset any of the men that worked in the Grey Buildings on Abu Musa. Life could get very bad for Hamid and his men if those men became unhappy. They had a schedule, and Hamid was but a component in the machine that produced according to that schedule. If things were not delivered on time, those men got angry. If anyone spoke of the work they did, they got angry. And when they got angry, Lt. Col. Pakvar got involved. No one wanted that.

Hamid had seen firsthand what happened when the rules of

secrecy were broken. They had forced Hamid to watch the punishment of someone who had threatened their secrecy. Pakvar had looked him in the eye and told him that the same would happen to him if anyone ever found out what he knew. That was almost three years ago now.

Pakvar was Quds Force—the elite Special Forces branch of the Army of the Guardians of the Islamic Revolution. English-speaking countries referred to it as the Iranian Revolutionary Guard Corps (IRGC). Men in Hamid's unit whispered that Pakvar had spent much of his time in Iraq, leading guerilla units in training, and planning attacks against US troops. He had arrived on Abu Musa four years ago, with the foreigners.

That was when the construction started. The Grey Buildings went up in a matter of months. Shipments of electronics and personnel arrived in a flurry. Sometimes by plane. Sometimes by ferry. On rare occasions, the shipments would be transported like they would tonight. Hamid knew that these shipments were one of the biggest secrets Pakvar's men held.

The Grey Buildings were three stories tall and had very few windows. A grey stone exterior. No other markings. This was strange for the Iranian military. Normally there would be propaganda plastered up on just about every bare surface.

None of the men Hamid worked with knew what went on inside these buildings. The men who worked inside the Grey Buildings almost never left. They always arrived on their transports at night, wearing masks, and departed in the same fashion. Food preparation, resupply, and trash collection to the structures had strict procedures that the IRGC support staff had to follow. It allowed the buildings to remain completely closed off to the rest of the island.

There were many rumors about what went on there, of course. Some said it was a secret Iranian military base to spy on foreign ships in the Persian Gulf; others claimed that it was a nuclear weapons facility or a chemical weapons research lab. Half of the island was an Iranian military base, so it made sense for the Iranian government to locate a secret installation there.

Abu Musa was located at the western end of the Strait of Hormuz, in the hot waters between Iran and Dubai. Every day, oil tankers and warships passed the island on their way in or out of the Gulf. Over the past few decades, Iran and the United Arab Emirates had had several disputes over who actually owned the land. Then Iran had stationed military personnel there, and the disputes didn't much matter. The Iranian Air Force had begun placing jets there in the mid-2000s.

Hamid had joined the IRGCN over fifteen years ago and had risen to the rank of chief petty officer. He had always liked the ocean, growing up near Jask, another Iranian oceanside city. When the chance to work on patrol craft had come up, he had jumped at the opportunity. Years of hard labor, baking in the hot sun while on these patrol boats, had taken its toll on him. But he still loved being at sea, regardless of the mission that they trained him for.

He looked at the large-caliber machine gun that sat on a five-foot stand on the aft deck. These sailors that Hamid commanded had probably chanted "death to America" with their teenage companions during boot camp. They probably looked at that weapon and were eager for the chance to use it in combat. Hamid wasn't sure when his personal beliefs had begun to stray from the politics of his organization, but they had.

Perhaps it had been the first time he had looked up at a US Navy aircraft carrier steaming past his patrol craft at twice his speed. The sheer size and formidability of those floating city-sized ships made Iran's patrol craft seem like some silly joke.

But Hamid didn't think that was why he had lost faith in his country's regime. The futility of preparing for war against a great foe had not changed his beliefs. More likely, his internal beliefs had changed when his wife had given birth to their first child. Hamid had spent his days on the steamy waters of the Gulf, and his nights placing his finger into the tiny, perfect hand of his new son.

The man that Pakvar had murdered in front of him that night had a son, too.

Hamid still heard that poor boy's screams in his sleep. It had been late at night, three years ago. Hamid was tying up his patrol craft to the dock. Pakvar was standing at the end of the pier and called him over. They drove to the Grey Building and Hamid finally found out what lay inside.

Pakvar brought Hamid down a series of concrete stairs, deeper and deeper underground. Hamid couldn't believe how far down the structure continued. They passed rooms filled with computers. Thousands of computers. Small square boxes, fans humming. No monitors. They were lined up on shelves, stacked three rows high. Every room had wires and piping connected to the network. There were very few people who actually worked here, Hamid realized. Whatever this place was, it did not appear to be what any of the gossipers on the island had thought.

When they arrived in the dungeon-like room Pakvar had been taking him to, Hamid covered his mouth in horror.

There was an Asian man and his family, each naked and bleeding, sprawled out next to each other on the cold concrete floor. The Asian man was older. He looked to be in his fifties. The woman that Hamid assumed was the man's wife lay next to her boy. None of them moved. A few of Pakvar's goons stood over them, machine guns in hand. The Asian man looked up at them all, terror in his bloodshot eyes.

Pakvar clutched Hamid's arm and said, "Today you begin

working for us. You will provide us with logistics transportation using your patrol craft. All of our activities need to remain confidential. Is that understood?"

Hamid nodded. He looked at the family on the floor.

Pakvar leaned forward and whispered into Hamid's ear. "No one can know of our secrets." He turned to one of the uniformed men in the room and nodded, his thick and dark eyebrows furrowed as he shouted a command. Then the family was dumped alive into some type of oven. Pakvar walked to the wall and flipped the switch. He stared at Hamid as he did it.

The screams were like nothing Hamid had ever heard. He looked away, the taste of bile on his tongue, his knees weak. The heat from the oven made him sweat.

When the flames overcame them and the screams subsided, Pakvar walked up to Hamid. His words were like ice. "This man tried to tell others of what we were doing here. You cannot. You can take your boat and flee across the sea at any time. But I am told that you have a family residing on this island. I promise you this: if you ever speak of what you see us do...or if you ever flee... your family will suffer this fate that you witnessed here tonight."

Hamid's eyes watered, both from the furnace and the horror. He nodded agreement.

As they walked back up the steps, he found himself wondering just where the smoke exited the building. Would others on the island notice the smokestacks? Not this late at night. Were there bits of human ash floating up into the air and then falling into the sea? Would his ash someday be scattered into the sea the very same way? A dull, helpless feeling overcame him.

After that night, every day had been a prison sentence. Hamid became the ship driver for those who worked in the Grey Buildings on Abu Musa. His normal chain of command knew that he was getting his orders from Lt. Col. Pakvar—and they knew not to ask any questions. On a typical day, Hamid would patrol the coastal waters of Abu Musa and then return home to his family at night.

But about twice a month, a message would arrive that he was to report to the Grey Buildings at a certain hour. There, Pakvar would give him a rendezvous location and a time. Out into the Gulf he would travel. Sometimes he was to bring supplies to the rendezvous point. Sometimes he was to pick something up. Always at night, and always in secret.

Usually, these transfers had been conducted with other small vessels. Smuggler speedboats from Dubai or somewhere else on the other side of the Gulf. An occasional passing tanker. Fishing vessels. Once it was a tug.

Sometimes he was tasked with personnel transfers. Those were interesting. Hamid was pretty sure that none of the men and women he transported were Iranian. They always wore masks, and they never spoke to him. Hamid had always gone alone and had kept quiet about what he saw.

Tonight was different, however. Tonight he was not alone. Something about tonight was extra important. Pakvar had made that clear. Hamid was sorry that he had to drag these young men out to help him, but Pakvar had made it mandatory. There was some heavy equipment tonight.

"Hamid!" Youthful excitement in the voice.

Hamid looked down at the main deck and saw his sailors looking out into the dark water. An enormous submarine mast rose up out of the water, twenty-five meters ahead of them. It came almost straight up, froth and swirls of black water reflecting the night sky above as it rolled off the submarine's hull. It was bigger than any of the Iranian Kilo-class submarines that Hamid had seen at Bandar Abbas.

"Is that what we are here for?"

"Eyes out front. Mouths shut. Do as I say."

"Yes, Chief," the men said in unison.

A hatch opened and red light spilled out of it. Then a stream of men climbed out, holding on to grips on the mast and heading down to the platform area on the front of the hull. They all wore dark masks with small eye and mouth holes. Hamid could hear a few of them speak to each other. Chinese, he was pretty sure. The same language that the foreigners in the Grey Building spoke.

A voice called across from the submarine in thickly accented Persian. "We are ready to receive."

Hamid called back, "Stand by to take lines."

He took his patrol craft out of idle and inched it forward at one knot of speed. He called to his men, "Throw over the fenders."

The two sailors threw over the long white rubber cylinders. They splashed in the water and floated, cushioning them as the submarine impacted the patrol craft.

Hamid yelled, "Cast lines."

Masked men on the hull of the submarine held out their hands, waiting.

Hamid's two sailors threw bow and stern lines towards the men on the submarine. The men on the submarine wrapped them around some type of cleat and headed over to the patrol craft. The two vessels were joined. For a moment, the groups stood, staring at each other.

A red spotlight shone down from the mast, illuminating Hamid's patrol craft. He could make out two men standing behind the light. One of them fixed a bulky machine gun to a turret on the mast. The other man, adjusting the red light, shouted orders to his subordinates below. Two of the men on the hull set up a small gangway that allowed the men to walk from the submarine hull to the forward deck of the patrol craft. The submarine sailors quickly moved onto Hamid's ship and began picking up the supplies.

Hamid pointed to several dozen cases sitting on the aft deck of his vessel. "It's all here."

The men didn't say anything; they just began lining up to transfer them back to the submarine. Before long, they had formed a chain of twenty men. They passed the cases of supplies to one another, hand over hand, moving each box onto, and then into, the submarine. They moved fast.

Hamid looked up at the men behind the red searchlight. They reminded him of prison security men in a guard tower, watching over the yard while the prisoners worked.

Every day since that night is like a prison sentence.

About halfway through the transfer, several of the masked men carried one particular wooden crate that Hamid recognized as important. This was the heavy equipment that Pakvar had emphasized must get aboard the submarine. He had been told that this crate was more critical than any other piece of cargo on board.

DM-B3 Mono Pulse RADAR was stenciled on the outside of the crate.

Hamid didn't think that the Chinese needed radars like this on their submarines. This radar was used in an Iranian cruise missile. Why they wanted that monstrous piece of equipment underwater, he had no idea. He walked back into his ship's pilothouse.

The unloading process took about twenty minutes in total. Hamid made sure that his sailors helped where they could and stayed out of the way when needed. They each worked up quite a sweat in the humid Gulf air.

Hamid heard a crackle on his ship-to-ship radio and climbed the ladder back up to the pilothouse. He listened for a moment but didn't hear anything. He scanned a few of the Iranian military frequencies and heard nothing. He then set the radio back on the bridge-to-bridge radio frequency. Nothing. Then he realized that the volume was almost all the way down. One of his young sailors must have turned it down without Hamid noticing. They should know better than that. He moved the dial up and immediately heard a voice speaking in English.

"Vessel in the vicinity of ..." The voice gave a latitude and longitude and then there was nothing but a static hiss. He knew enough English to understand what they were saying, but the transmission cut out before he could make out the latitude and longitude they provided.

He looked at his marine radar. It was an old machine, and one that was notoriously unreliable. He studied the green radar sweeps. Each pass of the radar line highlighted a smudge of green just to the south of their position. *That* was a surface contact—a ship.

"This is US Navy Warship..." More static.

The radar contact was one nautical mile away. Could that be who was calling on the radio? If so, they had seemingly appeared out of nowhere. Or was it possible that he was hearing a transmission from far away? Could the contact on his scope just be a bit of trash in the water, thrown overboard by a passing tanker?

The transfer was almost complete when the men behind the red spotlight began yelling in what Hamid assumed to be Chinese. The chain of men scattered like ants. The man holding the machine gun was waving his arms and then yelled something down into the submarine.

One of Hamid's young sailors called to him. He looked scared. "Chief, what's going on?"

Hamid said, "Make preparations to get underway." His heart beat more rapidly.

The man on the sail of the submarine screamed and pointed into the night. Hamid peered in the direction he was pointing, but all he saw was darkness. The Chinese submariners each bounded up the ladder of the sail, trying to get the last of the supplies into their vessel.

Then a bright white light became visible on the southern horizon. When the light changed intensity and illuminated the water between it and the two vessels, Hamid realized what it was. The white light was a high-powered searchlight, mounted to whatever that radar contact had been. It soon illuminated the submarine and Hamid's patrol craft.

Hamid's hands went to guard his eyes.

Up on the mast of the sub, the masked men pulled back on the machine gun's horizontal cocking handle. The chugging sound of a fully automatic weapon erupted through the air. Hamid could see the recoil of the weapon and heard the metallic clang of shells as they hit the hull of the submarine.

The sub shook suddenly, vibrations transferring over to their small patrol craft. This wasn't the machine gun. This was something much more powerful. White foam rose in the water all around them. He realized that the submarine's screws were turning. She was moving. Hamid yelled to his sailors, "Get clear! I'll start up our engines."

The foreign men had dropped the last of the boxes and were hurtling their bodies back belowdecks into the sub. The two men on the top of the mast packed up their gear, dropped out of sight, and shut the hatch behind them.

The submarine's lights were extinguished. Hamid and his two young sailors were left in the dark, their ears ringing from the small-arms fire. The Iranian patrol craft floated slowly away from the sub.

"Hamid, what do you want us to do?" one of his sailors asked. The boy had just taken in the lines and was standing near the bow. He was shaken.

Behind him, out of the distant darkness, a brilliant segment of yellow light arced towards them. It looked beautiful at first. Like a shooting star hovering silently over the black abyss of the Persian

Gulf. Then Hamid realized what it was. The shooting star would soon transform into a violent tongue of flame.

The silent light show became a torrent of white-hot metal ripping through the patrol craft. When it came into contact with their vessel, hell awoke. The sailor that had just called to Hamid disappeared in a burst of wet reddish spray. Hamid and the other sailor dove behind the small superstructure of the boat. Destruction erupted around them as rounds hit the hull.

Pressing his body down and facing aft, Hamid could see the heavy machine-gun fire that missed his ship. The yellow tracers skipped on the surface of the water like stones on a river. They then bounced up into the night sky and disappeared as the tracer rounds ran out of energy.

The submarine drove away from them. Hamid watched its mast sink below the surface of the water.

In one of the few coherent thoughts he was capable of, he wondered just who was firing at them. Then he heard the earsplitting sound of his patrol craft's own machine gun. It was so loud that his chest thumped and his molars rattled with every round that it fired.

He peeked from behind his hiding spot and saw his lone remaining sailor standing behind their patrol craft's forward-mounted weapon, gripping it with both of his hands and squeezing the two-handed trigger. Hamid was paralyzed with fear. He couldn't think. He just wanted to be home, with his wife and child.

He clenched his jaw so tight that it hurt. When he thought that their attackers had ceased fire, another group of tracer rounds scattered around them, and then the patrol craft once again burst into chaos as bullets tore through it. Something exploded near the engines and a ten-foot flame rose from the aft end of his boat.

The return fire stopped. Hamid looked around the pilothouse and saw that his second sailor had been killed as well. He smelled something awful and realized that he had soiled himself. Hamid wasn't sure when that had happened.

His ears still rang, but he could just make out the sound of large diesel engines getting closer.

The tracers had stopped. The pungent smell of gunpowder and diesel fuel filled his nostrils. He looked around in the direction the engine noise was coming from. It was a warship, or a large patrol craft. He couldn't make out what nationality. They would be here shortly.

Hamid realized what that meant. He thought of Pakvar and of what he would do if he were captured. Hamid realized that he couldn't allow that to happen. His family's safety was at stake. For a moment, he thought of trying to take his own life.

In the reflection of the moonlight, he could now make out the mast and superstructure of a US Navy destroyer racing toward him.

He needed to get away. Perhaps if he could just escape before they arrived to search his boat, they wouldn't find him. Hamid walked up to the bow of his ship and looked it over. It was torn up and burning. He reached down and grabbed an orange life vest and strapped it on. He could feel his boat listing badly, and he imagined that it must have been taking on water. He wasn't sure how long it would stay afloat.

He climbed up the ladder to the pilothouse and clutched a radio in his hands. He turned the knob all the way to the right and began to let out a distress call. But the sound on the radio was unlike anything he had heard before.

It was a definite radio transmission, but it was electronic junk. He changed the frequency, but it was the same on every other channel.

At first he thought that his radio was broken. One of the American bullets must have hit the antennae. Or perhaps someone was jamming it? Why would the Americans do this? It didn't matter. He would not be able to send a distress signal.

His only hope was to be rescued by one of his fellow IRGCN sailors. There was no telling what Pakvar would do to his family if he were taken by the Americans.

Hamid removed the small life raft from under the starboard storage area and pulled the inflation cord. The yellow single-person raft immediately filled up with pressurized air. He walked over to the rim of his boat and placed it in the water, ready to hop in.

He took one more look over at the remains of his two sailors. The aft end of the patrol boat was taking on a lot of water now. He took his first step into the lifeboat.

Then the world went white and silent.

* * *

He came to moments later, unsure how long he had been uncon-scious. He floated in the sea, dozens of meters away from where he last remembered being.

Through bloody, blurry eyes, he saw the remains of his patrol craft. It had been obliterated. Small flames covered what was left. He turned away, trying to swim, then realized that he was missing an arm.

Horror struck him upon the discovery, but he was pleased to find that he felt no pain. Just a coldness that was sweeping through his body. He looked away from the fiery wreckage.

He could just make out a strange object in the distance, protruding out of the water. It was barely illuminated by the flames of his own vessel. The object looked like a pole sticking up from the sea.

Hamid tried to think. He was getting colder and more tired.

But he knew that shape. What was it? It was far away, and through the blur and disorientation, he could barely process the thought.

A periscope. It was a periscope.

He thought of what Pakvar had whispered to him that night. The night that had started this prison sentence. He'd whispered it just before throwing the switch and burning that poor man and his family in the oven. Hamid realized that the Chinese submarine must have fired upon his vessel. They, too, had followed Pakvar's code.

No one can know of our secrets.

2

Al Dhafra Air Base, UAE
Three Weeks Later

Chase Manning watched as a dark green military pickup truck raced towards them, leaving a cloud of desert sand in its wake.

The man he was with nodded towards it and said, "I think somebody's looking for one of us."

Chase examined the vehicle through his protective sunglasses. "Fun's over, I guess. Back to work."

He double-checked that his MP-5 was in SAFE, and then placed it on the wooden bench before rolling up his target and collecting his shells. He thumbed through the sand to make sure he got them all.

"Christ, Chase, you ever miss?"

His companion, also a member of the CIA's Special Operations Group, looked at Chase's target. A group of holes was scattered in the very center of the inner black circle.

He smiled at his friend. "Not unless I mean to."

"Guess I owe you another beer."

"How many do you owe me now?"

"Too many. Who taught you to shoot?"

"The Navy."

"Ah. Don't say things like that. It makes it so much worse."

Chase chuckled. Almost all the SOG guys were former military. Most were former Army. Military branch rivalry jokes were commonplace.

The green Ford F-350 came to a halt just behind where they were standing. They were the only ones using this gun range. A uniformed US Air Force technical sergeant got out.

"Chase Manning?"

"Yeah?"

"Sir, they need you over at Center. I can drive you, sir." He motioned to his vehicle.

Chase nodded. "Thanks. I'll be right with you." He finished cleaning up and said goodbye to his friend.

Chase got into the passenger seat and asked the sergeant, "Any idea what it's about?"

The sergeant, sitting in the passenger seat next to an airman, said, "Sir, a man by the name of Elliot is on his way to meet with you. That's all I know."

"Got it. Thanks, Sergeant." The only Elliot that Chase knew of was the CIA's station chief in Dubai. He had never called on Chase personally, and it would be very unusual for him to do so. He usually had minions do that work.

They began speeding over the desert road toward the other side of the base. Chase saw the enlisted man glance at the end of his gun.

"Is that a silencer?"

Chase said, "Yup."

"Why do you use a silencer at the range?"

"Practice how you play. That's what I've always believed."

"Sir, you mind if I ask you what outfit you're attached to?"

"Sure, Sergeant. You can ask. I just can't answer."

The man rolled his eyes as if to express that he should have known better and remained quiet the rest of the way.

Seven minutes later, Chase entered the Joint Tactical Control Center, the US-only building where several hundred American servicemen worked each day, managing the American military's tactical picture in this part of the world.

Chase entered through two layers of security before he got to the CIA's section of the building. The CIA security man looked up when he entered. Chase recognized him.

The security man said, "ID?"

Chase removed the microchipped government-issued ID that hung around his neck. The duty officer slid it into a card reader and then handed it back to Chase.

The door behind him buzzed, and Chase entered a large dark room with flat-screens on the wall and dim blue lighting. About a dozen people were inside, most hovering over tactical displays or talking on headsets. The displays on the walls showed various images. Live feed from drones throughout the area of operation. Digital maps. Green lines for national borders. Red and blue shapes representing military units.

It was freezing cold in the room. The temperature was kept very low in order to ensure optimal performance for all the high-tech computers and electronics. Most of the people working there had on winter jackets. To Chase, just coming inside out of the desert heat, it felt great.

The duty officer was a redheaded woman of about thirty. Chase thought her name was Doris, but wasn't sure enough to call her by name. He remembered her from when he had first arrived on this base, almost a year earlier. Just after his mother's funeral. That seemed like a long time ago.

Upon completion of his CIA training near Williamsburg, Virginia, Chase had been transported to Al Dhafra Air Base in the United Arab Emirates. After some initial orientation training on base, he had been moved about the Middle East on various assignments. He had served on missions targeting ISIS leadership and supply lines in Syria and Iraq for a few months. Then they had flown him to East Africa, where he had participated in operations disrupting the terrorist groups Al-Shabab in Somalia and Boko Haram in Nigeria.

Some of the time, Chase felt like there was little difference between the type of work he had done with the SEALs and the type of work he now conducted on behalf of the CIA. At other times, the differences were starkly apparent. His chief complaint was that he felt like he was in a corporation and not a tactical unit. There was more politics. More political correctness. And there was a definite rank-based class system in the Agency. This frustrated Chase, but he didn't feel like there was anything he could do about it.

Chase stood before the woman whose name he thought was Doris, and she gave him a once-over. She had the slightest hint of a smile. Rosy cheeks in the cold air.

She stood behind a desk with several landline phones, each with different labels. "Elliot's on his way to see you. I'm to have you call him as soon as you are available. Apparently he wants you in Dubai tonight. Not sure what it's about."

"Yeah, I got that from the Air Force tech sergeant. Anything more?"

She shrugged. "Just that it was urgent."

She picked up a white phone labeled US Embassy Dubai, Station Chief. "Yes, sir, Manning is right here. Roger, sir. Here you go." She handed Chase the phone.

"Manning."

"Chase, this is Elliot."

No last name required. Elliot was a man of great importance in Chase's world. As the station chief in Dubai, he was in charge of over fifty agents scattered throughout the operating area, and he was the senior ranking CIA agent in one of the most active regions of the world. He also happened to be a friend of Chase's father, which hadn't hurt Chase's station assignment.

"Yes, sir, how can I be of service?"

"I'll be quick. Your expertise is required. I need you in Dubai tonight. I'm getting on a plane. Pack your things. Be ready for me to pick you up in one hour."

* * *

The U-28A was the military version of the single-engine turbo-prop PC-12. The Air Force loved its versatility and used it as a Special Operations transport for small numbers of passengers. It had the horsepower to get them there fast and could take off and land on very small runways. If there was a remote part of the world that was hard to get in and out of but at least somewhat flat, Air Force Special Operations could likely get you there quickly in a U-28A.

This one was painted dark grey, and Chase watched as it rolled up to the passenger terminal, its reverse thrust buzzing wildly before it shut down. The door opened and Elliot Jackson stepped down the ladder.

He was a tall black man with close-cropped grey hair. He wore rimmed glasses that tinted automatically in the sunlight. He walked up to Chase and shook his hand. He had a firm fireman's grip. The kind of handshake that told Chase that Elliot Jackson was a man's man.

"It's good to see you again, son."

"Thank you, sir." Chase had his black travel duffle bag slung over his shoulder.

Elliot said, "Go ahead and throw that on the plane. Then let's go find someplace quiet to talk for a bit." Chase wondered what subject of conversation would require the station chief to fly twenty minutes at around two thousand dollars per flight hour. He could have had Chase drive the ninety minutes and meet him somewhere in Dubai. Either it was good to be king, or the conversation was going to get interesting.

A moment later, they walked into a building marked *Base Operations*. It was a passenger terminal for Americans going in and out of the UAE via military transport. Several dozen US Army soldiers were sprawled about the waiting area, sleeping next to their bags while wearing their boots and cammie uniforms.

Chase and Elliot found a quiet air-conditioned room down the hall. A briefing room that the pilots used to prepare for their flights. There was a whiteboard and a stack of charts sitting on a plastic table. An old TV hung from the ceiling. A digital aviation weather forecast scrolled across the screen.

Elliot motioned for Chase to take a seat. "Your father is in town tomorrow."

Chase said, "Is he? I didn't know."

"You heard about his job change, right?"

"Yes, I did. It's...unfortunate."

"Yes, it is."

Elliot was tapping his fingernails on the table. "Iranian-US relations are at an all-time low right now after the Abu Musa incident."

"They weren't so great before that."

"True. I'm just saying that your dad didn't do anything wrong, Chase. He just happened to be in command of someone who did. Happens to the best of us."

Admiral Manning was the one-star in charge of the *Harry S. Truman* Carrier Strike Group, the lone US aircraft carrier strike group in the region. As such, he was responsible for all the actions of the ships under his command. Including the US Navy destroyer, the USS *Porter*.

Iran had accused the US Navy of sinking one of its patrol craft off the island of Abu Musa three weeks ago. One of the lookouts on the *Porter* claimed he saw a submarine next to the Iranian patrol craft. The crew of the US destroyer also stated that the Iranian submarine had started firing first, a claim that made the entire US story seem far-fetched. US intelligence had confirmed that all of Iran's subs were in port. Due to the hazy and humid weather conditions, the US Navy video from the *Porter* was inconclusive.

There was still confusion surrounding what had really happened, but the bottom line was that both the US ship and the Iranian ship had fired rounds at each other. The Iranian ship had exploded, killing all three of its crewmembers. There were no American injuries. The Iranians were furious, and the American politicians had issued apologies the next week. Admiral Manning had apparently become the fall guy.

"Mr. Jackson—"

"Elliot."

"Elliot, may I presume that you didn't come here to make me feel better about my father's career situation? And may I further presume that, as far as I am aware, station chiefs don't normally come flying out to have conversations with lowly Special Operations Group men like myself? Would you say that is accurate?"

"Yes, Mr. Manning, that is accurate." A soft smile.

"May I ask why you came down here?"

Elliot sighed and contorted his lips as if he was mulling something over.

"I've known your old man for quite some time. He's loyal, and I'm willing to bet that his kids are too. Plus, I read your file. You were a top performer with the SEALs. I knew that you must have been. You had to be, to get picked for SOG. But still...your record was shinier than most I see."

"Thank you, sir."

"Chase, I've got a task for you. And it's a delicate one, to say the least."

"I'm all ears."

Elliot stood up and walked over to the window. Chase could hear the roar of a twin-engine fighter jet taking off outside. Seconds later, a second roar followed as another jet took off behind it.

Elliot waited for the noise to quiet and said, "Chase, we have a leak."

Chase raised an eyebrow.

"You're familiar with the Dubai Financial Summit?"

"Somewhat. I just got back from Iraq a few days ago, so I'm catching up on my news."

He grunted. "Mark my word, son. The Dubai Financial Summit is the biggest thing to hit this part of the world since they struck oil. China's new version of the World Bank, the Asian Infrastructure Investment Bank, is rolling in here as one of its primary backers. The most powerful countries in the world have each sent their financial gurus. They'll go over trade deals and talk about oil production in the region. But the main event is going to be this new currency exchange they're setting up." He looked at Chase. "You know what an exchange is?"

"Like a stock market exchange?"

"Right. Like that. Only this one is for money. People trade money. Well, banks trade money. I trade baseball cards."

Chase smiled. Elliot was a likeable guy.

Elliot said, "So the Emirates and a few global investors are building this new monetary exchange. A few countries in the Middle East have agreed to try something out. They're restructuring their national currency so that they are backed by bitcoin. You heard of bitcoin?"

"Sure."

"Of course you have. You're young. A lot of people thought bitcoin would end up being a fad, but it's gaining a lot of traction."

"How does bitcoin fit into this?"

"I'm not an expert, but as it was explained to me, a type of currency—whether it's a euro or a dollar or whatever—it's just paper. Actually, what's more likely is that it's just a bunch of electrons on a server somewhere. What gives that currency a value is when people agree to give it value. You catch my meaning? Well, sometimes, people get nervous and one type of currency looks more stable than another. So all those traders—banks, mostly—will pile their money into the stable currency and out of the risky currency."

"Sounds like the stock market."

"It is just like the stock market. And just like the stock market, there is something behind the investment. Something that backs it, that gives people a reason to believe in its value. Or a reason to get spooked. In the case of the stock market, it's the company. If the company keeps making money and earning profits, people believe that the company's stock has value. But money isn't like that."

"I thought it was backed by gold. Doesn't the US Treasury have gold at Fort Knox or something?"

"A lot of people share that misconception. But in actuality, the US dollar has not been redeemable for gold since the 1930s."

"So then what backs it up?"

"Fiat."

"The Italian car brand?"

"Yes. The Italian car brand." He shook his head. "No...not quite. Where'd you get your degree again?"

"The Naval Academy."

"Figures. A fiat currency is a type of legal tender that isn't backed up by a commodity...the opposite would be a commodity currency, like one backed up by gold. The dollar is backed by the full faith and credit of the US government."

"Well, that's a scary notion."

"Well, not when you consider the alternatives. Better the US government than the others, I'd say."

"True."

Chase's eyes looked up at the ceiling, moving rapidly as he thought. "So in this case, bitcoin is the commodity."

Elliot nodded, proud of his pupil. "You got it. The Dubai Financial Summit is about to create a new currency. A commodity-backed currency, backed by bitcoin reserves. A whole lot of heavy hitters in the I-banking world are investing in this. But the biggest investor is this Chinese version of the World Bank I was telling you about, the AIIB."

"So what's the problem?"

"There are a few. Right now the US dollar is king. We as Americans don't ever want that to change. Another issue is that bitcoin is untraceable. So as these countries change their currency to be backed by bitcoin, that apparently means that new currency is a lot less traceable than others. That's the way it's being set up right now, anyway."

"Isn't the US fighting that?"

"No one's asking us. But trust me, we're protesting. One important part of this is that a currency needs a host. It's kind of like a new product launch. You need a test market as a proof of concept. It makes adoption much faster."

"So who's the test market?"

"There are two. Iran and the UAE. Iranian rials—that's their currency—would basically be tied to bitcoins. The theory is that eventually, many Iranians could just switch over to using bitcoin altogether. This could have a big economic impact if it proves successful."

Chase frowned. "I'm surprised that the UAE and Iran were

able to agree to partner on this. I thought that everyone on this side of the Gulf hates Iran?"

Elliot said, "Iran's got some rising-star politician who's actually related to the ayatollah. Name's Ahmad Gorji. From what I understand, he's a pretty reasonable guy. His ideas are progressive, but it seems he's given a lot of leeway because...well, because when you're related to the Supreme Leader, you get a lot of leeway. Might be the perfect mix. The ayatollah has put him in charge of Iran's bitcoin-backed currency. He might make a difference in relations around here. The Emirates like him. So they're willing to allow use of this type of money in the UAE as a secondary currency."

"I'm guessing that we don't like this. The UAE is one of our strongest allies. We probably don't want them getting cozier with Iran."

"That's partially true. Although the State Department has an interesting theory that it could actually help us in the long term. An economic beachhead that would spur on democracy in Tehran. I'm skeptical."

"Me too."

"But in the short term, the issue is over tracking funds. Iran supplies weapons and funding to several terrorist groups around the world. Mainly Hezbollah. We estimate that last year Iran gave the equivalent of almost two hundred million US dollars to Hezbollah."

"That doesn't sound like a recipe for peace."

"Well, here's where bitcoin comes into play. Today, the US and our allies can slow down and freeze many of Iran's terrorist-funding transactions. But bitcoin is untraceable. We already believe that terrorist groups, and nations of ill repute, use bitcoin to transfer funds when they don't want us to know about it. But with this new currency backed by bitcoin, and wider adoption of bitcoin, it could open the floodgates so that countries like Iran could start transferring much larger sums of money to some very bad people. And not only to Hezbollah, but also to terrorist cells around the world. Today, the US could stop Iran from funding a terrorist cell in New Jersey. But if this new currency system is set up and we can't monitor transactions, it would be much easier to fund terrorists anywhere in the world, including the US. This could become a very real threat to our national security."

"I see."

Elliot said, "And lastly, the US doesn't like the idea of China launching a competitor to the World Bank. That weakens us and empowers China. This is the AIIB's first real move. So what do they do? They go and fund this new currency exchange between Iran and the UAE...I mean, they might as well be pissing in our rose garden."

Chase leaned back in his seat. He cocked his head and said, "Well, I imagine that there are certain American entities in Dubai that are very busy keeping an eye on this Dubai Financial Summit."

He gave Chase a knowing look. "I imagine that there are."

"Elliot, if you're so busy with all that, why did you fly out here to see me?"

He sat back down and placed his hands on the coffee table. "Chase, have you ever been to the American consulate in Dubai?"

"That's where your office is, right? For your State Department job?"

Elliot nodded. "Let me tell you something. There is no need for a US consulate in Dubai. We have an embassy in Abu Dhabi. The reason we have a consulate in Dubai is because we get more Iranian citizens in there asking for American green cards than any other location on the planet. Some are businessmen who oversee state-run organizations. Some are would-be defectors with military experience. I've got three interrogation rooms with two-way mirrors in that consulate, and a staff of ten managing daily interviews. It's been a great source of human intelligence over the years."

"Sounds like a good operation."

"Consulates are often the best places to collect intelligence. And the best intelligence is what we get from human sources."

"That's what I was told during my training at the Farm."

The CIA station chief smiled. "Two days ago a guy came into our consulate in Dubai. You know who it was?"

"Who?"

"You know that Iranian politician I just told you about? Ahmad Gorji? The one who's spearheading the Iranian participation in the Dubai Financial Summit?"

"Yeah."

"It was his personal assistant."

"What did he want? He wants a green card too?"

"No. That wasn't what he wanted."

"What, then?"

Elliot Jackson narrowed his eyes and leaned forward. "Well, Chase, as it turns out, he wanted *you*."

3

Chase frowned in disbelief. "I don't understand. I've never met any Iranian politician's assistant."

"I don't expect that you have. But still, he used your name. He said it. *Chase Manning*. He waited until we were alone, of course. Even asked me to turn off any cameras. Said it would be in my best interests. I didn't listen, but maybe I should have, knowing what I now know."

"What do you now know?"

"So here this guy is, just flown in from Tehran. His boss is a big deal, so he's probably pretty damn busy. He's probably using his only hour of free time in between meetings to make his way through Dubai to the American consulate. God knows what kind of tricks he had to pull to get there without drawing attention. Hell...I hope he did, anyway. For his sake. Then he asks for one of my Special Operations Group rookies. You. A former US Navy SEAL who's been off fighting ISIS in Iraq for most of your first year on the job." Elliot paused. "I didn't know what to make of it. The guy told me that he wouldn't talk to anyone else. Then he told me that he had some very important information that he was to give to you."

Chase shifted in his seat. He didn't like the tone that Elliot was using. "Sir, are you suspecting me of anything?"

Elliot said, "No, of course not. But I generally like to be in the know about all our human assets in the area. So if there is something you need to tell me, now's the time."

Chase's palms were sweating. He hadn't done anything wrong. He wasn't sure why he felt nervous. Perhaps it was because he couldn't prove that he hadn't done anything wrong. He held out his hands. "Look, Mr. Jackson. I swear to God that I have no idea how this guy got my name."

Elliot waited a moment. It was uncomfortable. "I asked this guy a lot of questions. At first he wouldn't answer. He said he would only talk to you. I told him that you weren't available, but that I would see if I could arrange a meeting soon. Then, he told me a story."

"What did he say?"

"He told me about a CIA operation in Dubai that had been uncovered by the Iranians. He let me know that I have a leaky ship."

"Could he prove it?"

"Yes, he could."

"How do you know he was telling the truth?"

Jackson said, "You know the new bitcoin-backed currency we were discussing?"

"Yes."

"Currencies need central banks. This new bitcoin-backed currency will have its own central bank located in the Dubai financial district...collocated within Dubai's own bitcoin exchange market. The whole thing is about to go operational any day now. And the US is not invited to the party. I've been working on a project with Waleed Hajjar, UAE intelligence, for about a year. We have been able to place a reliable asset in the IT department of the bitcoin-backed currency's central bank. He will also be linked in to the new bitcoin exchange once it starts trading next week."

"Sounds like a damn good source."

"That's what I was hoping."

"But?"

"But, it appears that the Iranians now know about him. Our new Iranian friend told me his name. Therefore, I have a leak."

"You said that you were working with UAE intelligence. How do you know they aren't the ones who have the leak? That seems more plausible."

"Because the Iranian knew the CIA code name for our source. That was information which was never shared with Waleed."

Chase raised his eyebrows. "I see. Any ideas on who the leak might be?"

"Honestly? No, I do not. That's what scares the shit out of me. Langley is sending me a few counterespionage specialists. They arrive the day after tomorrow. They'll help with plugging the hole. There's a special place in Hell awaiting this person when we find them."

Chase looked out the window. Another pair of jets was taking off. "So...I still don't understand why this guy asked for me. Did he tell you?"

"He didn't say. But we agreed that I would set up a meeting between you two." Jackson rubbed his temples. "Look, I realize that this is highly unorthodox, but I'm going to need you to work with UAE intelligence on this. I've already spoken to Waleed. I trust him. As much as I can trust anyone in this line of work. I'm loaning you out to him while we clean house at Dubai Station."

Chase nodded. "Understood. Whatever you need."

"Once we scrub a few agents clean and make sure they are not compromised, I'll send you someone to provide backup. But for now, do not speak to any Agency personnel about what you are doing in Dubai. Understood?"

"Yes."

"If you need help, I'll authorize contract assistance for you. But not agents."

"No problem. What will I be working on with Waleed?"

"Our asset in the Dubai financial district has some data we need. I can't send any of my people now, because I can't be sure whom to trust. In three days, you need to make contact with him and get something from him."

"Get what?"

"It'll be a memory stick, or an external hard drive. Something like that. We need it. It will allow us to monitor transactional data within the bitcoin-backed currency network."

"Why do we need to wait three days?"

"Because we need the exchange to start operating for us to get our information. Our source created a program that…" He made a face like he was trying to figure out how to explain it. "It's like this. Say there was a hole in one of your backyard gas grill propane lines, right? You could spray some soapy water around the lines and see if any of the bubbles are moving around. That would show you where the problem was. But it would only work if the gas was flowing. Same situation here. The program we have to identify where any illegitimate activity is coming from needs the funds to be flowing. The exchange opens in forty-eight hours. So three days from now, we agreed to get the first delivery of data. I need you to get me that ASAP once he makes the handoff."

Chase nodded. "Okay."

Jackson took out a phone from his pocket and handed it to Chase. "Use this. It's encrypted, and it only has one number on it. Mine. I'll text you with information as I get it. Please do the same. If you have sensitive updates, tell me that we need to meet and I'll arrange for you to be picked up."

"Alright. How do I get in touch with the source in the Dubai financial district?"

"Waleed knows. He'll help you with that. The other thing I need you to do is to meet up with Ahmad Gorji's assistant. Try to develop either him or Gorji himself as an Agency asset. Find out why he wanted to meet with you. Then report back to me."

"Okay."

"That's all for now. Like I said, I'll try to send you an agent to back you up in a few days."

"No problem."

"Alright. Grab your bag. We'll fly to Dubai right now. There will be a car for you when we get there." Elliot stood. "This is your first time working with the Emiratis, right?"

"In this capacity, yes."

"Well, prepare yourself. They're what you and I would refer to as high rollers."

* * *

The US Air Force turboprop flew from Al Dhafra Air Base to Minhad Air Base in less than twenty minutes. Chase wondered why they couldn't have taken the ninety-minute car ride, but he wasn't complaining. Minhad, like Al Dhafra, was officially UAE property. Unofficially, there was a heavy international military presence at both locations.

A well-polished black Lexus sedan waited for him on the runway as he and Elliot departed the aircraft. Nicer than the reception he typically got. In Iraq he had been picked up by a '93 Toyota with no air conditioning. Elliot said goodbye and walked toward an unmarked white van. The side door slid open, and he disappeared inside.

Chase looked at the Lexus. He was going to like working for the Emirates.

The driver looked Arabic, although Chase doubted that he was Emirati. They imported their help here in Dubai. The man spoke in thickly accented English. "Good evening, Mr. Manning. Please, I take your baggage."

Chase handed the man his black duffle bag. The driver looked around as if he was expecting more. Seeing none, he cast Chase an odd look and held the rear door open for him. Moments later, they were racing along Dubai's main highway.

The driver didn't speak during the entire thirty minutes it took them to get to their destination. It would have been a boring drive except for the view. At first, Chase could see nothing but the enormous reddish-brown sand dunes of the desert. Then the dark outline of the Dubai skyscrapers appeared through the haze of the sky. The magnificent cityscape went on as far as the eye could see, crowned by the tallest building in the world, the Burj Khalifa.

The setting sun's reflection lit up the Burj Khalifa like a torch. The giant structure towered over the rest of the city's skyscrapers. And these were buildings that would have otherwise been considered enormous. It wasn't the first time Chase had been to Dubai. But it didn't matter. He couldn't help but marvel at the Burj Khalifa each time he saw it.

As they drove inside the city limits, Chase's view switched to the modern monorail-style train system, luxury cars, and bright city lights. They passed enormous four-level shopping malls and plush high-end restaurants. Many of the hotels had palm trees covering their rooftop pools and bars.

When the car stopped at an intersection, Chase watched the cross-section of people walking the streets. It was a mix of European tourists, international businessmen, lower-class workers (mostly from India), and the local elite. Groups of Arab women adorned in black flowing robes walked into street-front shops. Most of the Arab men were dressed in bright white robes, with a variety of head garb. Everyone was sweating in the desert heat.

It was almost dark by the time Chase arrived at the hotel. As they pulled around the long driveway, he saw a glimpse of the beach behind the hotel. A thin rim of the setting orange sun peeked above the ocean. Chase saw a group of bikini-clad women sipping cocktails at the poolside bar. Definitely not Iraq.

His Lexus came to a stop and Chase stepped out into the hot, moist air. Neat rows of imported palm trees towered overhead. He thanked the driver and threw his bag over his shoulder. He then walked toward the hotel entrance, past a row of luxury cars parked on the red-and-white brick driveway.

Bentley. Maserati. Lamborghini. Ferrari. Porsche. Chase was drooling on the inside. He liked cars. He owned a Ford Mustang. It was a few years old, but it was what he could afford. The Mustang was nice. It was like dating a pretty girl. But these cars were super-models. Out of his league.

His polo shirt and khakis began to feel inadequate. But it was all he had.

He looked up at the name inscribed on the hotel. The Four Seasons Dubai. Chase entered the large glass revolving doors and felt a soothing cool air cover his face and arms. A sweet floral scent filled the air, and an artificial waterfall cascaded down ahead of him. Across the way, a man wearing a tuxedo played Rachmaninoff on a Steinway grand piano.

The lobby was filled with wealthy-looking patrons. Chase's eyes followed a group of Western women in stiletto heels, black dresses, and expensive jewelry. They were escorting several Emirati men in the traditional white robes and headscarves, wrapped with black headbands. Part of him wondered if they were pros. Supposedly the prostitution industry was in full swing here.

An Indian woman wearing a hotel name tag appeared in front of him. She spoke with a British accent. "Mr. Chase Manning?" She had a brilliant white smile.

"Yes?"

"Right this way, sir. Mr. Waleed Hajjar has asked me to take any luggage that you might have and show you to the Hendricks Bar as soon as you arrive. If you would please follow me."

Chase handed her his duffle bag, which she in turn placed on a roller. She slid it behind the front desk. He then followed her down a hallway covered by a high arched ceiling with gold trim. The Hendricks Bar was inside the hotel, at the end of the hallway.

Dubai law had a wonderful loophole that allowed alcohol to be served at hotels. It was banned almost everywhere else. All of the bars, and most of the best restaurants, were co-located within their finest resorts.

They arrived at a fifteen-foot-high wooden doorway. A dark interior lay beyond it. The pudgy doorman in a grey suit retracted a purple felt rope from gold stanchions. They walked in, and Chase thought that the word *bar* didn't quite do this place justice.

He was used to working-class watering holes. Places with names like The Greasy Spoon. The Rusty Nail. This was not one of those places. This was something else entirely.

The Hendricks Bar had high ceilings and rich mahogany walls. There were no beer taps. The world's most expensive liquors lined the single shelf. Magenta cushions adorned each of the bar stools, and a five-foot vertical wall of light surrounded the bar like an enormous lampshade, illuminating the room with a soft yellow glow. Miniature candlelit chandeliers seemed to float down from the high ceiling. The walls were lined with expensive-looking canvases.

The servers were all skinny Asian women who wore tight purple dresses. Their attire matched the décor of the room. Each of them was very pretty. Chase was reminded of an article he'd read that had said the Emirates Airline was one of the few in the world that, due to an apparent lack of legal or political constraints, hired its flight attendants primarily based on looks. Political correctness be damned, Chase had to hand it to the

UAE—they sure knew how to make things aesthetically pleasing.

The hotel hostess that had brought Chase to the bar took him toward the rear corner of the room, then politely nodded and left.

Chase found himself staring at a tall Arabic man in a dark suit. The man stood next to the corner table, half-hidden by a set of decorative curtains. They eyed each other as Chase approached. He had a hard look about him. He must be security, Chase realized as he saw another man sitting at the curtained table behind him. The security man moved to block Chase from getting any closer.

Then the man sitting at the corner table said something in Arabic, and the security man took a few steps back towards the wall. The man at the table rose. He wore a white button-down shirt with a dark blue suit jacket. No tie. The top button was undone and there were sweat stains under his arms.

"You are Chase Manning?"

Chase nodded and shook the man's hand. "Yes. Mr. Waleed Hajjar?"

"Please, call me Waleed. You have good pronunciation. Have you taken Arabic?" His grip was firm, and he shook for about two seconds too long before letting go.

Chase said, "A little."

"But you do have an accent. Did an Iraqi teach you Arabic?"

Chase smiled. "Yes. I spent some time in Iraq. And my teacher in the US was from Baghdad."

"Ah. I have a good ear, I think. Now, please have a seat."

Both men sat at the table. One of the pretty waitresses came over and used a long-stemmed match to light the wooden table's lone candle. Waleed said something to her in Arabic that Chase couldn't understand, and she walked away.

For a moment, neither man said anything.

Waleed began. "Mr. Jackson told you why you are here?"

Chase looked to his side before speaking, trying to see if anyone was in earshot.

Waleed said, "You are worried about privacy? Don't be. No one will hear this conversation. I come here often for business meetings. My security team is watching the other patrons of the bar closely. We know the names of everyone in here. And the host knows not to seat anyone near my table."

He pulled the curtain over the table entrance and they had the illusion of being in a large tent.

Chase said, "I'm told that my company has had unexpected outflows of information, and that recent events require action on our part."

"The Iranian that came to your consulate...he asked for you."

"That is what I'm told."

"Do you know why?" He raised an eyebrow.

Chase shook his head. "I do not."

Waleed rubbed his chin and said, "Interesting."

The waitress came back with a wheeled cart. She removed a large bowl of hummus and a plate of steaming-hot pita bread from the cart and placed it on the table. Then she laid a plate of falafel next to the hummus. Next she placed two old-fashioned glasses on the table and poured a double scotch into each.

Waleed asked, "I assume you drink alcohol?"

"I suppose one wouldn't hurt."

Chase thought that while regulations might not specifically call for it, it would probably be insulting not to have a drink with Waleed. Plus, he hadn't had a drink in several months. He wondered about the whole Muslim-no-alcohol thing, but decided not to ask. Just like every religion in the world, people had different levels of practice.

The waitress left the bottle of scotch on the table. Macallan. The bottle had sharp angles. It looked very modern and expensive. Like everything else in this city.

Chase grabbed a piece of the pita bread and dug in. He hadn't eaten in hours.

"Tell me, Mr. Manning, what do you know about the history of Dubai?" Waleed sat back in his chair, taking another sip from his glass.

"It is a relatively young city. It grew very rapidly over the past two decades. And it is one of the more...progressive...cities in the region."

Waleed smiled. "Yes, we are the liberals of the Middle East. But that is sort of like being the fastest turtle. An impressive thing... but only among other turtles. Compared to America, Dubai is quite strict. I know. I've been to America. I liked it very much." He raised his thick eyebrows as he spoke. His face was very expressive. "But you are right, we are also a young city."

Chase nodded politely. "I've also read that the population and real estate growth here has been incredibly impressive."

Waleed seemed to consider what he would say. He said, "Let me ask you something. Do you know why Dubai grew so quickly? Do you know what the catalyst for growth was?"

"I assume it was oil money."

"You would be wrong. It is a common misconception. Many Westerners think this. However, the true reasons for Dubai's growth are these two things—our airport, and the aftermath of the September eleventh attacks on the United States."

Chase cocked his head. "I haven't heard that before."

"Most people haven't. Most Westerners think that, like many of the other kingdoms in this part of the world, we are rich from our oil. Not quite. We discovered oil here in the 1960s. But compared to some of our neighbors, it wasn't a huge find. In the early seventies, Sheikh Rashid tasked the then-young Sheikh Mohammed with building an airport. He brought in experts from the West— an old British Airways executive would help found what you now know as Emirates Airline. Have you flown it before?"

Chase shook his head. Most of his flights had been on Air Force transports or Army helicopters. "No, I haven't had the pleasure."

"It is a truly world-class airline. In the 1980s, both the airport and the airline opened the door to tourists. By the 1990s, we had built tax-free zones for shopping and dozens of extravagant hotels. It was the only place like it in this part of the world. And with the airport, it was now accessible to a great many people. Businesses began to see that in a region of war and terrorism, there was a shining beacon of peace and prosperity."

Chase waited for him to finish his story.

"Unfortunately, it took the atrocities of September eleventh to spur major capital inflows to Dubai. For after September of 2001, your nation passed the Patriot Act. I was in America at the time. Not a good place to be an Arab during those days. But you see, in the 1990s, the oil-rich nations of the Gulf States would take their money and invest it in American ventures. After the Patriot Act, however, that became less appealing. Too much of a hassle for Middle Eastern investors. No one wanted to go through all the paperwork and deal with the risk that the US government might decide to freeze his assets. So...what were the wealthy families of the Middle East to do with their money? Where could they invest?"

"They invested in Dubai."

Waleed nodded. "They invested in Dubai. That peaceful land of shopping and tourism that I was just telling you about. But tourism could only take one's money so far. And that's all Dubai was at the time. Up until the year 2000, it was just a tourist destination. A very appealing one, sure. But with the amount of money that was beginning to pour in, we could do so much more than just tourism. Diversification was important to the Emirates. So was planning for the future."

Waleed sipped his drink. He said, "Someday, the oil would

either dry up or become obsolete. While Dubai didn't make its money that way, many of our investors did. So how would we sustain ourselves when that happened? How would we ensure prosperity for our kingdom?"

Chase could see how proud Waleed was of this story. It was his family's story, Chase realized. Elliot Jackson had told Chase that Waleed was related to the Dubai royal family. He continued to speak for a while about their great rise from the hot and barren sands of the Arabian Gulf.

Chase was impressed. He had seen the pictures of what this city had looked like only a few decades ago. Then it had been just a few buildings along a desert coast. But today's Dubai was a masterpiece of modern architecture, and a rapidly growing center for several industries.

Waleed continued, "That was his stroke of genius. Sheikh Mohammed knew what ruled investors' hearts: fear and greed. So he gave the world what it needed. Reassurance. Confidence. He carved out sections of land within Dubai and made them legal zones for certain types of businesses. They would be protected by Western-style laws. Entertainment companies. Technology companies. Real estate. And—what is most relevant to this conversation—financial companies. We brought in McKinsey. Do you know McKinsey? The consulting firm?"

"Yes. It's a very good company. I have a friend that works there. He's one of the smartest people I know."

"They helped us design the structure for Dubai International Financial Centre—not the buildings, but the actual financial and legal entity. Soon, all of the big banks came. This Financial Centre became the engine that pumped in more and more capital investment. In the 2000s, all one could see in this city was the miles and miles of skyscrapers with cranes on top of them. The real estate market was in a feeding frenzy. The Iraq war was increasing the price of oil. And all the while, the capital inflows were pouring into Dubai. It was a furious race to create the new capital of the Middle East. A peaceful, tolerant, and luxurious city. It was, and still is today, a symbol of hope for the region."

Chase gave a polite smile as he washed down some falafel with a sip of scotch.

"Tell me, you have been to many places in the Middle East. Do you feel safe in all of them?"

He'd been shot at in four different Middle Eastern countries. "Sure. As long as I'm armed."

Waleed smirked. "Well, let me ask you, do you feel safe in Dubai?"

Chase thought about it. "I do. It reminds me of a Western city. Clean and modern. Although this is more luxurious than almost any city in the West."

"It is more luxurious than *any* city in the West. I've been to most of them."

"You're probably right."

Waleed said, "I love this city. And I want to protect it. I raised my family here. My two sons know nothing other than the peace and prosperity of modern Dubai."

Chase could feel that there was a tension in Waleed's tone.

"The brilliance of Dubai's design is the vision that our leaders showed. They knew that oil money could only take us so far. Someday, this world's hunger for oil will dry up. Or the wells themselves will. When that happens, many cities, and even entire nations around this region, will suffer greatly. They are not prepared for that change."

"But Dubai is?"

"Absolutely. Less than five percent of our economy is from oil income. The rest is from industries that are growing and bringing in the best and the brightest from all over the world. We have become self-sustaining."

"Impressive."

"I love what it stands for. It is much like America, in many ways. A symbol of hope in a troubled world. A place where leaders with great vision created something special. Something that could grow into greatness." Waleed paused. His thick eyebrows narrowed as he leaned forward. "Now we must protect it."

"Protect...Dubai?"

"Yes. Because I believe that Dubai as we know it is in great danger."

"Why do you think Dubai is in danger?"

Waleed said, "Chase, tell me...are you familiar with the Iranian military unit known as the Quds Force?"

Chase knew of that unit very well. When he had operated with the SEALs in Iraq and Afghanistan, it was rumored that the Iranian Special Forces group known as the Quds Force was supplying and even assisting the anti-US militias.

A congressional hearing in 2015 revealed that as many as five hundred American deaths could be linked to Iranian-made explosively formed penetrators, or EFPs. While the US was trying to stabilize Iraq and Afghanistan, Iran was helping to kill American troops stationed in both countries.

One of the things that always bothered him about the media coverage of the wars in Iraq and Afghanistan was that they seemed to pay little attention to the fact that Iran helped provide the funds and technical training to harm the US military.

Chase had witnessed the use of several of these EFPs during his deployments. One such explosive device had shredded a Humvee in a convoy that he was a part of, killing two of his brother SEALs that had been riding in it. They later found evidence that Quds Force personnel had supplied those weapons.

The anti-American militias that Quds Force had been equipping weren't just Iraqi freedom fighters. They were a mix of jihadists from around the region. Some of the things that Chase had witnessed these groups do were pure evil. They maimed and killed civilians they thought were cooperating with the Americans. These violent acts were often carried out in public, as a scare tactic, and as a way to demonstrate power.

There were stories of fathers being shot in front of their children. Wives stoned to death in front of their husbands. Chase had once seen a four-year-old boy without a hand. When he asked one of the locals about it, they had said that his father had shaken the hand of an American soldier, and that the boy's injury was the result.

In Chase's experience, only the weak and scared felt the need to prove their power by harming those without the means to protect themselves. His time in Iraq and Afghanistan made him realize that there were truly evil people in the world.

Before going to war, he had only read about atrocities like that in the news. But seeing a TV news report or reading about an incident online was one thing. Witnessing these brutalities was another. There were truly wicked men in the world. Everyone might have been born equal. But the types of people that would cut off a child's limb to send a message to a village—these men were his enemy.

Chase said, "I'm familiar with the Quds Force."

"There is an Iranian military officer that is a member of that organization. His name is Lt. Col. Bahadur Pakvar. He has a particularly brutal reputation, according to our intelligence."

"What does he have to do with Dubai?"

Waleed took his phone out of his pocket and flipped through a few images before holding it out for Chase to see. "Bahadur Pakvar was spotted in Dubai two weeks ago. My sources tell me that he has been looking into several employees of the Dubai Bitcoin Exchange."

Chase lowered his voice. "Were any of those employees our source?"

Waleed nodded. "I believe so. Mr. Jackson and I had hoped

that it was the result of sloppy tradecraft by our asset. But Elliot told me about the Iranian politician—Gorji—how his assistant came to visit the US consulate. His revelation suggests that Iran knows about our man. And it appears that they have infiltrated the CIA in Dubai."

"So you are worried about his well-being? Why not just pull him?"

"We need to wait until the exchange goes operational. Otherwise he is useless to us. We want to ensure that our monitoring systems are set up appropriately. If so, we will be able to track the new bitcoin-based currency and monitor the reserve bank. If not... well, we aren't comfortable with that situation."

"I thought the UAE was part of this new currency? Why aren't you comfortable with the setup?"

He shifted in his seat. "The UAE's participation is complicated. It is essentially a big trade agreement. A step toward peace in the region. Iran will be the big winner in the short term, if this new currency shift helps to stabilize their inflation rate."

"So again, why are you concerned about this? I guess a better question to ask would be—why did the UAE agree to participate in the first place? The Persians and the Arabs have been rivals for...well, forever, right? Why would...?"

Waleed shook his head. "It's about more than just Iran-UAE relations. The Dubai and UAE leadership want to move our country forward. That is their first priority...that our nation has a prosperous future. This Dubai Financial Summit, and all of the agreements that will be a part of it, are backed by China's new competitor to the World Bank, the Asian Infrastructure Investment Bank. The newest, largest investor backed by one of the world's only two superpowers. I told you that my leadership was filled with visionaries. They want to have the AIIB on their side. Do you know what they fund?"

"What?"

"Infrastructure. Roads, bridges, airports, trains...fiber-optic cables and data centers. Expensive investments. Things that the UAE will need to fund if it is to continue to thrive. So the UAE leadership wants to keep them happy. This is their first investment in the Middle East. The man the Chinese have sent over, Cheng Jinshan...you have heard of him?"

"I can't say that I have."

"A savvy investor. A multibillionaire. He is the one pushing the Chinese to finance in all of this bitcoin-backed currency. He is the reason this is all happening. And I'm somewhat embarrassed to admit, he is the reason that my leadership is falling all over themselves to ensure that there are no hiccups. My job is to keep us safe. The decision has been made to proceed with the Dubai Financial Summit Agreements. I voiced my concerns. Now I need to make sure that there is no Trojan horse built into the system."

"I understand."

"So you see...I can't pull out our source in the Dubai Bitcoin Exchange. We need him, and his information."

"Can he just email it to us?"

"No. There can't be an electronic trail. It will be a face-to-face meeting. It's set up to occur in three days' time. You'll accompany me and transport the information back to your team."

"So how do we keep this Pakvar fellow from getting hold of your man?"

"In my opinion, we need to find Pakvar first."

"And how do we do that?"

"We ask your new Iranian friend. I suspect he can help us."

Chase took another sip of his drink. The ice clinked in the glass as he placed it back down on the table. He said, "The one that asked for me? The politician's assistant?"

"That's the one."

4

Chase awoke to a ringing phone next to his soft bed at the Four Seasons. Bright sunlight shone in from behind the curtains. He squinted and could make out the beach. A few tourists were already sunning themselves outside.

He picked up the phone.

"Good morning, Mr. Manning. I trust that you are enjoying your stay at the Four Seasons?"

It was Waleed.

"Very much."

"Excellent. I have asked them to send up your breakfast. Please plan to meet me at ten o'clock in the lobby. From there, we will leave to meet Gorji's assistant. It will be your show."

"We have a meeting set up already? How did you manage that?"

"I have many friends in this city. There is little that I cannot do."

Chase agreed to meet him and hung up. He looked at his watch. It was just before eight. He opened his duffle bag and threw on his running shoes and a gym outfit. He spent the next hour working out. The hotel's fitness center had hardwood floors, brand-new equipment, and a view that overlooked the Gulf. It was empty. And it was heaven, for a gym rat like Chase.

When he came back, a cart had been wheeled to his room with several plates of hot food. Assorted chilled juices. Smoothies. A grilled tomato. Spiced hashed browns with eggs benedict. A full basket of fresh fruit. Another full basket of croissants and muffins. Three different types of sausages. And a large container of hot coffee.

Perhaps Elliot was right about the high roller thing. This was somewhat better than what he had grown accustomed to while fighting ISIS in Iraq. He turned the TV on to a news channel and ate.

"The Asian Infrastructure Investment Bank officials have hinted that further talks are underway with several Asian countries regarding future adoption of the new bitcoin-backed currency. The value of bitcoin has been climbing steadily over the past few weeks to new record highs.

"In other news, Iranian naval vessels have continued to step up their activity level in the Straits of Hormuz and the Arabian Gulf. One Iranian missile boat conducted a test fire of unguided rockets only fifteen hundred yards from the US aircraft carrier Truman. *The USS* Porter, *the ship at the heart of the recent controversy, is still in port in Dubai. US officials say that she will remain there until the investigation and repairs are finished."*

Chase listened to the story and sighed, thinking about his father. It was a damn shame that he was to be the scapegoat in this mess.

He finished eating, showered, and got ready for the day. At ten o'clock sharp he walked into the hotel lobby wearing khakis and a button-down shirt. Waleed's security man was waiting there. He directed Chase to a running black Mercedes S600, just outside the hotel entrance. The driver opened a rear door for Chase. Waleed was sitting in one of the rear seats, reading on his tablet.

"Good morning, Mr. Manning."

"Good morning. Where are we going to meet him?"

"Near the fountains."

"Now?"

Waleed nodded.

The driver and security man got in the front seats. The V-12 engine whirred to life. Seconds later, the sleek black car sped through the city. They headed towards the towering Burj Khalifa.

Once there, Chase followed Waleed. Under the Burj Khalifa's shadow sat a nine-hundred-foot-long man-made pond. Enormous fountains sprayed from the pond, shooting hundreds of feet up into the air before they plummeted back into the aquamarine water below. Hundreds of tourists were gathered to watch. They held their phones up, taking pictures and video.

Chase said, "It reminds me of the Bellagio in Las Vegas."

Waleed replied, "It should. It was the same builders. We paid them several hundred million US dollars to make this. It's one of the biggest landmarks in the city."

Sweat began collecting on Chase's forehead. It was, as always, incredibly hot. Chase was glad when Waleed kept walking past the fountains and into a beige building with the words *Souk Al Bahar* written on the entrance.

The Souk was situated just next to the Dubai Mall. In contrast to the Dubai Mall's modern, luxurious feel, the Souk was richly decorated, yet kept a traditional Arabic theme to it. Arched ceilings and gold decorations gave it the appearance of an Arabic palace or a temple. It was filled with small gold and diamond shops. Every price here was negotiable, Chase knew. Both the customers and the storekeepers loved the game of bargaining for the best deal.

Waleed pointed to one of the shops. "There. He is inside. I will wait here."

"You aren't coming?"

"No. He didn't ask to see me. It's you that he wishes to speak with. I will keep an eye out for any sign of trouble."

"Alright. I'll be back in a few minutes."

He entered the jewelry store and headed to the back of the shop, where he saw a frail man in a suit watching him. The man had a nervous look. There was no sign of anyone else in the store, including the shopkeeper.

"Mr. Manning. Good day." The man held out his hand and Chase shook it. "I represent Mr. Ahmad Gorji."

"Yes, I've been told."

"I have been asked to make contact with you on a very serious matter."

Chase said, "Please excuse my caution. But how do I know that you truly represent Mr. Gorji?"

"I assume that by now, your Mr. Jackson has looked into my background?"

He had. Chase said, "We know that you work for Mr. Gorji, as his personal assistant. I recognize the picture I was given, so I know that you are who you say you are. But I don't know that you actually *speak* for Mr. Gorji. Why has he not come himself?"

The man thought about that. "I understand. I promise you that I am loyal to Mr. Gorji. Mr. Gorji *does* wish to speak with you in person. But this will be a great risk for him. You must understand —a man in his position…he needs assurances from you before he will agree to a face-to-face meeting."

Chase said, "And why does he want to speak with me?"

The man looked around the empty shop. Nervous eyes. He took a step closer to Chase. His voice was barely a whisper. "I am to give you the following message."

"Alright, I'm listening."

"You already know that you have a traitor in your organization. We gave Mr. Jackson the CIA code name of your source within the Dubai Financial Exchange. We do not know who your traitor is, but we know that there are certain parties that are trying to find out his identity."

"Who is trying to find out his identity?" Chase hoped to get knowledge of Pakvar.

The man held up a hand. "I am to tell you that we have a list of others."

Chase froze. "A list of other what?"

"Other traitors."

He tried to appear calm. "Please elaborate...tell me more."

"There is a list of names. Americans. Each of them is an expert in their field—defense, intelligence, politics, military strategy, and satellites. Communications and information technology. Many subjects that would be of great value to an enemy of the United States."

He looked around again and then back at Chase. Fear in his eyes. As if he was afraid someone was about to come in and take him away.

"Go on."

"These people are providing information to help plan an attack on the United States."

Chase's eyes narrowed. "They're giving secrets to Iran?"

"Not exactly. Mr. Gorji wants peace. Many in Iran do not. There are multiple circles of power in the Iranian nation. But I assure you, this list of American names is not the property of the Iranian government."

"Who has the list? Who is it for?"

"People on an island."

"What island?"

"Abu Musa."

"Then it is Iran."

"No. Mr. Gorji has come across this list. But this list, and its purpose, are not supported by the Iranian government. Our two nations have enough problems between us. Mr. Gorji recognizes that if Iran is ever to prosper, we must repair our relationship with the West. We are telling you this as a sign of good faith. And because we need your help. Some of the people involved *are* Iranian. But please be assured, the people who created this list are *not* Iranian."

"Then who are they?"

"I don't have that information."

"Does Gorji?"

He didn't answer.

Chase scoffed. "You said they were planning an attack. What is the target?"

"I do not have that information."

"When is the attack planned?"

"I do not know."

"Why would a group of Americans do this? Why would they betray their country?"

"I don't know that either. It is best that you speak with Mr. Gorji."

"Do you know who the person is that provided our source at the Dubai Financial Exchange to Iran?"

The man said, "I have told you, this is not the Iranian government that is working against you. But I still do not know who in your organization is responsible for the leak."

Chase crossed his arms. "What can you give me?"

"Mr. Gorji wants to trade this list. The list of additional names is what he has. This is the help that we can provide."

Now the negotiation.

"Didn't you just tell me that this was in good faith?"

"Notification that the list exists has been given in good faith. Delivery of the names of your American traitors...that will cost you."

"What does Gorji want in return?"

"The people that have created this list...the people on Abu

Musa...they have become a problem for Iran. We would like to provide you the entire list in return for American assistance in resolving this issue."

"What does that mean? Assistance in resolving this issue?"

"The group that generated this list of American traitors—we would like to see them displaced, without Iran having to take any action."

Chase tried to follow. "I don't understand."

"Mr. Gorji can explain further. We just need to know that you will consider helping us. Then I can set up a meeting between you and Mr. Gorji."

"Why would Gorji want the US to remove this group on Abu Musa? That island, if I'm not mistaken, is under Iranian control. Why would Gorji want—"

"It is not just Mr. Gorji who is asking."

"Who else, then? Who else is asking for our assistance?"

"Mr. Gorji's superior."

"And who is that?"

He cleared his throat. "The Supreme Leader of Iran."

Chase paused. Then he said, "You're telling me that the Supreme Leader of Iran is asking for help from the United States? Have you seen the news? Iran is claiming that we just sank one of your patrol boats. The IRGC Navy just test-fired rockets fifteen hundred yards from a US aircraft carrier in the Straits of Hormuz. To put it bluntly, Iran officially hates us."

"Mr. Gorji does not wish for US-Iranian relations to suffer any more than they already have. He has the ear of the Supreme Leader. Please believe me, Mr. Manning, this request comes from the highest level."

Chase looked him in the eye. He looked like he was telling the truth. "You told us that there was someone looking for our man in the Dubai Financial Exchange. I need to know more about that."

He looked at his watch. "I must leave."

"Tell me first, is this person a man named Pakvar? Do you know that name?"

He looked more worried. "I do."

"Is that who is after our source?"

He nodded. "I believe so, yes."

"Do you know where he is? Where we can find him?"

"He is not the type of person you want to find, I should think. But I am aware that he is in Dubai."

"I need to know where."

"I will speak with Mr. Gorji. If God wills it, he will provide you that information as well. I do not know Pakvar's location. Thus, I cannot help you with that today."

He turned to leave, but then reached for something in his inner suit jacket pocket. "I take it that you wish to continue this conversation with Mr. Gorji?"

"Yes, indeed."

"Then I am to provide you with one more thing, Mr. Manning. Have you asked yourself why we wanted to speak with *you* in particular?"

"Of course."

"And what answer have you come up with?"

"I have none. I have no idea why you asked for me."

"I am told that there are several members of your family that work with classified military matters."

Chase flushed. He hadn't expected this skinny bastard to bring up his family. He kept his voice under control. "What's your point?"

"Mr. Chase Manning, I am authorized to give you one name on this list. A word of warning. Whatever name is on this paper, do not contact this person. If you do, we will not provide you the rest of the names."

Chase clenched his jaw. "Then why provide us with this name? You can't expect that we'll do nothing with it."

"We expect you to look into the veracity of our claim. If you find that this person is indeed providing classified information to a group outside the US government, then you will know that we are telling the truth. We do not have the means to research this. But you may. However you do this, remember: you cannot communicate with them. This risks alerting the Abu Musa group, and places Mr. Gorji in danger. If we find out that you have communicated with this person, we will no longer provide you the other names."

He handed him an envelope. "Don't open it until I leave. Then burn it. We will be in touch." He walked out of the store, quickly.

Chase's heart pounded as he opened the envelope and looked down at the single name written in ink.

David Manning. His brother.

5

Chase ate dinner alone in his room, waiting. He had texted Elliot an hour after he had finished with Gorji's assistant. The day had passed without a reply.

The mobile phone that Elliot Jackson had given him buzzed on the night table.

A text message read: *Sending a car to pick you up. 15 min.*

Chase walked back out of the Four Seasons Dubai and into the dark parking circle. Even after the sun had set, the humid air was still incredibly warm. He waited on the steps of the hotel. The sounds of honking horns and city traffic filled the air. To the east, the white lights of the Burj Khalifa made it look like a metallic rocket about to launch into the hazy night sky.

The sound of high heels echoed on the brick walkway behind him. He turned and saw two large eyes staring at him from behind a headscarf. Beautiful eyes. The eyes of a woman who had worked for the CIA for many years, and had recently been promoted to the number three position in Dubai.

"Hello, Chase." He could see her modest smile, half-hidden behind the headscarf.

"Hello. I wondered if I would run into you."

She stood very close to him. Her fingertips crept over his right hand. She stared into his eyes for a moment, neither of them saying a word. They didn't need to. He wondered if anyone was watching them. Public displays of affection were forbidden here.

She tilted her head ever so slightly. "Shall we?"

"After you, Miss Parker."

Chase got into the passenger seat of Lisa Parker's Toyota sedan, and she accelerated onto Jumeirah Road.

He had first met Lisa a few months after arriving in the UAE. He had been called to Dubai Station for a weeklong training session. It was mostly classroom stuff. Briefs on the geopolitical situation. Updates on the regional terrorist cell habits and practices. But there were a few skills improvement classes. One of these was entitled Unarmed Combat Refresh. Lisa Parker was the instructor.

She had gone over hand-to-hand combat techniques, as well as escape and evasion best practices. It was an all-day class, half of which was spent in a rented-out private gym.

Lisa embarrassed a lot of men during those few hours. She was the only female in a group of very macho men. There were five students, four of whom were from the Special Operations Group. The last part of the training called for the men to demonstrate some of the techniques she had taught them—on her. Chase watched her demolish them one by one. She flipped the first guy, a 220-pound former Delta operator, onto his back before he knew what hit him. As each man finished with her, they were allowed to leave. She left them all humiliated and in tatters. And these were men who had a good deal of training and real-life experience in hand-to-hand combat.

Lisa was *very* good. Chase also found her extremely attractive. Her tight workout attire was distracting, to say the least.

Chase was the last person in the group to go. This also meant that Lisa and he were alone, facing each other on the floor mat, when he made his attempt to take her down.

Chase gave her a sheepish grin. "You know, I just watched you kick those guys' asses, and I've got to tell you, I am one hundred percent positive that they were all much tougher than I am. Would it be possible to just assume that you will whip the hell out of me? If it's all the same to you, we could call it a day now and go grab a drink or something."

She smiled back at him. Big, beautiful eyes. "Or something?"

Chase wasn't sure what to say to that. Was she being forward and showing interest? Or was she offended and giving him more rope to hang himself with?

She said, "Do you know who I am?"

"You're the toughest woman I've ever met is who you are." He took a step toward her, a playful glimmer in his eye. His senses were heightened, muscles tense. He would try to get close enough that he could get her in a grappling move. Maybe a half nelson.

She stood relaxed, feet shoulder-width apart, hands at her hips. Not a care in the world. "It would be inappropriate for me to be seen out in town, getting a drink with you."

"Why's that?" He took another step towards her. Whether she was interested in drinks or not, this might distract her enough that he could get the first move on her before she used any of that judo shit.

"Because I am, I believe, what you would describe as very *senior* to you."

Chase began to rethink both of his advances. "I'm sorry if I—"

She dropped to the floor and spun, her leg swinging around and clipping his feet out from underneath him.

He fell hard, landing on his back, the wind knocked from his lungs. She was *really* quick. As he groaned on the floor, he saw her walking away. He guessed that she wasn't interested after all. He closed his eyes in pain. Then he heard the heavy metallic sound of a deadbolt lock.

She stood over him. He was still on the floor, stunned. She said, "I'm not interested in drinks. But perhaps I will take you up on the 'something.'" She kept her eyes locked on his as she crouched down and straddled him.

That was how their very physical and very secret affair began. Chase had asked around about her in the days following. She was a very gifted woman. A rising star within the CIA's Political Action Group, she had been stationed in Dubai for two years prior to their meeting. She was smart, and spoke several languages fluently. A talented recruiter of foreign assets, she had a knack for getting people to spy for the United States, whether they knew they were doing it or not. And she had earned a lot of respect from the SOG team members for handling herself well in several firefights.

Chase and she had seen each other maybe a dozen times now. She called the shots. She sent him an email with a time and location. Lisa knew when he would be able to get time off without even having to ask him. Usually they met at a Dubai hotel. They'd chat a little over dinner and drinks and spend the rest of their time in bed. The relationship filled a need for each of them, but they also kept up an abnormally strong set of boundaries.

Chase hadn't told anyone that he was seeing her. And he was certain that she had done the same. They never spoke about their past, beyond surface-level stuff. It was intentional on her part, he was pretty sure. And he was taking his cues from her. If she wanted anything more than this, he was pretty sure that she would let him know. The problem was, the more they saw of each other, the more emotionally attached he got. He had no idea where this was going, if anywhere. But he didn't want to blow it by saying something that he shouldn't.

Now, in the car on the way to see Elliot, he presumed, he

wanted to ask her how she had been. He wanted to ask her a lot of things. He stole glances at her out of the corner of his eye, so as not to appear too eager. He had thought about her a lot when he was in Iraq. They had exchanged a few emails, but it had been very superficial. He felt a bit used, but he didn't want it to stop.

"Where are we headed?"

She glanced at him and then looked forward, taking a sharp turn. "To see Elliot."

"I know. Where?"

She didn't reply.

This was a typical response from the Political Action Group agents. They saw themselves as the real CIA agents. The cloak-and-dagger types that clinked martini glasses with foreign dignitaries and picked up envelopes at dead drops. To them, Chase was one of the other types. The machine-gun-toting men that had a reputation for being less cerebral and therefore only needed to know enough to pull the trigger at the right time.

Chase was in his second year as a member of the CIA's Special Operations Group. Together, the PAG and SOG formed the two halves of the Special Activities Division. While many jobs in the military and intelligence machine were mundane office jobs, the Special Activities Division was where the action was...at least, in the CIA. SOG was considered the paramilitary wing.

Plucked from the most elite units of the military, members of SOG were selected because they were smart, capable, and deadly. In his opinion, they needed to know every bit of information that the "regular" spies knew. Yet members of Lisa's community ran the CIA. They were promoted faster and higher. It was the way things were. As a PAG agent, Lisa was a member of this superior "master race" within the CIA's organization.

Chase wasn't too worried about his promotion potential within the CIA. He wasn't looking to make GS-15, and he didn't want to deal with the bullshit that the executives dealt with. Just look what was happening to his father. He was a scapegoat for the politicians in Washington. Chase preferred to serve his country well, and without public reward.

The other card that Chase had in his back pocket was that he was still a reserve officer in the US Navy. He was in his second year with the CIA now, and hadn't done much with the reserves. But in another month, he was scheduled to start actively drilling with SEAL Team Eighteen, the reserve unit that he had joined up with. While that wasn't going to be a vacation, to say the least, it would be a nice change from the culture of the CIA.

Lisa drove across the bridge onto the Palm Jumeirah Island.

In 2001, the land that they were now driving on had been nothing but water. But eight years of dredging and construction had produced an island in the shape of a giant palm, with 320 miles of coastline, twenty-eight hotels, and thousands of luxury residences. Each leaf on the palm tree had rows and rows of extravagant housing, restaurants, resorts, and shopping.

Lisa sped down the main street that encircled the island. Chase watched a monorail glide by on a concrete structure above them. Everywhere Chase turned, there were rows of identical palm trees, expensive cars, and luxury residential properties. The wealth here was incredible.

Lisa took a sharp right turn and drove down a ramp and into a two-car garage beneath one of the townhomes. The garage door shut behind them. For a moment, they were alone in the quiet darkness.

She touched his cheek and leaned close to him. "It's good to see you again."

He whispered, "You too." He looked into her eyes, but made no move to get closer.

A trace of her sweet perfume found its way into his nostrils. It reminded him of the last time they were together. His heart beat a bit faster as she closed in. Her lips grazed his ear as she whispered into it. "Perhaps tonight we could get a drink after work?"

She moved back and looked into his eyes, waiting for his answer.

"I'd like that."

The smallest of smiles, and then she left the car and headed into the residence. He followed. Entering the home, Chase saw that the dwelling had been set up as a listening post. All of the windows and doors were covered. There were interior rooms with soundproof walls, digital security locks, and enough electronics to service any surveillance requirement that the CIA and other agencies they were working with might have.

Elliot sat on a worn leather couch, watching what looked like a live video feed of a sizeable hotel conference room. He stood up as Lisa and Chase approached.

Elliot shook his hand. "Thanks for coming out." Chase looked around the room. There were several people with ear sets on, typing into laptop computers. Lisa stood next to them, a curious expression on her face. Chase began to wonder if Elliot had told her why he was here.

"Lisa, we'll be just a few minutes."

She had taken the headscarf down and let it hang around her neck. She raised her eyebrows and said, "Of course. I'll be right here." She didn't look like she was too keen on being left out of the conversation.

Elliot walked down the hall and opened a door. The room was bare save for a lone table and four chairs. It could have served as a secure conference room. Or an interrogation room. Chase entered and took a seat at a small wooden table. Elliot closed the door behind them.

Chase said, "You haven't told Lisa Parker what I'm doing here?"

He shook his head. "Not yet. I intend to, once the counterespionage guys clear her. But there's protocol to follow and I cannot be too careful." He clasped his hands together, his elbows on the table. "Alright, fill me in on everything."

Chase recapped his conversation with Waleed, and let Elliot know about Pakvar. When they were finished, Elliot looked upset. He pulled out his phone and typed a few keystrokes. He held up the screen and Chase saw a face.

Chase said, "That's Pakvar?"

Elliot nodded. "I received a report that he was in Dubai earlier today. This guy is bad news, Chase. I don't want him anywhere near our man. We need that data. If they launch this bitcoin-backed currency and we aren't able to get transaction information, we're essentially going to have a growing financial black market out there that we can't monitor or control."

Chase nodded. "We need to talk to Gorji, as well. I met with his assistant. The one that came to see you at the consulate."

"Already? When did you meet with him?"

"Earlier today. I sent you a text."

He looked down at his phone. "Ah. I guess you did. Sorry, things are crazy here right now." He shook his head. "There's just a lot going on. Did you find out why he wanted to meet with you?"

Chase had been deciding what to say next all day. He was torn between potentially hurting his brother's reputation and career, and doing his duty. He knew that David wouldn't voluntarily provide information to any entity that he wasn't supposed to.

"I've been pretty conflicted about this. Elliot, I swear to God there has to be some mistake. Or this is part of some Iranian misinformation operation or something. I don't know..."

Elliot frowned. "Spit it out."

"The reason that Gorji apparently wanted to speak with me is because of my brother. Do you remember David?"

Elliot frowned. Elliot had been long-time friends with Admiral

Manning, David and Chase's father. He had met David before, but
didn't know him. "I remember your brother."

"We've got a bigger problem than just one leak in Dubai. They
claim to have a list of Americans that are providing some group on
Abu Musa with classified information. Gorji's assistant claims that
Gorji wants to meet with me personally. Says the Supreme Leader
of Iran wants to make a trade. This list of Americans for our help
in getting rid of this group on Abu Musa. The proof that the list is
authentic is that my brother, David, is on the list. They think that
if we look into it, we'll be able to verify that he's doing something
he shouldn't be."

Elliot's face contorted. "Excuse me?"

Chase repeated everything that he had been told, careful to
emphasize that his brother would never betray their country.

When Chase was finished speaking, Elliot leaned back in his
chair. He didn't say anything for a while. He just looked at the
wall, thinking. Then his eyes went back to Chase. He said, "It must
have been hard for you to tell me about this, Chase. But you did
the right thing."

"I don't know what to do. They said that we can't communicate
with David or the trade is off."

"Why did they say that?"

"They think it will be too high-risk. It might alert whoever has
penetrated Dubai Station."

Elliot nodded. "Chase, I don't know what Gorji is up to. I don't
know if this list is real, or how they got the name of our man in
Dubai. But...do *not* contact your brother David. Do you understand? Not until we figure all this out."

Chase grudgingly said, "I understand."

"Meet with Gorji. Soon. Let me know when you go to see him.
I need to run this one up the chain. This is turning out to be much
bigger than I thought."

"And about Pakvar?"

"We're trying to locate him. See if Gorji can help with that when you meet."

"Will do."

They got up and walked back out to the living area, where the equipment was set up. Lisa stood across the room, speaking to a group of CIA surveillance technicians. Her eyes locked onto Chase. They held each other's gaze for a moment. Busy conversations went on around them. Neither of them showed any emotion as they looked at each other. But Chase could feel a craving inside himself. He wondered if she was thinking of the same things. Then a landline phone rang loudly, the spell broke, and they continued on with what they were doing.

Chase turned to Elliot and said, "May I ask what is all this for?" He motioned toward the electronic eavesdropping equipment.

Elliot pointed at the big TV screen, the one showing the live feed of the hotel conference room. "There wasn't US representation at the Dubai Financial Summit. It's a closed-door session among the big investors. But the director wants us to make sure we know everything that's going on there." The director he referred to, Chase realized, was the actual director of the CIA. This must be getting a lot of attention back in Washington.

Lisa appeared next to them. She said to Elliot, "There have been sweeps of the room by three different intelligence services so far."

Elliot said, "I'm guessing that you would have told me if anyone found one of our devices?"

She gave a coy smile. "Oh, was that important?"

He smiled and said to Chase, "You see what I'm dealing with here?"

Lisa gave a sly wink. "Relax. I've got you covered."

Chase looked at the TV screen. It was HD-quality video from

two different angles, and while the volume of the TV was low, there were captions being typed at the bottom of the screen.

"How did you guys pull this off?" Chase asked.

Elliot looked at Lisa. She didn't answer. Then she said, "Well, tonight's show is about to begin. Chase, I'll give you a ride back when we're finished. Why don't you have a seat?"

Elliot sat back down and Lisa pulled up a chair. Chase remained standing, reading the captions at the bottom of the screen.

The conference room filled up and different groups began speaking. Chase picked up the gist of it. A large Chinese investment was being made into the new financial exchange in Dubai. It would open up more opportunity for global investment in the region. So far nothing stood out to him that would be suspicious.

He watched as an Arabic man in a flowing white robe finished speaking. The man then walked down from the podium and sat in the front row.

A short Chinese man hobbled up to the stage.

Chase asked Lisa, "Who's that?"

"*That* is the man everyone is here to see."

* * *

Cheng Jinshan was ready for this moment. This was the culmination of decades of careful planning. His meteoric rise in the business world, and equally impressive—although unpublicized—rise in the world of Chinese government power brokers had made this all possible. But this was not just business. It was not just politics. This was war.

He took a drink of water from his glass and looked out at the room. There were only fifteen or twenty men here. No women. The American ambassador had no doubt been quite irritated that she had been not invited to this gathering, but it would not matter.

"Gentlemen, thank you for allowing me—*a mere investor*—to speak and dine with such great statesmen and economists as each of you. It is you who are the nation builders, the thinkers, and the world makers. I am but a humble businessman."

There were smiles on the faces of the spectators. Many of them knew Jinshan well, including the Chinese ambassador. Those who did know him were aware that he was a very accomplished individual. The word *mere* would never be used to describe one such as him.

He gave a devilish grin. "What is money?" He grasped the edges of the wooden podium and looked around the room. "There are some that would tell you that money is only created by men who produce. It is the great equalizer in this world. These same people would have you believe that money can only be exchanged in the fair trade of goods, because both parties must agree on the price. The novelist Ayn Rand, in one of her books, said, 'To trade by means of money is the code of the men of good will. Money permits no deals except those to mutual benefit by the unforced judgment of the traders.' And I think that this could be true, except for one thing. We don't all use the same *type* of money. And of that great king of currency, the US dollar...none of us in this room have any control over its regulation. I suggest that the world is *not* currently set up for mutually beneficial trade.

"While I am only a simple businessman, I am a businessman that knows a great opportunity when he sees one." His audience smiled, some of them with a few seconds delay after the translation finished in their earpiece as Jinshan spoke in his native tongue, Mandarin.

"What we are about to embark on is a great investment for the bankers of the world, but also, what one can only hope will be a great rebalancing for the citizens of the world. Each of you, no doubt, is now well acquainted with the details of cryptocurrency. A few years ago, when bitcoin first came to us, I thought it to be nothing more than a passing flavor. How simpleminded that thinking was. The great transformations of technology always seem preposterous at first glance. Especially to simple old men like myself."

He looked down at the wooden podium, then back at his audience. More polite smiles.

"There are representatives here tonight from many countries. Each of our countries claims its own national currency. We trade our goods, services, our stocks and our bonds in each of these national currencies. And then we trade the actual currencies themselves. We trade our yen for dollars and our euros for rubles. Back and forth and forth and back again."

He raised his voice. "A shell game. And a fickle one at that, with few real advantages. But there is one big one. If you control the king of all currencies, the world is yours to rule. This major advantage is claimed by a nation that is not represented here tonight in this dining hall. The United States dollar is king."

He paused for effect.

"We can complain all we want, but we know it in our hearts to be true. As long as the rest of the world rushes back to the dollar as the global reserve currency, we are slaves to America."

He took another sip of water. He could see that some of them were on guard. Everything had been cordial and superficial in the speeches that came before Jinshan took the stage. Now he was upping the ante. Ears perked up. The nations friendly to America probably didn't want to be associated with someone who wasn't. Well, that notion wouldn't last much longer.

"Gentlemen, I'm an old man. I'm *tired* of this game. Because unless you can control the dollar, which none of us in this room can, then we're each at a disadvantage."

Some nods from the Russians and the Iranians. There was no love lost between America and those groups. The Emiratis looked torn.

"But I'm not here to put any country, even America, at a disadvantage. What I propose to do, with the help of everyone in this room, is to *rebalance* the field. In the past few months, my country's currency has decreased in value by quite a bit. Our stock market has suffered devastating losses. Around the world, we are likely on the verge of yet another economic downturn. And in many countries, inflation pummels the value of our money." He motioned to the Iranian delegation. "A loaf of bread in Tehran was much cheaper a few years ago, was it not?"

One of the Iranians nodded somberly. Another nudged him and he stopped.

"But I say to you, no more! We now have the first volley in the battle for global economic stability. A *digital* currency reserve. One with no national master, its value rooted in indisputable mathematical fairness, not the whims of the bureaucrats. Iran and the UAE will begin backing their currency with bitcoin reserves. As we all know, the Dubai Financial Exchange, which will also trade raw bitcoins, will open within the next forty-eight hours. This has spurred growth in the value of bitcoin itself, and these two brave nations will prosper."

He took another drink of water. He clasped the edge of his podium and leaned in as he spoke. "Now I have some news. I am very excited to announce here today that we have begun negotiations in Beijing for our own country to follow suit. I wanted those of you in this room to hear it first. China, too, will begin holding reserves of bitcoin. Over the next year, we will begin a transition from central regulation of the RMB to a bitcoin-backed currency. It is our hope that the rest of the world will follow. No longer will one nation dictate financial terms to the rest of the world. Bitcoin is as fair a currency as gold. It is scarce, it is secure, and most importantly, it is not regulated by any one government. It is our hope that this practice of using bitcoin to back national currencies will evolve into a single, global, decentralized currency. When that happens, an economic rebalancing will follow."

* * *

"Holy shit," Elliot said. He was on his phone and walked away, into the other room.

Phones began ringing in their room. Everyone began speaking more loudly. Chase could tell something very big had just happened, but he didn't fully understand it.

Elliot looked at Chase and waved him off. He covered the receiver on his cell phone and said, "I need to take this. Call me or text me when you have something more."

Chase gave him a thumbs-up.

Lisa stood up next to Chase. "Well, I knew it would be entertaining, but I didn't realize quite how much so."

"What are the implications of this?"

She raised her eyebrows. "If what Jinshan just said is real, that would be huge news. China shifting to a bitcoin-backed currency would be a game changer."

"How so?"

"When this gets made public, which will probably be any minute now, the sheer volume of Forex trading will drive the value of bitcoin through the roof. That will virtually guarantee stability for other countries that want to follow suit."

"I don't understand. What do you mean, follow suit?"

She said, "Let me put it this way. This could be the first domino in a chain of events that would ultimately dethrone the American dollar. If everyone starts shifting to a bitcoin-backed currency, and then eventually to a single global currency, that could really hurt the United States economically."

"I see." Chase watched the others scramble around the room, speaking on phones and to each other in anxious voices.

Lisa said, "I can take you back now. These guys will be busy getting copies of this speech to everyone who needs it in our government."

"You're leaving? Amidst all of this?"

"Yup. My work here is done."

"And what work was that?"

She smiled. "Who do you think got the video feed in there?"

On the TV, the crowd of dignitaries rose to their feet. They exited the conference room in groups of twos and threes. The screen shifted to a view of a very fancy-looking bar. There were ornate gold-decorated marble pillars, crystal chandeliers, and rows and rows of liquor. So much for the Muslim rules on alcohol.

Chase said, "Where are they?"

"Atlantis—The Palm."

Chase felt like it was wrong for them to leave now. "Isn't there something we could be doing?"

Lisa said, "Just let it play out. This part is neither of our jobs. Come on. Let's get out of here." She brushed her hand up against his, ever so slightly. "Now, are you ready for that drink?"

* * *

Three hours later, Lisa lay naked on top of him. Strands of her long black hair hid one of her eyes. Her smooth skin glistened with sweat. They had caught their breath, their session of love-making finished for now.

Blue moonlight illuminated her apartment bedroom. Chase could hear the late-night sounds of the waterfront out the window. The beach tourist district lay several floors below.

Her fingertips traced the muscles from his shoulder to his bicep. A slow, admiring caress. She said, "I don't mean to ruin the moment, but I need to say something."

"Yes?"

"I just want to make sure you understand that we can't tell anyone about this. Especially not Elliot. You know that, right?"

He looked into her eyes. "I haven't told anyone. And I don't intend to."

She didn't smile, but her eyes did. She said, "I know very little about you."

"I think you've obtained quite a bit of knowledge."

"I mean personal things. I know very little about you personally."

"Have you read my file?"

She said, "I always read up on my marks."

"Is that what I am?"

She got up suddenly, her glorious bare body standing over him while he remained on her floor mattress. She held out a hand. "Come on."

She grabbed the sheet from the bed and a water bottle from the refrigerator. A few moments later they were sitting on chairs on her balcony.

It was a private overhang. No one could see them. Chase could just barely make out the outline of waves crashing against the shore. They sat there, drinking water in silence and looking out at the stars.

She said, "Why'd he bring you here?"

"Elliot?"

"Yes."

Chase looked at her. "A special project."

"I know about the leak."

He didn't say anything.

"Did he tell you not to talk to me about it?"

He felt an uneasiness come over him. A conflict of interest. He already had a pretty big one of those to worry about with his brother.

Chase said, "I'm not supposed to talk about what I'm working on."

"I won't place you in the horrible position of answering the girl you were just sleeping with whether you trust her or not." She wasn't smiling.

"I appreciate that."

She said, "Elliot didn't turn off the cameras in the consulate interview room. One of my subordinates reviews all the interviews that take place there. He brought the one with Gorji's assistant to my attention."

"Why didn't you tell Elliot?"

"He probably already knows that I know. But everyone must follow the process, right? He's following procedures. He can't talk to anyone who works in Dubai Station about it until counterespionage clears them. Tomorrow or the next day I'll be cleared and he'll brief me on everything. Then maybe I'll come to your closed-door meetings."

She winked. Her feet were perched up on the small glass coffee table. The sheet that she was using to cover herself fell a bit to reveal one of her long, toned legs.

"So then what do you think I'm doing here?"

"I'm not completely sure. But if I were him, I would need immediate help with any operations related to the leak. Or to Iran."

"Isn't that everything?"

"He can't shut all the operations down. Procedure says that he is to isolate only the operations that are directly compromised by the leak. Therefore, my money says that Elliot's got you working with the Iranian—Gorji's guy—to find out what information he's got and what he wants for it. Blink twice if I'm close."

He smiled. She was too smart. A thought occurred to him. "Is this why you took me here? To ask me about this?"

She feigned a look of hurt. "You couldn't really believe that."

"I don't."

She smiled. "Oh, alright, my dear. I'll quit pumping you for information."

Then she rose up and walked over to him, the white sheets falling down to the floor. She climbed on top of him, not saying a word. He felt her hands caress the back of his neck.

She whispered, "Well...maybe a just bit more..."

6

Chase opened his eyes to the sound of Lisa grunting nearby. A black pull-up bar was fastened to her closet door. She was cranking out sets of pull-ups. A lot of them. She changed grips every few seconds, swaying, and then starting up again. Her back muscles were very well defined. She wore only a black sports bra and tight runner's shorts. Not the type of outfit that she could get away with if she was to go outside on the streets of Dubai.

He got out from under the covers of her bed and found his clothes strewn about the floor. He grabbed them and headed towards the bathroom. He threw the shower on and found a disposable razor in one of her sink drawers.

"You got any shaving cream?"

"It's under the sink," Lisa replied, all business. She was on to a set of push-ups. She didn't look up at him.

Steam fogged up the mirror. He wiped it away with his hand. He shaved and showered, wondering if she was going to join him. She didn't.

He got out of the shower, dried off, and got dressed in the clothes he had arrived in. He checked his watch. The *Truman* should be moored by now. It was supposed to reach the pier at dawn.

Chase walked into the bedroom. Lisa held her body in some sort of plank yoga move on the floor. She watched him as he walked up to her. He said, "I'm going to get going."

"Would you like a ride? I'm almost finished." No hint of emotion in her voice. She was like a machine.

"No, that's alright. I'm going to just grab a cab. I was actually going to run an errand before heading back to the hotel."

"Alright. I'll see you later, then."

No kiss. No embrace. Chase had no clue how to treat this. He had never met a woman that had been this detached the morning after. "Okay. Thanks." He walked out the front door and took the elevator to the bottom floor.

He headed out of the lobby of the residential high-rise and into the sweltering heat of the city. There was a coffee shop across the street. He ordered a cup of black coffee with two sugars and picked up an English-language version of a newspaper called the *Khaleej Times*.

He flagged a cab and hopped in. Another black Lexus taxi. They were everywhere.

The driver spoke very little English, but Chase was able to convey that he wanted to go to "Jebel Ali...to the Navy ships." The driver nodded and they started off. Chase scanned the headlines of the newspaper and sipped his coffee as they drove.

The articles were mostly about the Dubai Financial Summit.

Monumental Agreements with Iran and UAE Pave Way for New Financial Exchange, read one headline.

Another story raved about this new politician Iran had sent over to broker the deal. A key paragraph in the story read:

Mr. Gorji's progressive politics would normally be hammered down by members of the Iranian regime. But experts credit his marriage to a favored niece of the Iranian Supreme Leader for supercharging his political stock. Some are even suggesting that he may be a presidential hopeful in the next Iranian election. Whatever the case, he has certainly shown the cunning and charm needed to bring together the leaders of the Gulf Nations in this monumental financial summit. One can only hope that this will lead to further peace and trade between nations that have traditionally been at odds.

There was nothing yet about China moving to bitcoin reserves for the yuan.

The cab turned into the port of Jebel Ali. It was bustling with activity. Through the windows, Chase could see stacks and stacks of containers. The containers were being craned onto the large commercial vessels. There were countless ships. Merchants, oil tankers, automobile transports, and natural gas tankers were in various stages of the transportation cycle. Jebel Ali was the largest man-made harbor on earth, and one of the top ten busiest ports on the planet.

They arrived at a ship unlike any other on the pier. The USS *Harry S. Truman*, one of ten active American nuclear aircraft carriers. The *Truman* was a supercarrier, over one thousand feet long, almost as wide as a football field, and as tall as a twenty-four-story building. It towered over the pier, casting a shadow over the many sailors and port logistics contractors that were scurrying below.

Chase paid the cab driver and gave him a generous tip. He marched toward the security gate.

As he walked, Chase could see many of the ninety aircraft in the carrier's complement. Some were packed in like sardines on the hangar deck, which was visible through a series of mammoth openings in its hull. The rest were lined up neatly on the flight deck overhead. Rows of F/A-18 Hornets, E-2C Hawkeyes, and MH-

60 Seahawk helicopters. Many of these aircraft had a set of enlisted maintainers crawling on top of them. These men and women conducted the crucial maintenance needed to keep them flying in the harsh salt air of the Arabian Gulf.

"Can we help you, sir?"

A pair of Navy MPs stood at the security gate, an iron turnstile in between them and Chase. There was a pair of US Marines about fifty feet further down, one with an M-60 on a tripod.

Chase took out his wallet and held up a US Department of State identification card. CIA protocol did not allow him to bring his US Navy-issued Department of Defense card.

"Good morning. My name is Chase Manning. Would you be able to call the *Truman*'s duty officer and let them know that I'm here? I believe that they'll be expecting me." It was easier to leave out the fact that he was an officer than explain why a Navy reservist had a State Department ID card. *Well, you see, boys, I'm kind of a super-secret agent...*

The MP looked over at his companion, who nodded. Then they waited in the sweltering heat. The gate guards were chugging water every few minutes.

Chase thought about what he had learned in the past day. Could David really be giving secrets to the Iranians? Or to whoever was on Abu Musa? And just who was this group on Abu Musa that the Iranians were too scared of to get rid of themselves?

Chase was partly ashamed of himself that he hadn't called his brother. He felt wracked with guilt for not warning David, but his duty came first. Even so, it didn't make any sense that David would be involved in something like that. Chase needed to think about what to do before taking any action that could be irreversible. He told himself that this would all get cleared up.

Chase's brother, David, was a family man. He lived in the suburbs of Northern VA. He had a mechanical engineering degree from the Naval Academy and worked as an analyst for new infor-

mation technology and systems. That sounded boring to an operator like Chase, but the subject of David's analysis was often
anything but. He worked for In-Q-Tel, a firm that invested in technology that the defense and intelligence community was interested in developing for their use. It was essentially the CIA's
venture capital firm.

Chase missed David and wished that he could see more of
him. He also needed to see his two nieces more often. Hell—not to
mention visiting his sister and father. Life always seemed to get in
the way. But unlike David, Chase's sister and father were more like
him. They were deeply invested in their careers of service to their
country. Careers that often took them overseas.

Their older sister, Victoria, was a Navy helicopter pilot
stationed in Jacksonville, Florida. Chase thought he remembered
that she would be going on deployment soon. He wasn't
completely sure, but he thought that she had picked up some
good-deal Eastern Pacific cruise, although it might not seem like a
good deal to her. She would want to be where the action was. She
would want to be here, in the Middle East. Providing air cover for
aircraft carriers as they transited through the Straits of Hormuz.
He should send her an email to check in.

Staying up-to-date on his family's status had been easier when
their mother was alive. She had been the hub of the wheel. The
one that kept everyone else in the know, and smiling.

Her passing had brought the siblings closer for a while. The
emails were a bit more frequent. The phone calls to his brother
and sister, while still few in number, were much more meaningful
in content. But that wore off. Once again, it was getting harder to
stay in touch. Especially for Chase.

He could never really say what he was doing. His siblings
didn't really even know that he now worked for the CIA. They
thought that he was with a Department of State security team.
The story he told them was that he protected VIPs. His father

pretended he didn't know about the job, but Admiral Manning was an old friend of Elliot Jackson's, the Dubai Station chief, so he probably knew. Elliot had been the one who had recruited Chase from the SEALs, and subsequently gotten him stationed in the Dubai area of operations.

The last time Chase had really spent time with his family was on leave for their mother's funeral. That leave coincided with Chase's completion of his training at the CIA's various schools for its Special Operations Group assets. Chase spent that time in the D.C. area—mostly with his brother David and his family.

Athletics and working out always came naturally to Chase and Victoria. But David had been more of the bookworm. After their mother's passing, however, David was struggling pretty hard. Chase had always used running as a way to meditate and de-stress. He hoped that encouraging the habit would help his brother, and by all accounts it had. Chase had helped train David for his first road race, and took pride in his brother's increasing interest and success with triathlons.

Chase had fond memories of that month with David and his family. He was a good brother and a loyal patriot. He had also gone to the Naval Academy, although he had been honorably discharged from the Navy for medical reasons. Chase found it inconceivable that David would betray his country. There had to be more to the story.

Chase was stirred out of his reminiscing by an approaching US Navy commander. The man, who wore the digital blue camouflage uniform with a silver oak leaf on the front of his cover, walked up to the gate. He had a Surface Warfare insignia pin on his chest and looked to be about as happy as one would expect after pulling duty on a day when his ship had just pulled into port near Dubai.

"Are you Chase Manning?"

"I am."

"Petty Officer, please log him in as my guest and get him a pass. I'll escort him."

"Yes, sir."

As he and the commander walked, Chase looked up at the carrier. He had been on board an aircraft carrier several times during his days as a SEAL. They were floating cities. Five thousand people, living on top of each other for nine months at a time. The galleys had to cook food almost around the clock. One whole deck of the ship was reserved for cooking and eating. Grown men and women in triple bunks, with only a few inches of space between each other where they slept. A small locker for all one's belongings. Almost zero privacy. Waiting in line to use the bathroom or a treadmill. The deafening sound of jets launching and recovering all day and night. That was life on a carrier.

He could see the three 20mm Phalanx Close-In Weapons System mounts. They looked like R2-D2 with an enormous Gatling gun protruding out. They were used as a last resort for shooting down inbound missiles. Deep in the hull, there were two Westinghouse A4W nuclear reactors on board, and the ship could steam more than three million miles before refueling.

They walked up the gangway stairs, climbing thirty feet or so just to get high enough to walk across. The commander looked back at him and said, "So when did you get in to Dubai?"

Chase said, "Just recently." No need to elaborate. The commander likely thought that he was a civilian.

"Well, it sure was nice of you to make it out," he said. "Given the circumstances."

Chase didn't reply.

They climbed up aluminum stairs to reach the gangway. Just before crossing the gangway to the hangar deck, the commander halted, turned, and saluted the flag. He then returned the salute of the armed enlisted man waiting to check both of their IDs as they came aboard. The petty officer gave the commander a funny look when he saw Chase's ID, but the commander told him that it was okay.

Chase continued following the commander as they went through throngs of men and women who were waiting in line to leave the ship on their much-deserved liberty. They came to a large grey steel hatch and twisted open a two-foot steel bar to unlatch it. They entered through it, closed and locked it, then climbed into a vertical shaft with ladders going all the way up and down the ship. Chase was already several steps behind. Carriers were a maze if you didn't know where you were going. The commander was half-walking, half-climbing up the ladder well.

"Sir, can you hold up?"

The commander stopped in between ladders.

"Before we see him, I just wanted to ask you a question. If you don't mind, perhaps we could keep it between us?"

The commander looked around. They could hear echoes of people clanking up the metal stairs from several decks below. "Sure."

"Can you tell me what happened? The real story?"

The commander shifted. He put his hands on his hips and looked Chase in the eye. "There's an investigation going on, son. So, no, I really can't. But know this. I've served under your old man for almost three years. He's a hell of a warfighter, and a great leader."

"But?"

"But...it's a kinder, gentler Navy. And your father rules with an iron fist."

Chase said, "I'm aware."

The commander smiled. "I'm sure you are." He checked his watch. "Listen, your old man's taking the fall here. But there isn't an E-2 through O-6 on this ship that wouldn't give his left nut to take his place if it meant saving your dad's ass. He's loved by his men, and with good reason. He makes us work hard, but we're better for it. He's the last of a breed. They don't make 'em like that anymore."

Chase nodded. "Yeah. Thanks, sir."

"No sweat. Sorry, bud. Your dad's a good man. Everyone in the battle group knows it. And if it was up to us, he'd be staying." The commander turned and they continued on up.

Several decks up, they opened another hatch and Chase stared out onto an expansive flight deck. It was like standing on a huge parking lot surrounded by a vast drop-off in every direction. It was incredibly hot up here. The sun cooked the dark surface of the flight deck, and the men and women who worked in it.

He followed the commander to one of the helicopters, an MH-60R. A young sailor in a blue vest and an older man in a flight suit were lying on their stomachs on top of the metal aircraft. They both had protective headgear on, and they were perched about twelve feet up from the deck of the carrier. The man in the flight suit had a single white star on each shoulder.

The commander cleared his throat. "Sir, he's here."

The admiral looked down. A slight smile formed on his sweat-soaked face.

Chase didn't really know what to say. "Hi, Dad."

"That will be all, Commander," Admiral Manning said. "One moment, Chase." He said something to the mechanic he was with and then started climbing down the helicopter.

The commander turned to leave and then whispered to Chase, "That's something else about your old man. I've never seen a flag officer turn the wrenches with the young enlisted guys like that. As busy as he is, that's unbelievable. He cares about his men, and he sits with them in the trenches. I hope that one day I'm half the officer that he is." The man shook his head as he walked away.

Admiral Manning got down and took off his protective head-gear and gloves, then embraced his son. For a brief moment,

Chase thought he saw sadness in his father's eyes. Then the steel look crept back over him.

"It's good to see you, son. Thanks for coming. Elliot contacted me and mentioned that you might be in town."

"Yes, he asked me to send his regards."

"He's a good man."

"Are you hungry?"

Chase said, "Sure."

"Follow me."

They walked down several decks. Chase followed his father. Everything looked the same. The entire ship was one big maze of tubes and pipes, passageways and ladders. How anyone could find their way around an aircraft carrier was beyond him.

Then the admiral opened a blue door with a gold placard marked *CSG HST*. Commander, Strike Group, *Harry S. Truman*.

His father sat behind an ornate wooden desk. His computer had a big red SECRET sticker just below the keyboard. The phone rang as the two men sat down on opposite sides of the desk.

His father picked it up. "Manning."

A pause while some young ensign, no doubt pissing himself because he had to speak to the admiral, gave him a report.

"Okay. Thank you."

Admiral Manning hung up, then picked the phone back up and dialed a five-digit number. "Hello, CS1, this is the admiral, how are you this morning? Would you be able to rustle up some breakfast for two? Thank you kindly. Have a great day, CS1."

After he placed the phone back down, Chase asked, "Have you heard from David?"

"Yes. I spoke to him and Lindsay on the phone this morning, actually. He tells me that the new baby is doing well. I just missed her birth, unfortunately. We had to leave that week. That is one aspect of all this nonsense that will work out in my favor, I suppose. I'll finally be able to see my granddaughters."

Chase squirmed in his chair. "Dad, I'm very sorry to hear about—"

"Don't." The admiral held up his hand. "There's nothing anyone can do about it." He pointed at the star on his shoulder. "This whole thing is a crapshoot anyway. There were better men than me that didn't make O-6. All you can do is prepare and be ready when fate comes a-knocking."

They sat in silence for a moment. Chase said, "What about Victoria? Have you heard from her?"

"She deploys this week, actually. I sent her an email. She didn't write back."

"Probably busy."

"Probably."

No one in the family could articulate exactly why or when Admiral Manning's relationship with his daughter had grown strained, but it had. Perhaps it was because they were so much alike. Both fierce leaders, always wanting to be in control and make their own way. Victoria resented any suggestion that her success in the Navy had come from either her father being an admiral, or her sex being female.

She was just like their father, Chase thought. She kept her emotions inside, and her sense of self-worth was derived from her career. She never bragged about her successes. That wasn't what drove her. She wanted command. As often and as high up as her bright career would take her. And Victoria wanted it based on her own merit.

Father and daughter had gotten into more than a few arguments over the years. They were each too proud to back down, when that happened. Ironically, Victoria was probably the thing in life that Admiral Manning was most proud of. And now she wasn't returning his emails. Chase would have to say something to her.

The door opened and two enlisted men in black culinary

uniforms with CSG HST MESS inscribed across their chests wheeled in a food cart. They placed a sterling silver pot of coffee on a small table next to the desk. Then they laid out two place settings and placed plates with eggs, sausage, toast, and jam on the table. The toast looked like cheap white bread from a grocery store, and the sausage looked like a rock. It wasn't the Four Seasons. But the men that delivered it were doing their best with what they were given.

"Thanks, guys," said Chase.

The admiral thanked them as well, and then they were off. Chase and his father ate.

They continued making small talk about Chase's brother and sister. The admiral was happy to hear that David was doing well at his civilian job in D.C. It was no secret that he wasn't thrilled that his son had resigned his commission. It had been conceivable that he could have stayed in the Navy as a restricted warfare officer. He could have been in the supply corps or perhaps the construction battalion, often referred to as the Seabees. But David had not been interested.

Their mother had supported his decision. And she had been thrilled when David had settled down in the D.C. area, less than an hour from Mrs. Manning's home. The admiral rarely made it back there.

Admiral Arthur Louis Manning IV was a career Navy man, and he was damn good at it. A warrior at heart, he had made no secret about where his priorities lay. It was his job to protect and serve. It was their mother's job to raise their three gifted children. There would be time to spend with his wife and family after he retired. Or so they all had thought. Mrs. Manning had spent the last years of her life caring for her only grandchild, David's first daughter. Mrs. Manning had died unexpectedly a little less than a year ago. Heart disease.

Admiral Manning said, "So, I know that you can't talk about it, but how are you liking your new line of work?"

Chase smiled. "At the State Department?"

His father tilted his head. "Come, now. I won't ask for details. But I knew Elliot when he first entered the CIA out of the Navy. And I know my son."

Chase nodded. "It's an adjustment. Different than the teams. But I like it. It's...it's like I'm playing a different sport. It still requires certain skills. I just need to develop a different set of them than I was using with the SEALs."

"That's a good analogy. I've always found that when the Navy moved me to different assignments, it would take the first few months to really get acclimated to the new role." He paused, a bit of sausage on his fork, halfway to his mouth. "I'm proud of you, Chase."

Now Chase was really worried. His father never spoke like that. Chase said, "Dad, can you at least tell me what happened?"

His father looked like he was pondering it. Then he looked at the wall, as if he was seeing it play out in his memory.

"I'm not supposed to—but my guess is that your clearance is at least as high as mine. I got a report of a submarine and an Iranian PC boat right next to each other off of Abu Musa. I sat next to the battle watch captain during the entire event. It boggles the mind to think that so much of our command and control is via typed instant messages back and forth between our units. Yet that's the way it happens nowadays when the shit hits the fan. I swear it was easier in the Cold War. People still used radios back then. And they're supposed to still, but it's redundant and slower to do so. Now we just watch events unfold in real time in little bits of text. If we're lucky, there is a video feed, but so often there is not. A surfaced sub. That's what the initial report was."

"I heard that. But I thought that signals intelligence confirmed all Iranian subs were in port."

The admiral nodded. "They did. More than just SIGINT. We actually have satellite pictures of each and every Iranian submarine. So the Pentagon has concluded that there *was* no submarine off Abu Musa. CENTCOM believes that the lookout on the *Porter* was seeing things. But the good general has never served aboard a ship."

"I take it that you disagree."

"I've made my case to Fifth Fleet and CENTCOM. But I had no video evidence, no pictures, to back up the sailor's sighting. Iran says we fired first at one of their innocent patrol boats, destroying it unprovoked. The men and women on that destroyer will tell you a different story. But they're being told to keep their mouths shut while the investigation is going on."

"That's crazy. Why?"

"Because when you play the game at this level, it's about more than just the simple truth. It's about the infinite political ramifications. The politicians feel that it's in our best interests to take it on the chin here. There is a lot of pressure to improve the US-Iran relationship. A lot of pressure."

Chase shook his head. "I can't believe that. I mean...I can't believe that our own leadership would go with Iran's story over what our own sailors saw."

"Perhaps if there was more compelling video evidence. But there is not...so this little incident is going to be swept under the rug, and we're going to let the Iranian military harass us just a little bit more in the Arabian Gulf. Courageous Restraint. That's what we're calling it now. It's in our doctrine. Hell. I support the decisions of those men that pulled the trigger. They knew what they saw. Whether there was a sub or not, it doesn't matter. If they were being shot at, they had every right to fire back. You can't second-guess the men on the ground, especially if you weren't there."

"I hear you."

The admiral looked at his son and said, "Sometimes I think that I was meant for a different time. No officer worth his salt ever really wants to be at war. But sometimes I think that I would have been better suited to the days of real sea combat. Not this institutional hogwash that I have to deal with today. I'm not meant for the diplomatic side of the Navy. And that is the type of man that becomes a four-star today."

Chase said, "I'm sorry, Dad." He didn't know what else to say.

"It's alright. I appreciate you coming to see me. I'll be flying back to the States tomorrow, tail between my legs. I'm relieved, effective immediately. They aren't calling it that. Not with me. They're letting me save a little face. I'll be replaced with a two-star that has experience with Fifth Fleet Carrier ops. Good guy. He'll do well."

"Where are they sending you?"

"Norfolk. They're going to put me in charge of the *Ford* until I retire."

"The *Ford*? Isn't she almost operational?"

"Not quite yet. She's still in sea trials. I'll be a figurehead. I'll be like the Queen of England for America's newest state-of-the-art supercarrier. With no enemy in sight. They're putting me out to pasture. I'm not sure why they're giving it to me, but I'll take it."

Chase suspected that his father still had good friends in high places, and that the *Ford* was their way of throwing him a bone. His father had never been the same since his mother died. A part of him had gone with her. The other admirals knew that. And whether his father admitted it, he was a part of that good old boy network. He was just an unwilling participant in it.

They finished their breakfast and made more small talk over coffee.

Chase said, "Dad, do you mind if I ask you something?"

"Of course. Go ahead."

"Have you ever had a situation where one of your good friends was suspected of wrongdoing, but you thought he was innocent? And you had the power to influence the outcome?"

He gave him a funny look. "I'm sure something like that has happened. But you know where I stand. It doesn't matter if they're a friend. If they did something wrong, they should answer for it."

"What if you weren't sure if they really did anything wrong, but turning them in would ruin their career?"

"What are we talking about here?"

"Just a hypothetical. I need to play a little catch-ball."

"I'm not going to be telling you anything you don't know already. Go to your friend and find out the truth."

Chase hesitated. "What if it were a close friend? Even family?"

He looked alarmed. "Chase...what are you talking about?" The admiral crossed his arms and looked at him out of the side of his eye. "You know where I stand on family too. Family always comes first. Everything else is a game. Now will you tell me what's going on? Who are we talking about?"

"Just a problem a friend has. I just wanted to get a smart old man to give me some sage advice."

The admiral laughed, but he looked like he didn't buy it. He did let it go, though, for which Chase was grateful. He looked at his watch again and asked his father if he would have any free time in Dubai before he left. Perhaps they could meet up in the city? His father politely declined. They walked out to the pier and bid each other goodbye.

Walking down the pier toward the white government duty van that would take him back to Dubai, Chase's phone vibrated.

"Manning."

"Chase. It's Waleed. Where are you?" He sounded tense. Upset.

"Good morning, Waleed. I'm—"

"I'm texting you an address. Get here as soon as you can."

"Why, what's happened?"

"It looks like we were too late. Pakvar got our man."

7

24 Hours Earlier

Cheng Jinshan looked across the desk of the best oncologist in Dubai. He was also one of the best in the world, but that was not why Jinshan had sought him out for this examination. It was for his discretion. Jinshan knew that there were people in China who would love to know that he had a deadly form of cancer. He had made many enemies while serving as the head of China's Central Commission for Discipline Inspection—the government body that had been formed to root out all corruption in Chinese politics. These enemies would use his cancer against him. He could not allow that.

"So you are sure? There is no other test that you need to run to confirm this new information?"

The doctor shook his head. "I'm sorry. But I have seen this many times."

"But...what you were saying about the survival rate. Is there further testing that could allow me to know where I sit on the spectrum?"

"Given when we identified this, the one-year survival rate for this type of cancer of the pancreas is approximately twenty to twenty-five percent."

"And if I am within that twenty-five percent? How long could I possibly have?"

"The five-year survival rate is about five to six percent."

"Does this include surgery?"

"Unfortunately, the malignancy has progressed beyond the point where surgical removal is possible. We will continue to monitor it to see how fast it is growing. The treatment that I would recommend is a combination of radiation and chemotherapy. The goal of this treatment is to relieve painful cancer sites and slow the rate of tumor growth."

Jinshan looked past the doctor, out his window. The tall buildings of Dubai sprang up around them. "I thought I would have more time."

The doctor said, "With treatment, you can maximize your time, Mr. Jinshan. That is my recommendation."

Jinshan got up and held out his hand. "Thank you, Doctor. I will be in touch."

The doctor shook his hand. "How long are you in town? We will need to set up a schedule for treatment if that is how you elect to proceed."

Jinshan nodded somberly. "I understand. I will be in town for a few more days. I will contact you." He walked out of the office and was immediately flanked by two security men and his personal assistant. While his assistant no doubt had many important things to tell him, he had the good sense to remain quiet after this appointment.

When they finally got into his car, his assistant said, "Lena Chou has requested to speak with you, sir."

He was staring out the window. "Did she?" He turned, a glimmer of life in his eye. "When is she available?"

"I hope you don't mind, but I have made arrangements for a phone call with her now. She told me that it was very important."

Jinshan said, "I want to see her in person."

His assistant gave him a surprised look. "A face-to-face? In Dubai, sir? Is that wise?"

Jinshan looked at his assistant coldly.

"I'll set it up right now, sir." He looked at his watch. "She had to be in the north of the city to meet with Mr. Pakvar. We'll have to go there." He said something to the driver, and he turned the direction of the vehicle.

Jinshan turned back to the window, watching the buildings as they traveled by.

Cheng Jinshan was a very busy man. As a successful businessman and investor, he had influenced the fledgling AIIB to finance the Dubai Financial Exchange. He oversaw the operations of a very secretive Chinese cyberwarfare organization. After some behind-the-scenes arm-twisting, he had been appointed by the Chinese president as head of the Central Commission for Discipline Inspection. This had allowed him to root out the politicians and government appointees that he felt would not serve China well in the coming shift to a wartime nation. Jinshan had also masterminded Lena's soon-to-be-created American Red Cell on a Chinese military base island in the South China Sea. He was a busy man, indeed.

A busy man's most precious asset was his time. Something the doctor had informed him he would soon be out of.

* * *

Jinshan's car parked in the parking garage of one of the less-crowded buildings near the Dubai World Trade Centre.

Lena stood alone in the dark garage, her arms folded across her chest. Jinshan's car door opened and his assistant and security men got out, allowing Lena to enter. The soundproof glass between the driver and the rear seat was up.

"It is good to see you, my dear Lena."

She smiled. "And you, sir."

"What did you need to speak with me about?"

"I need your guidance and assistance. Mr. Pakvar and I are now in possession of a man who we believe was working for the CIA. A source, not an agent."

"You believe? Why are you not sure?"

"The information that we have uncovered points to a small operation between Elliot Jackson, the Dubai Station chief, and a Waleed Hajjar, a UAE intelligence officer. As far as I know, they were the only two people who had any knowledge of this source."

"What is the significance that would have you bring this to me?"

"This source placed an NSA-written worm within the Dubai Financial Exchange. It would allow the American government to gain tracking information on all bitcoin and bitcoin-backed currency transactions."

Cheng Jinshan frowned. "I see," he said. "I must say, I am disappointed that they would take this action. It leads me to believe that they may be aware of what our Abu Musa team has been doing. But I am pleased to hear that you have this source in your possession. Tell me, Lena, what guidance do you seek? Please be clear for a simple old man."

"I plan to extract the required information from him to ensure that we can proceed as planned with the Abu Musa operation. I will have him provide us any information on the NSA-created program. I will need to get you this information so that your cyberwarfare team can reverse-engineer it. With luck, we can turn this into an advantage."

He considered this a moment. Then he said, "Approved. Anything else?"

"No, sir." Jinshan could see that she knew something was up, or else he would not have requested to see her in person. But she was patient and disciplined. She remained quiet.

"Lena, you have been one of my greatest successes over the years."

"You are too kind, sir."

"I have received notice that an important piece of hardware did not make it from the Iranian patrol craft to the submarine that has been working on the underwater fiber-optic cables."

Lena's eyes narrowed. "How does that affect our schedule?"

"We may no longer have the ability to physically link in our Abu Musa network to the cables."

"That is concerning."

"Yes. We will need to look for other opportunities to tap into the Dubai Bitcoin Exchange."

"I will explore all options and keep you informed."

"Thank you, Lena." He sighed. "What of the Red Cell? Is everything still on track?"

"Yes, sir. Operations commence within the month."

"Good."

"Is everything alright, sir?"

He looked at her, a sadness welling up inside of him. "Yes, everything is fine. We just need to ensure that we execute on time."

* * *

An hour later, Lena sat cross-legged on the folding chair, staring at her prey.

She loved watching their eyes as they began to figure out that they had no hope. She could never tell anyone this, of course. Others wouldn't understand the source of her pleasure, although she was sure that she wasn't alone. Pakvar here, for instance, killed for pleasure. She was sure of it. But the crowds that she normally ran with were more...proper. Thus, she had to keep these moments of inner delight to herself.

The two men Pakvar had brought with him were doing fine without her help, so she could sit. Their prisoner was suspended naked in midair by a rope tied to the rafters of the half-finished building. His wrists bound, his body dipped into the empty fifty-five-gallon polyethylene drum. His mouth was taped shut.

They all wore protective clothing and safety glasses and had access to gas masks.

With all the construction in Dubai, it was easy to find a location. There was one man in the hallway, monitoring the elevators and stairways. But this high up, visitors wouldn't be a problem. They had shut off the security cameras just prior to arrival. This floor of the building was unfinished. The floor-to-ceiling windows that would make up the exterior of the skyscraper were absent. It gave the impression of being up in the clouds. While their floor was expansive, it fell off into the air like an infinite pool, dozens of stories up. The wind would help with the ventilation.

Pakvar's men handed out gas masks. They even placed one on their prisoner, removing the tape over his mouth.

Lena stood, looking at the man. She put one finger over her lips to indicate that he was to remain quiet.

Pakvar's men had four hot plates set up. They were using industrial-sized cooking pots—unpressurized. This meant that they would only be able to get the lye to just above boiling. That was okay, but the process would take longer. The bottles had large red-and-yellow warning markings on them. The men poured the liquid into the large pots and heated it until just above boiling.

Lena spoke to the prisoner. "I want you to answer some questions. If you do this, you will live. If you do not answer my questions, or if I think you are lying to us, I will begin pouring the lye into this drum. It will be very unpleasant." Pakvar had put his phone down. He stood behind her, arms crossed.

The naked prisoner nodded.

"Do you work with the Americans?"

No movement.

She put a glove on, walked over to one of the pots of boiling liquid, and carefully carried it over to the fifty-five-gallon drum. Pakvar took the other side and they poured the liquid into the drum. It sloshed around the bottom and began to coat his feet.

The man screamed inside his mask.

Lena said, "This is a highly basic liquid. Do you know what that means? If you understand chemistry, you will know that a very strong base can dissolve your flesh."

The prisoner's eyes were streaming with tears. Through the mask he said, "Please let me go."

Lena tilted her head, smiling under her mask. "The process is much more effective if you can heat the lye to at least three hundred degrees Fahrenheit. We are heating up gallons of it. After all, we don't want this to take all day."

She held her hand out to the boiling vats. The Iranian men stood staring back at them, their eyes impassive. Pakvar looked at his watch.

Lena's heart beat faster. She enjoyed the chase, but it appeared that this would be a quick victory. This man was clearly broken. "Do you work for the Americans?"

He nodded and whimpered. "Yes."

"What were you going to give them?"

"An external hard drive. With data from the Dubai Financial Exchange. Where I work. It would give them access to transactional data, so they could see where the money is flowing."

"Who were you going to provide this information to?"

"I don't know him by name. I just know the time and location where we were supposed to meet."

"Where is this hard drive now?"

"It is in my apartment. Under my bed, in a box."

"Is it locked?"

He nodded. "Yes. The key is on my key chain."

She looked over at the Iranian men. One of them walked behind the set of hot plates and grabbed one of several duffle bags. Inside the bags were all the contents from his apartment, which they had removed in the early morning. The Iranian man came back with the box and a key.

Lena said, "This is it?"

The prisoner nodded. He yelled, "It burns my feet! Please make it stop burning!"

She peered over the top of the drum, seeing his feet, red and slimy. The basic solution was eating through his skin. His toes were a bloody mass.

"Please listen. Is this all the information? There are no copies?"

He said, "Yes. That's everything. The Americans didn't want me to make any copies."

She looked at Pakvar. He opened the small wooden box. It looked like a jewelry case. He removed the lone object inside, the external hard drive. Then he walked fifty feet away, near an open window, and removed his mask. He took out a laptop from his pack and booted it up, then plugged in the hard drive to the laptop.

Pakvar held his phone to his ear. He said, "It's me. I'm logging in now. I need you to check something out. Let me know if it's everything we need, or if you think there is more."

Lena looked back at their prisoner. This was everything. She could tell by the fear in his eyes. He was giving them all that he knew. He would sell his own mother right now.

They waited in silence. Pakvar holding the phone. The other two Iranians cooking the lye. Everyone wearing gas masks. The prisoner crying, naked—his fat hairy chest heaving. Bloody toes swirling in the pool of reddening hot sludge below.

At last, Pakvar said, "Okay. We'll call you if we need anything else."

He pressed the screen and placed the phone back in his pocket. He looked at Lena. "Natesh thinks we're good. He said that this should be it."

"That was quick." She smiled and looked back at her prey. "As much as I would love to stay, I have to leave." Then she turned to Pakvar. "Please take the bags of his belongings and burn them. Not here. Finish questioning him and don't leave any evidence."

Pakvar looked at the man and grinned. "Time to finish our work here. The nice lady is leaving." The only noise in the room was the sound of the boiling liquid and the sobbing man.

He looked at Lena and said, "Please, will you let me go? You said that if I cooperated, you would let me go."

She smiled and tilted her head. "Yes, I did say that. But you see, in my position, sometimes I have to tell lies in order to tease out the truth. I am most sorry."

He cried harder. He said, "Why are you doing this?"

She took a deep breath. She looked thoughtful. "To help forge a better world."

Then Lena winked at the soon-to-be-dead man and walked out.

A part of her wanted to stay and watch. The part of her that no one could understand. The next pot would get the liquid up to midcalf. It would be excruciating pain. But pretty soon after that the blood would begin to drain from his upper extremities and he would lose consciousness. All the fun would be over. Alas, she just didn't have the time.

8

"Are you alright?"

"I will be."

Chase took another sip from his glass. Lisa had arrived at his hotel fifteen minutes ago. They were done with work for the day, and he was in need of something to take his mind off what he had seen.

He stood in the pool, the water chest-high, his arms laid out over the white-and-gold mosaic tile on the edge. He held his glass with both hands. She sat down on the rim of the pool next to him, wearing a black halter swim dress and looking great in it.

They sat there for a while, not saying anything. He directed a thousand-yard stare into the ocean. Chase was glad for the quiet. He was disturbed by what he had seen today and needed to be with someone. But he wanted to let the alcohol and the cool pool water do its work on him a little while longer before they talked about it.

She saw that his drink was done. "What's your room number and what are you drinking?"

He told her the room number and said, "I'll take an old-fashioned. Get yourself one too, if you want. It's better to drink with company." He offered a weak grin.

She returned from the pool bar and set the glasses down on the tile. Then she gracefully plopped into the water next to him. She went under, wetting her long black hair, and threw it over her shoulders. He watched her swim back up to the side of the pool. She was very well put together. More than just sexy. She looked like a natural athlete. That was probably what had first attracted him to her.

She saw him checking her out and smiled. Then her look changed and she took a sip from her drink. "You can tell me about everything now. The counterespionage team cleared me today. You can check with Elliot if you need to."

The look in her eye suggested that she was hoping he would trust her.

He was drained, and a little drunk. He decided to trust her, so he told her the gist of it. He'd spent most of his day at the crime scene. Waleed had received a call earlier from one of the Dubai police detectives who had been told to inform him of any violent crimes, and they'd arrived at a skyrise that was still under construction.

"Pakvar and his goons had strung him up from the rafters."

"Who's Pakvar?"

"An Iranian that we're after. Connected to this Abu Musa business."

"The Navy stuff?"

"No, not that. Something else. We had a source that we were going to get information from. A man that Elliot had planted within the Dubai Financial Exchange. When we got to him, he was hung over a plastic barrel and...it was sickening." Chase looked out over the water.

She said, "If you don't want to talk about it, it's alright."

"They used some type of acid, I think. The lower half of his

116

ANDREW WATTS

body had melted away. You could actually see the bottom half of his skeleton in places."

Her hand went up over her mouth. "Oh my God."

"He had something he was supposed to give us that would let us monitor the new exchange. We had given him some software to load into their system. It was going to help us monitor any bitcoin-backed currency. They carved something in his chest, too. It looked like it might have been an American flag. They were sending us a message. It was just a bloody mess. I don't know what kind of people would do something like this."

"That's awful. Were you able to get what you needed from the man before they killed him?"

"No." He realized he was being a bit too loose-lipped. "We probably shouldn't talk about it anymore."

"Alright." She rubbed his back muscles and around his neck. Then she took his glass and placed it down on the edge of the pool. She took his hands and wrapped his arms around her. They kissed in the pool, oblivious to the world around them.

She asked, "Am I helping you get your mind off it?"

Chase said, "It's certainly helping." He reached for his drink and took a final swig, crunching one of the ice cubes in his teeth. "Let's stay out here all night."

She laughed. "Fine by me."

A poolside servant came by and they asked for two more drinks and a menu for food. An hour later, the sun was setting and they had finished off two more rounds of drinks, as well as a platter of appetizers. They stopped talking about work. Well, about their current work anyway. They traded stories about their past. About old assignments and duty stations. Funny stories and interesting events from previous missions. Chase realized that her work and attitude were very similar to his own. She was a warrior, driven by a sense of duty and honor. He admired her very much.

A custodian lit tiki torches on the perimeter of the pool as night crept closer.

"Would you like to take a walk on the beach?" he asked.

"Sure."

They bumped into each other as they stepped, giggling drunk as they walked along the sand. About a half mile down, Lisa sat down in the light surf and Chase came up next to her. A handful of people swam in the beach in front of them.

Lisa said, "Tell me about your family."

So he did. Chase told her all about their Navy history and his father being the admiral who had just been relieved of command. He suspected that she already knew that, but she seemed to be surprised and impressed. He also told her about their mother dying and Victoria being deployed and David...

"What do you mean, he was on the list?"

Oh shit. He shouldn't have let that slip.

"It was..." He tried to find the right words, but he had consumed too many drinks. Plus, it was just so much easier to tell the truth. "I met with Gorji's man. He said he had a list of people that were going to give information to them on the island."

"What island?"

"Abu Musa. What other island is there?"

She shrugged.

"Anyway, so apparently this list of Americans contains the names of informants. Traitors or something. So then before he leaves he gives me an envelope. He says that the reason they wanted to speak to me is because I know someone on the list. That I can verify that the list is real, because the person I know will be able to prove it or something."

Lisa seemed much more sober than he did, which was both extraordinary and concerning. She said, "And you're saying that your brother David was on this list?"

"He handed me the envelope, and the name David Manning was written on it. Yes."

"Hmm." She looked down at the sand for a moment and then said, "And what did Elliot say when you told him this?"

"He said not to talk to David. That he had to run it up the chain or some bullshit. I feel like such a traitor. He's my brother. He would never do anything like that. I have no idea if there really is a list or why he would be on it. Even Elliot knows that it might be some misinformation play. But I've got to keep quiet for now. It was either betray David or my country. I guess I'm just too well trained."

She raised her eyebrows. "I see."

"What do you think I should do?"

"Well, legally I would suggest that you obey Elliot."

He sighed. He knew that she was right.

"But personally," she added, "I wouldn't leave it alone, either."

He said, "What *would* you do, then?"

"Do your homework and gather more information. But I wouldn't say anything to David. Whether he is or is not doing something that he shouldn't be, you talking directly to him would not be appropriate. Where did you say he works?"

"A company called In-Q-Tel."

"Right. Okay, I'll tell you what. I'm headed to D.C. in a few days for work. I'll be there for a couple weeks."

"Really?"

He was surprised. She hadn't said anything to him until now. Not that she had to. It wasn't like they were dating or anything.

"I know someone at Langley who interacts with In-Q-Tel. I could have him discreetly check up on David for you. If he turns anything up, I'll bring it back to you and we can talk about next steps. If my contact doesn't find anything, then there is probably nothing to find. Either way, I don't agree with Elliot's suggestion that you leave it all to him. I couldn't do that, if it was my family."

Chase nodded. "I mean, after Elliot runs it up the chain, I think that we'd be doing this sort of thing anyway, right? Doing our due diligence on him and anyone else on that list."

"Exactly. Consider this a professional courtesy. If Elliot finds out, I'll tell him that we didn't want to bother him with it since he's got so much going on."

He felt a wave of relief spread over him. "Thanks, Lisa."

She leaned forward and kissed him. "No problem."

She pulled him up from the sand so that they were standing again, and then into the water. Chase hoped that Lisa could bring him good information, which would clear David. As they floated in the waves, buoyant in the high-salinity Gulf Sea, he tried not to think of the horrors that he had seen earlier in the day.

9

Chase took another painkiller and guzzled water down before getting out of Waleed's car. He was just about over his hangover from the drinking he'd done with Lisa the night before, but he needed to be completely clear-headed now.

As Chase followed Waleed into the Mall of Dubai, he could hear the Muslim call to prayer echoing over outdoor loudspeakers from a temple a few blocks away.

It was his first time here, and the mall was every bit as impressive as he had heard. As they walked inside, he passed by an indoor ice rink, a hundred-foot-high indoor waterfall, multiple luxury hotels, a train station, movie theaters, and a long line that led to tours of the tallest building in the world, the Burj Khalifa.

Tourists were everywhere. The place was packed. Lines were long, but the diverse crowds were smiling for the most part.

"Where is this meeting spot?"

Waleed pointed up ahead. "There. Let us go."

Chase looked down a long blue tunnel. It was part of the indoor aquarium, which lay on the other side. The tunnel was all glass, rising up around him in a circle of aquamarine. Small sharks and schools of tropical fish swam over and around him.

Chase walked into the middle of the thirty-foot-long tunnel. Gorji's assistant waited at the far side. He indicated that they should follow.

Coming out of the aquarium tunnel, the three men walked along the giant glass aquarium wall. To their left, a two-level metallic grey observation deck wrapped around the giant fish tank, the throngs of onlookers illuminated by the blue light. Those observation decks were just a part of the mall, extending from the stores nearby. To their right, the glass wall of the aquarium rose up at least fifty feet. It radiated a dancing spectrum of beautiful blues. Exotic fish, rays, and the occasional shark swam by large sections of bright coral. It was a loud scene, with children hollering and tourists talking and snapping pictures with their smartphones.

Gorji's man walked into one of the stores on the lower level. It was a slender cigar shop. A custodian had been standing at the door, and he shut the entrance behind them, locking the door and flipping over a Closed sign.

He directed Chase to the humidor room, where a skinny man with curly black hair and a rich suit perused the most expensive cigars. Gorji.

"I thought it would be just you," Gorji said, not yet looking at Chase or Waleed.

He spoke in polished English. His assistant had closed the door behind them. Waleed, Chase, and Mr. Ahmad Gorji of the Islamic Republic of Iran stood alone in the humidor room. Cigar boxes were stacked up in rows, four high.

Chase said, "Mr. Waleed Hajjar is working with me on this."

Gorji turned to look at them. "He is UAE intelligence. They can't be trusted." He selected a long, thick cigar and held it up to his nostrils, inhaling deeply.

Waleed was smiling widely. So was Gorji.

Chase said, "What's going on?"

Waleed and Gorji embraced and then began speaking rapidly in Arabic. It was too fast for Chase to follow.

Waleed looked up at Chase. "Now you know. And you are one of a very few who do. Ahmad is a dear friend. We grew up together."

"Grew up together? Where?"

Waleed said, "In Iran. I was born there. My father died when I was young. My mother immigrated to Dubai when I was just a boy. She had relatives here. She remarried. For many years, Ahmad and I kept in touch. But recently, we have been forced to be more discreet with our friendship."

"Does Elliot know about this?"

Waleed shook his head. "I do not want to risk anyone knowing about this."

"And that's why you had him approach the CIA instead of you?"

Ahmad Gorji said, "This is how I knew where to approach the CIA. I decided that this was the best course of action. I am privy to intelligence documents in my country. I knew that you were stationed in the UAE, and that your brother was on the list. It was the only way I knew of to prove to the Americans that my information was legitimate. I assume that you have examined your brother's communications?"

Chase frowned. "I'm looking into it. But we are taking your claim seriously based on the Dubai leak that you uncovered."

Gorji said, "So you haven't evaluated your brother's activities?"

"Not personally."

"Why, may I ask?"

"You may not."

Gorji looked at Waleed, then back at Chase. "I can tell you with certainty that he was on the list I saw. I don't know your brother, but I understand your loyalty to him. Based on my knowledge of the situation, however, I strongly believe that he will be giving information to the men on the island. That is what I was told by my source on Abu Musa."

Chase said, "Let's talk about that. What is going on there? On Abu Musa?"

Gorji gestured to the group of thick leather chairs in the center of the room. "Come, sit with me for a moment. I am tired of standing and this will take some time to explain." The three men sat.

Gorji said, "What do you know of the name Satoshi Nakamoto?"

Chase said, "I recognize the name. He is supposedly the creator of bitcoin, right?"

Gorji nodded. "In 2008, a person or group of persons published a white paper describing the bitcoin digital currency. The document was published under the name Satoshi Nakamoto."

Waleed said, "I heard that the name Satoshi was a pseudonym."

Gorji said, "Whether Nakamoto was really one person or many, no one knew. The modern legend that formed would have you believe that a single mysterious man began to collaborate with software developers for the next two years, at which time he handed over control of the source code and other important information to several prominent members of a now-loyal bitcoin community. This Satoshi Nakamoto created the world's first widely used digital currency. Bitcoin is untraceable and therefore untaxed. Every transaction is uploaded into the bitcoin network of users. Unlike paper money, which can be created by governments, bitcoins are in limited supply, one of their two value drivers."

Chase said, "What does this have to do with Abu Musa?"

Mr. Gorji held up a hand. "We'll get to that. The other driver of bitcoin's value is demand. This is basic economics. Supply and demand together will meet and support a given value. It is important that you understand how bitcoin is different than paper money. Let me ask you something, do you know how much money the US Treasury prints each day?"

Chase shook his head.

"I do. I have had to study these things in preparation for Iran's shift to the bitcoin-backed currency. The US Bureau of Engraving and Printing creates thirty-eight million notes a day. That's over five hundred million US dollars created by the American government each and every day. Now, the vast majority of that is used to replace what's already in circulation. They are making old dollar bills look new. But the point is, the American regulators and other national currency regulators around the world control the rate at which they pump money into their currency supplies. And what happens if you pump more money into a currency supply?"

Chase said, "Inflation."

"Correct." Gorji smiled. "As long as politicians and government regulators continue to print money faster than it disappears, the value of that money decreases. A dollar today will be worth less tomorrow. Another way of saying it is that a loaf of bread, or a car, or a house will cost you more tomorrow."

"But you are telling me that bitcoins are different?"

"That is right. Bitcoins, like gold or diamonds, are a scarce resource. And now that enough people have started to assign value to bitcoins, there is a sufficient demand that it can actually be used as a currency."

"I still don't see how something digital can be a scarce resource."

"Chase, how do you acquire gold?"

"Usually the process starts by meeting a very attractive woman. I guess that's what you called demand creation. Most women I meet are very demanding on that front. Afterwards, I go to a jewelry store."

The two other men laughed. Gorji persisted. "But how do you

get the gold? Not from the store. How do the jewelry makers get gold?"

"Gold mines?"

Gorji pointed at him. "Precisely. Mines. You see, bitcoins are based on a series of mathematical equations, many of which remain unsolved. These unsolved equations are like unmined gold. They are rare, sought after, and can be unlocked if you have the right equipment—which in this case is a powerful computer. The bitcoin code was written so that only twenty-one million bitcoins can ever be unlocked through the solving of these equations. Today, we have 'mined' about fourteen million of them. As each equation is solved, it unlocks another equation. Sets of them, really. And each equation gets exponentially harder to solve than the last. They are so hard to solve that they require more and more advanced computers to solve them. This has created a whole industry of bitcoin miners. Factories of computers linked together with only one purpose—solving the bitcoin equations to unlock more bitcoins."

"So who gets the bitcoins when they are unlocked?"

"Whoever mines them."

"How much are they worth?"

Gorji said, "Like I have said, supply and demand change. Last week, they were worth about four hundred dollars each. With the announcement of the Dubai Financial Exchange starting, the value has gone over six hundred dollars each. When word spread that China was going to back the RMB with bitcoin reserves, it went to fifteen hundred dollars, and it is still rising. And as the bitcoin supply runs out and demand increases, their value should continue to increase as well."

Chase said, "Remind me why this is relevant to my firm? Because it's untraceable?"

Waleed said, "Yes. People who use bitcoins don't need to ever involve a bank, because all transactions are stored in the bitcoin peer-to-peer network. When Satoshi Nakamoto published his white paper in 2008, bitcoins were just a collection of software and ideas. They were worth nothing. Then, a few early adopters began exchanging them for goods and services. Eventually, one man even purchased a pizza in bitcoins. He had to get another man, half a world away, to facilitate the transaction and exchange another currency for the pizza, but it worked nonetheless. Almost overnight, bitcoins had actual value. They were worth only a few cents at first. But like gold and silver and Dutch tulips—once more people began trading bitcoins, exchanges popped up. There were crashes and software glitches and arrests and scandals. But bitcoins quickly grew in value."

"A pizza, huh?"

"Yes. But there is an important lesson there. As new currencies are adopted, there must be an exchange to provide liquidity. Many do not trust the bitcoin network. They are afraid of keeping their money in bitcoins because they are afraid that it will disappear. Because it is digital." He shook his head and laughed.

"Why are you laughing?"

"Because everyone's money is held digitally today, most people just don't think about it. Banks are all online. And your money can disappear there just as easily. But people trust what they know. They trust the current system. But the Dubai Financial Exchange and the bitcoin-backed currency will change all that. This is what I believe."

"So you think that this will be the start of a truly wide adoption of bitcoin."

"I believe it will spur the global adoption of a decentralized digital currency, yes. Whether it is bitcoin or not, that could change. But for now, bitcoin is the most valuable and liquid option. This is the tip of the iceberg, as the expression goes. Mr. Jinshan calls it The Great Rebalancing. It will change the economics of the world. No longer will the United States have an advantage like it once did."

Chase said, "Mr. Gorji, I appreciate the education, but again, what does this have to do with Abu Musa?"

"I will explain. In 2013, the amount of bitcoin that Satoshi Nakamoto supposedly owned would have meant that he was a billionaire in US dollars. Yet no one had ever seen him. He had been almost completely silent on the message board that he once used to communicate to his bitcoin disciples. Why would a genius who had created such an innovative technology remain in hiding? How, in this day of social networks, video omnipresence, and twenty-four-hour newsfeeds, is it possible that such a rich and famous man's true identity is unknown?"

Chase frowned. "No one has ever seen this guy?"

He ignored the question. "Over the years, dozens of potential Satoshi Nakamotos have been 'outed' by the press. One was a legal scholar and cryptographer from the United States. Another was a Japanese-American physicist and systems engineer. One news source claimed that Satoshi was actually a group of exceptional computer programmers from several different nations."

"That's unbelievable."

"I agreed with that sentiment. A few years ago, Mr. Jinshan approached my country with the idea of shifting to a bitcoin-backed currency. Iran did not want to shift to a volatile currency without fully understanding its origins, no matter how bad our inflation was. So I was asked to investigate the true identity and whereabouts of Satoshi Nakamoto."

"What did you find?"

Gorji didn't answer the question. "Today, as millions of people around the world are beginning to adopt the use of this new digital currency, regulators and banks are scratching their heads, still trying to figure out who created it. Large American invest-ments banks are now investing in it. Bitcoin ATMs are popping up around the globe. They are in especially high demand in nations with declining currency. Popular websites are allowing consumers to pay using bitcoin. And all the while, its true origins remain shrouded in mystery."

Waleed looked intrigued. It appeared this was the first that he was hearing of Satoshi's whereabouts. He said, "Come, Ahmad, don't keep us waiting. What did you find?"

Gorji said, "So Jinshan approached the Iranian government with a proposition. Bitcoin was becoming larger, and he had a solution that would solve Iran's inflationary and economic woes. We agreed to allow one of Jinshan's companies to set up buildings on Abu Musa. A very secretive project that would give Iran an advantage if and when the bitcoin-backed currency project launched."

Waleed and Chase looked at each other, alarmed.

Gorji continued. "Jinshan funded the entire thing. He only asked for support from some of our IRGC components. We thought that it was strange, but the request was granted. He was a very smooth talker. They set up bitcoin mines on Abu Musa. Huge ones."

Chase said, "So that's what this is all about? Abu Musa has bitcoin mines?"

"Abu Musa has bitcoin mines. Enormous buildings filled with computers with a single task. Solve the mathematical equations that unlock new bitcoin blockchains. Jinshan split the profits with Iran. Once the Iranian leadership saw the promise of the investment, and at Jinshan's request, we gave him more control over the operation. A lot of things went on there that the Iranian leadership wasn't privy to. Let me ask you another question. Do you know where most of the world's bitcoin mines are?"

"No."

"*China*. Almost two-thirds of all bitcoins are mined in China. And about eighty percent of all bitcoin is traded in Chinese yuan."

Chase said, "So why would Jinshan want to open up new bitcoin mines on Abu Musa if they already have all of that going on in China?"

"Why indeed? This is the thought that bothered me a few years ago while I was in the midst of investigating Satoshi's true identity. So I began to conduct occasional inspections of the Abu Musa facilities."

Waleed said, "What did you find?"

"The bitcoin mines on Abu Musa are not just any mines. These mines have been set up to connect with the undersea cables that transfer information between the new Dubai Financial Exchange and the rest of the world. The bitcoin mines on Abu Musa are special."

"How so?"

"Believe me, I have been trying to find out, but even I don't fully know. But my theory is that this setup will allow Jinshan to artificially manipulate the currency. Either way, Jinshan's operation has become too secretive for his own good. Some of the IRGC members who work there seem to have forgotten where their loyalty lies. I believe you know one of them. A Lieutenant Colonel Pakvar."

Chase and Waleed looked at each other again, and then back at Gorji.

Gorji folded his arms. "Iran wants Jinshan's Abu Musa operation shut down. But we want the bitcoin-backed currency adoption to continue, without any illegal value manipulation. Which places us in a precarious position. How do we regain control of the Abu Musa facility without angering Jinshan, who has so much influence over the Dubai Financial Summit decisions?"

Chase said, "You want us to shut down the Abu Musa operation?"

"Any illegitimate parts of it, yes."

"How do you propose we do that?"

"I believe that there is someone who can help us. While inspecting the Abu Musa facilities, I met with a foreigner who was working there. Jinshan's bitcoin expert, I was told. From what I could tell during my limited exposure to him, Jinshan has essentially imprisoned this man on Abu Musa. I met with him years ago, before Pakvar got involved and security was tightened. I believe that this man would be open to defecting to America. If we can make that happen, he could help us ensure that the bitcoin-backed currency is free of malicious code. But I need his extraction to be an American operation. Otherwise Iran could suffer the wrath of Jinshan's anger. Can you help?"

Chase said, "I'll have to take this up my chain of command. But I think this would be mutually beneficial. Would you be able to get me access to this man? This expert?"

"I believe so. I have contacts on Abu Musa who are still loyal to me. I think that they could help me get him away long enough for you to extract him."

Waleed said, "So who is the expert?"

Gorji smiled. "Isn't it obvious? It is the man that I was searching for all along. The expert on Abu Musa is Satoshi Nakamoto."

* * *

They spoke for a few minutes more, hammering out details of their next communication. Waleed would stay in touch with Gorji through their normal channels. Waleed would receive a message indicating where and when Satoshi would be available. The rest was up to Chase and his team.

Chase said, "What about the list of American names? When can we see that, and how does that fit in to this?"

Gorji said, "I came across it during my most recent inspection of the Abu Musa facilities—a few months ago. A young man who was working with Pakvar mistook me for someone who worked on Abu Musa on a regular basis. An Indian boy in his twenties. He's actually an American citizen. Natesh, I believe his name was. I did not learn his last name. I don't believe he was supposed to speak of the list with me. I took a picture when he was not paying attention."

Chase shook his head. "That's how these things happen. Tiny mistakes."

Gorji said, "I will provide you with the list of American names once Satoshi's extraction is complete. That is the deal that I am authorized to make." He looked at both men. "I'm sorry that I cannot give it to you now. I serve many masters, you must understand."

Waleed said, "We understand. We will make this right. Inshallah."

They shook hands and walked out of the humidor room and toward the front of the store. Chase could see the blue light of the aquarium on the other side of the cigar shop's glass windows.

They walked out of the cigar shop and into the mall. Then Chase's world slowed down.

Chase had been in combat in Iraq and Afghanistan when he was with the SEALs. It was very different in those two theaters. In Afghanistan, battles in the mountains could be slow and deliberate. Firefights could take days or weeks. In the streets of Iraq, combat was much faster. It could be over in a matter of seconds. But in both settings, it was crucial to maintain good situational awareness, understand the terrain, and know the capabilities of one's opponent. Chase had been trained in observing the people and things around him until it became instinct to know when a firefight was about to erupt. Right now, his instincts raised the hair on the back of his neck.

Walking out into the blue light of the aquarium, Chase saw several men that didn't fit the tourist profile. The first was a hulking, dark-featured man that towered over everyone around him. Pakvar.

He stood in the middle of a crowd, glaring at Chase and his group. He held something under his jacket. A lightning-quick scan revealed at least two more men that were dressed like him and staring Chase's way. Both had their hands hidden behind clothing as well.

"Stop," Chase called to Waleed and Gorji.

They stood in the entrance of the store, swarms of people moving all around them. Chase felt under his sport coat to where his Sig lay in its shoulder holster. He unbuckled it and flipped off the safety, keeping his hand on the grip and his eyes on Pakvar.

Pakvar yelled something in Persian. His voice was loud and he spat as he spoke.

Gorji said, "I must go. He said I am to go."

Chase said, "What? Waleed, what did he say?"

"He told Gorji to leave, that he wouldn't hurt him."

Chase wasn't sure what to do about Gorji. Hell. "Go, get out of here."

After Pakvar yelled, a clearing formed around him as people realized that something wasn't right. One of Pakvar's men held Gorji's assistant by the collar. He threw him into the glass wall of the aquarium. Pakvar yelled something at Gorji and then looked at his man.

Chase's grip tightened on his weapon. There were too many variables. Three of them and one of him. They weren't firing yet, which meant that something was restraining them. Chase's CIA training had taught him to look for options and minimize the possibility of civilian casualties. He couldn't fire his gun here unless he absolutely had to.

Gorji stopped and turned when Pakvar called his name. Pakvar took his weapon out. A thick, boxy weapon with a long, straight magazine—it looked similar to a MAC-10. He fired a spray of bullets at Gorji's assistant. A two-foot flame shot out from the weapon and Gorji's assistant's white shirt filled with dark red holes.

The aquarium wall behind him began cracking and tiny streams of water spurted out. Gorji screamed and started to walk toward Pakvar, then stopped and thought better of it. He cursed Pakvar, turned and ran out of the mall.

Screams from the crowd. Hysteria. Tourists running. Mothers guarding their children, their heads still turned and watching Pakvar. Even the mall security guards ran.

A moment later, Waleed and Chase were left alone in the mall's wide-open floor space. The sounds of water shooting out from tiny holes and hitting the tile floor echoed through the room. Pakvar and his men were spread out about thirty feet away, Pakvar at Chase's eleven o'clock, the other man at his two o'clock position. The third man was behind them.

It was what Chase's trainers at the Farm would term a "less-than-ideal field-of-fire situation."

Footsteps sounded from the exit where the crowd had been running. A lone woman, covered from head to toe in a flowing black robe and burka. She walked through the group, seemingly oblivious to the violence that had just taken place. But she wasn't. A slit revealed eyes that Chase recognized, and they took in everything.

The five men all held their guns out now and were maneuvering. Pakvar and his men took slow steps to get a better angle on Chase. The woman in the black robe confused them and caused them to pause.

The nearest of Pakvar's men yelled something at her that could be loosely translated as "Get out of here, you stupid bitch."

She kept walking. They all watched her in curiosity as she walked up to the unsuspecting Iranian. When she was about ten feet away, she raised a Beretta and casually fired one round through the head of Pakvar's first man.

Chase dropped to the ground, twisted, and fired at Pakvar's second man behind him. Two rounds, center mass. He went down hard. No blood. Possibly wearing body armor. Chase fired another round and hit his temple.

Pakvar was open-mouthed in astonishment after witnessing the woman's action. He quickly sidestepped and hid behind one of the large white posts that rose up through the floor and provided stability to the mall structure. The woman ran toward Chase and grabbed his hand. Waleed, Chase, and the woman turned and sprinted through the mall.

Chase looked back and saw that Pakvar was starting to follow them. He fired a few rounds in Pakvar's direction and then took cover again. He turned to the woman. "Lisa, aim where I'm aiming."

He raised his gun and fired at the location in the glass where the cracks and holes had formed from the MAC-10 rounds. Chase emptied his chamber and saw more cracks spreading through the giant glass fish tank. Lisa's rounds finished the job. The pressure of the water forced the glass to shatter, and in excess of two million gallons of salt water thrust out from the shattered aquarium wall.

A violent wall of blue water surged from right to left. Chase watched Pakvar get swept away, then turned and followed his two companions as they ran through the aquarium tunnel and out to safety.

10

Al Dhafra Air Base, UAE
Three Weeks Later

Elliot said, "So I've got good news and bad news. What do you want first?"

They sat in a small room connected to the Tactical Operations Center. Chase said, "I always like to go with the bad first."

"I couldn't get you the air support I thought I would be able to get you."

"What was the air support you were going to get me?"

"I was trying to get you a helo insert. I thought I might be able to hook you up with the guys from the 160th and their stealth helos. The same ones that DEVGRU used for the Abbottabad raid."

"Didn't they crash one of those?"

Elliot frowned. "Yeah. Actually, now that you mention it, that's the same objection that they had when I asked about it."

"So then...this would seem like good news, not bad."

Elliot pointed at him and said, "I really appreciate the positive outlook you have. So, when was your last HALO jump?"

HALO stood for High Altitude Low Opening, a specific method of parachute insertion. Chase had completed many of those jumps when he was with the SEAL teams, but he was not current, and definitely not proficient enough for a night jump. It was a perishable skill, something one had to practice often to keep good at.

"It's been a while."

"Ever used a wingsuit?"

"Once. It was a cross-training exercise we did with the Army. They're pretty high-speed." Elliot was giving him a funny look. Chase said, "You want me to wear a wingsuit?"

"It's the best way to stay far enough from Abu Musa so that we don't raise any suspicion."

"How far can I travel on one of those?"

"The world record is fifteen nautical miles."

Chase said, "Assume I'm not the world-record holder."

"I think you should be able to at least get ten miles out of it. But you should probably talk to the pilots about the winds and all that. Listen, you're the Special Operations guy."

"Minor details."

"I got you a Cessna Caravan. An Air Force plane. They'll be your insert. But the wingsuit isn't what I'm excited about. The good news is actually my brilliant plan to get you extracted. I want you to know it was very challenging to get someone that was able to reliably transport you and our mystery passenger off of Abu Musa."

Chase said, "I'm sure."

"I mean, it was really challenging. Like, no contractors, government, or military guys were suitable for this. Too high a risk of getting caught. And in my opinion, a covert operation is like going to a crowded church on Christmas Eve. You always need a good exit strategy."

Elliot was using his hands as he spoke. He was really trying to sell this one. Whatever the punch line was, Chase didn't think he was going to like it.

"I'm sure you were able to come up with something..."

"Oh, I was. A crack team...well, more like an individual than a team...but he's got a great reputation for delivering whenever we've needed to smuggle guys into or out of Iran."

"Nice. So far, so good."

Elliot looked like he had something more to say. Something that Chase might not like. Chase said, "What aren't you telling me?"

"Well...about this guy...he's a little...how should I put it...he's a bit...junior..."

"What the hell does that mean?"

"You know, like a bit less experienced than some of the internal Agency support that you might be accustomed to."

"How junior?"

"Well, let's look back at the positives. He's been one hundred percent reliable in all the work we've sent his way. All three times. And—"

"You've only used him three times?"

"And he came at quite a discount from the private sector guys."

"So he was the lowest bidder? Is this really the mission that you're trying to save money on?"

"Plus, if you guys get rolled up by the Iranians, he has no ties to us, so it will be easier to completely disavow all knowledge. Of course, you guys will be totally fucked. But I'll come out squeaky clean. Brilliant, as far as I'm concerned."

Chase smirked. "This sounds like some top-notch planning on your part. So what's the downside?"

"He's sixteen."

"Sixteen?"

"Well, he'll be sixteen next month. He told me his birthday was coming up."

"Fifteen? You're having me get picked up from an island that Iran uses as a military outpost with a fifteen-year-old kid?"

"No. No, Chase. It's not like that. Well...sort of. Yes. But I'm starting to question your positive outlook." Elliot smiled. "We'll have a SOCOM Mark V boat pick you guys up once you're out of the twelve-nautical-mile arc."

Chase rolled his eyes. He stood up and looked at the nautical chart on the wall, the one that showed the Arabian Gulf. Abu Musa was only about fifty miles north of Dubai.

Elliot said, "Look, Chase, you're the one who convinced me that Waleed's man Gorji is legit. I went out on a limb to make this happen. If this Iranian bitcoin-mining operation really has some bigger nefarious purpose, then we need proof. Just like you said. And if this Satoshi character can provide us with that proof, then we need to bust him out of there. If you're not comfortable going, I could try to get some SOF guys pulled off their ISIS missions in Iraq and—"

"You know that won't work. It'll be too big of an op. It'll take too long to plan and get authorization for. We'll have to go through the president if we do that. Again. And you said that Langley barely convinced him this time. Plus, if we send a team of SOF guys and people start shooting, it will get messy. It's better to keep it just one or two people."

"Exactly. I knew you'd come around."

Chase snorted and rolled his eyes. Elliot was doing his best to use humor to his advantage.

"Fifteen. Jesus. Alright, tell me the details..."

Elliot smiled and opened his laptop. "Attaboy."

* * *

Chase sat in the back of the dark grey turboprop aircraft. The

Cessna Caravan was holding short of the main runway at Minhad Air Base, twenty miles to the southeast of Dubai.

It was pitch black outside. There was supposedly a quarter moon, but the dust and haze had completely hidden it. Chase checked his watch: 1:30 a.m. He could see the blue runway lights and hear the powerful engine as the pilots ran up the RPMs, conducting their pre-takeoff checks.

The copilot yelled back, "You all set? The flight should be about twenty-five minutes. We have our clearance. You good?"

Chase gave a thumbs-up. The copilot said something into his lip microphone and the other pilot said something back. The engine picked up again and seconds later they were airborne.

Chase had triple-checked his gear. Helmet with a clear visor. No smudges. He wanted to be able to see everything clearly as he parachuted into the least inhabited part of the island. His helmet was strapped on tight. He had a knife in a sheath that slid into his boot. His altimeter was matched up with the aircraft's barometric setting. Parachute. Quadruple-checked. AAD—automatic parachute activation device. Check. And one big, rubbery wingsuit.

He and the pilots were already breathing through oxygen masks. As a safety precaution, they'd pre-breathed oxygen for one hour prior to the flight in order to prevent oxygen sickness.

His backpack was filled with another twenty pounds of gear. A silenced pistol. A small amount of food and water. A few tightly packed medical supplies. A fully charged satellite phone and an extra battery. He had memorized the number to dial.

Phone calls.

Chase's jovial mood broke as he thought of a voicemail he had just listened to from his sister Victoria. She had called to inform him that their brother David hadn't checked in with his wife Lindsay in weeks. David had ostensibly been on a government-related work trip. When pressed, Lindsay had revealed that the work trip was related to some sort of classified government project. Could this be related to the mysterious list of American traitors the Iranian had mentioned? In the weeks since finding out about the list, Chase had still not contacted David, per Elliot's instructions. But now, after learning that David was off the grid, he was kicking himself for following orders.

Two days after the shoot-out at the Mall of Dubai, Lisa had traveled to Langley. She was supposed to use her source at In-Q-Tel to check up on him. But Chase had not heard from her since she left. Chase and Lisa had to go through a series of debriefs and provide written statements concerning what had happened. But between Waleed and Elliot, their names and faces were kept out of the press. Officially, the Dubai Mall shooting had been reported as a terrorist attack. No mention of Iran was made.

Chase tried not to think of his brother. He had to push away his fears of what might have happened to him. Whatever this list was, it was Chase's fault for not warning him. But before a mission like this, he couldn't afford any distractions. He needed to block those thoughts out and save it for when he returned.

The aircraft took off and climbed rapidly. The pilots turned off all the external lights and switched off their transponder once they were out over the Gulf. Fifteen minutes later, the copilot rose from his seat and gave Chase a thumbs-up.

The copilot opened up a plastic panel next to the door of the aircraft, revealing a dozen switches and circuit breakers. He flipped one switch, and a soft red glow light came on above them. The copilot looked Chase up and down, patting certain areas of his gear to make sure he was secure and double-checking his chute. He then clipped himself to a canvas belt that was attached to a steel link in the ceiling and reached for the door.

The copilot flipped another switch, and a yellow light lit up above it, illuminating the word *READY*. The pilot flying the aircraft saw this in his cockpit as well and started to slow down to 140 knots and fly into the wind. Chase could see the copilot flip another switch and then heard a hiss and felt the temperature rapidly drop. It would be well below zero up at this altitude, regardless of how hot it was on the desert surface below.

He checked his altimeter, which was strapped to his chest. The needle was spinning up to an altitude of twenty-two thousand feet.

Chase hoped that the aviators had placed him in the right spot. He had personally overseen the wind calculations when they were on the ground. He could angle the wingsuit and use aerodynamics to glide pretty far, but a lot depended on how high they were and what the winds were doing.

The READY light turned green.

The copilot placed his hand on the long metal door handle and then pulled it down and inward. A black void of hurricane-force winds opened up in front of him. Chase patted the copilot on the shoulder and stepped out, facing forward and crossing his arms tight over his chest.

Stepping into the wind, he felt like a linebacker had hit him as the relative wind pummeled him in the opposite direction. But that feeling was short-lived, as drag slowed him down and gravity took over. The acceleration vector shifted downward, and his stomach fluttered as he fell.

Then, as he spread his arms and legs and the airflow filled the sail of the wingsuit, he had the sensation of flying. Chase forced his limbs outward and angled himself so that he would glide toward the island below. Skydivers in free fall normally traveled downward at 120 miles per hour. Yet with the wingsuit, he was falling at a velocity of only forty miles per hour, and moving forward at over 140 miles per hour.

Abu Musa consisted of a smattering of village lights around the outside of the island, and an unlit runway in the middle. Intel reports said that the aircraft here almost never flew at night.

Almost never. He hoped that it would remain empty for him to land on.

For the first minute of his fall, he was above the haze. Looking up, he could see the moon and stars. He felt like he was floating in outer space. Below, there were several formations of lights. They were likely commercial ships. Oil tankers, headed to and from the Straits of Hormuz, probably.

Three minutes into his descent, he decided that the pilots had done a good job placing him where he needed to be. He was almost over the island. Now he needed to tighten his limbs a bit to decrease his lift and ensure that he didn't overshoot. As he did that, he began falling faster.

He checked his altimeter. Three thousand feet. Any second now, his AAD would deploy his chute. It was set for one thousand feet. If it didn't go off, Chase would pull it manually.

He felt a little flutter as the chute deployed and then a jarring slam when it fully opened, arresting his descent. Chase flipped down his night vision goggles and examined the runway. No lights, and no sign of any movement. Chase looked underneath the goggles at his altimeter every few seconds, trying to gauge his altitude.

The hard part about landing while wearing night vision goggles was the disparity between what his eyes told him was real and actual reality. It was like watching a video of what's in front of you and trying to walk up the stairs. Yes, you could see what was there, but it was very challenging to estimate the exact distance between your feet and the ground. The trick was to look out at the horizon.

Chase pulled on the chute's maneuvering lines to line up with the runway centerline as he descended. With about one hundred feet to go, he began looking underneath his goggles, using the lights of the island and the faintest hint of a horizon to estimate how close he was to the surface.

The green image of the runway grew larger and larger as he tensed his body for impact. He pulled to start his flare, slowing his rate of descent at just the right moment to cushion his landing. He felt his boots hit the runway and began running and taking in the parachute as he came down.

Moments later, he had stuffed the chute back into its container and moved over to a spot about twenty yards to the north of the runway. He checked his watch. It had been thirty minutes since takeoff. He would have about four hours until the sun began to lighten the horizon. That meant three hours until his extraction.

He took out a handheld GPS map and checked his location. He was right where he wanted to be. About a thirty-minute hike to the north side of the island, where the large buildings that housed the bitcoin-mining computers were. He removed his wingsuit and gear and stuffed everything into the duffle bag. Underneath, he wore a white cotton tunic and beige pants. The kind of outfit that a local fisherman would wear. Out of his supply backpack, he took a thin grey wool hat that fit tightly over his head.

He threw his backpack over his shoulder and began walking. He gripped a silenced Beretta and four extra magazines of ammo in a belt underneath his tunic. An eight-inch WK II Defense Dagger was tucked into its Kydex sheath, strapped to his boot.

Chase took his time making his way over the sand-and-rock terrain. If he kept on this heading, he would avoid alerting any of the island's civilian population that might have trouble sleeping.

To his right, at the far end of the runway, he could see evidence of the Iranian military. A few jeeps and a fuel truck sat next to an old Soviet-era jet. If that thing ever flew in combat, he wondered what would be a greater danger to the pilot—the enemy, or his own aircraft.

Ahead, Chase spotted two large concrete structures. There was a row of large generators and HVAC units that fed into the first building. They made a lot of noise, which should help him stay undetected.

Chase crouched down and took out a heavy set of thermal imaging binoculars from his pack. Looking through them, he noted that the heat signature from the first building was very strong. They had what must have been a hundred rows of servers in there, but Chase couldn't see any signs of people in the large building.

Each of those computers was speeding through a mathematical calculation that would help unlock the next blockchain of bitcoins. The more computing power these guys had, the more bitcoins they could unlock.

But why do this here? If what Gorji had said was true, and this operation was funded by Jinshan, why did the mine have to be here? This had been the subject of much discussion between him and Elliot. Gorji suggested that there was some mysterious link to the submarine cables running through the Gulf. They were still missing information.

Chase looked at his GPS and then back at his watch. He had time.

He took off his pack and set it in the dirt, then looked through the thermal binoculars again. Nothing. He lay in wait for almost an hour before he finally saw what he came for.

A figure left the first building and walked in his direction. No one else was in sight. Chase waited fifteen minutes as the lone man, who would be in plain sight if any security were to look that way, made his way towards him. Chase hoped to God that this was legit.

Finally, when the man was close enough to the rendezvous spot, Chase spoke. "Hello?"

"Hello?" a voice said in English. It was dark. Hard to see his face.

Chase stood up, still holding his weapon. "Are you here to meet someone?"

The man walked closer.

"Yes. I was told that you could help me. I was told to tell you that my name is Satoshi."

* * *

At a secluded, rocky shoreline of Abu Musa, Chase and Satoshi listened as the buzz of an outboard motor grew louder. Chase saw the narrow twenty-foot fishing boat pull up to the dock. A skinny dark-skinned boy waved.

"What's your name?" called Chase.

"Timmy."

"Timmy, huh?"

"Mr. Elliot said you pay me first."

Chase reached into his backpack and pulled out an envelope. He threw it to the kid. Timmy counted it. Five hundred US dollars. The kid said, "Okay, mister, you and your friend, get in the boat."

They sat on wobbly plastic seats that faced backward, toward the driver of the boat. Timmy cranked up the power and the bow moved up out of the water, then settled back down. Chase remained on guard, eying Satoshi, who looked scared. He didn't blame him.

The island of Abu Musa grew smaller behind them.

11

"Thanks for coming. Please, have a seat."

Chase thought Elliot's tone was quite formal compared to the way they had been speaking to each other lately. Their relationship, while always professional, had grown more and more comfortable as Chase had proven his worth. Now, Elliot had the look of a father about to give his son a stern lecture.

"What's wrong?" Chase said as he sat in the chair across from Elliot's desk. They were in a small office in the same building as the Tactical Operations Center, on Al Dhafra Air Base. Chase had been working on the post–Abu Musa analysis for the past few weeks.

"I need to let you know something. It's about Satoshi."

"What is it?"

"He's not really Satoshi."

"I thought we had established that. No surprise. That's not his real name, right?"

"You misunderstand. I have reason to believe that the man who you recovered from Abu Musa is not doing what he agreed to do."

Chase's eyes narrowed.

Elliot and his team had been working with Satoshi to remove any illicit code that had been placed in the Dubai Financial Exchange's bitcoin interface by the Abu Musa operation. Interviews with Satoshi confirmed that Jinshan had indeed set up an elaborate operation to artificially control the value of the bitcoin-backed currency. He intended to accomplish this via malicious code and a unique hardware connection to the underwater communications cables.

Waleed and Elliot had set the operation up almost as soon as Satoshi had arrived in Dubai. Once Satoshi agreed to remove the malicious programs hidden in the Dubai Financial Exchange, Waleed and Elliot had gone to work on a joint operation to get Satoshi daily access to its computers. It had taken a lot of hard work, but they had executed it flawlessly.

Each day, Satoshi's software fixes were uploaded to NSA laptops and taken to a building adjacent to the Dubai Financial Exchange. There, Elliot's NSA contacts had helped set up a long-range Wi-Fi connection to the computers of several employees in the building. They infected these computers with a worm that allowed Satoshi to anonymously edit the trading programs. While their computers weren't directly connected to any of the servers that handled the bitcoin-backed currency exchange, they didn't need to be.

Each night, when the employees who used the infected computers had gone home, the NSA's worm would start their computers up. It would send out electronic signals in any form that the host computer was capable of. Bluetooth, Wi-Fi, NFC. It would spread to other computers that were in range, forming a larger network of infected computers. Eventually, some of these computers became connected to external drives and hardware. On and on the spread of the virus went, until three weeks into the operation, they hit gold. One of the NSA-infected computers linked up to the trading server software. This triggered the network of computers to scan and transfer the information that Satoshi needed.

Several of these server-to-external-hardware connections were necessary before Satoshi could begin his work. This week, he had told Elliot, he was confident that his updates would start affecting the system. He had made two changes at Elliot's request. First, Satoshi had destroyed any of the Abu Musa code, which would negate Jinshan's ability to anonymously manipulate the value of the bitcoin-based currency. Second, he had implanted software that would allow the CIA to monitor transaction activity.

Waleed and Elliot had set up a secure workspace for Satoshi at the Burj Al Arab hotel. This also sweetened the pot for Satoshi's compliance. The NSA and CIA teams conducted all of their interactions with him in his hotel room. All the software fixes Satoshi was making to the Dubai Bitcoin Exchange were evaluated first by the NSA and CIA teams before being uploaded to the system. Satoshi had argued that this would greatly slow the operation down, but Elliot would not budge on this security measure.

Satoshi was essentially a prisoner at the hotel, though as prisons went, a room at one of the world's most luxurious hotels was about as good as it got. For his own safety and the security of the operation, Satoshi was confined to his room. Elliot had several members of the CIA's security team guarding him closely. Satoshi wasn't allowed to communicate with anyone unless Elliot approved it.

Jinshan had flown back to China. None of the bitcoin plot had been made public, but there was some back-channel communication between the US, the UAE, and the Chinese that made it clear Jinshan was no longer welcome in either nation. Strangely, there had not been any response from the Chinese government. Not even a denial.

Waleed had not heard from Gorji since Satoshi had been extracted from Abu Musa. He, too, was strangely quiet. All of

Waleed's attempts to contact Gorji and get the rest of the list had failed.

Chase said, "What isn't Satoshi doing?"

"Well, that's the funny thing. It appears as though our man Satoshi is not actually trying to remove code. He's trying to *activate* it. He keeps complaining that he needs live access to the servers, and that this secure, limited-access setup we've established is making it very difficult for him. Well, it's time I laid my cards out for you, Chase."

"Sir?"

"I never fully bought into Satoshi."

"What do you mean?"

"When something seems too good to be true, it probably is."

"You think Satoshi was some sort of Trojan horse?"

Elliot said, "Gorji comes to us with partial truths—your brother being on the list, a leak in Dubai Station—he establishes credibility, then follows that up with a problem that we can solve. It's classic tradecraft. But this ain't my first rodeo. So I placed safeguards on our side."

"Safeguards?"

"I could have given Satoshi access to the Dubai Financial Exchange. Actually, Waleed wanted me to. But that would have been exactly what the Iranians were asking for."

"But Gorji? I mean, he's a good guy, right?"

"Maybe. The truth is, I don't really know. But I do know that he came to us with a problem and asked us to take a certain action to solve it. He told us that the Dubai Financial Exchange was part of the Abu Musa operation. The only way to fix it was to get Satoshi out of Abu Musa and let him go to town hacking away at the secure code in the exchange servers. Chase, let me ask you, how in the *hell* did Gorji get Satoshi to just walk out of those secure buildings on Abu Musa?"

"He said he had a contact inside."

"But he also said that the Abu Musa operation was run by Jinshan's company, right? And that Pakvar was growing loyal to Jinshan."

"Something like that."

"So Satoshi's been enslaved by Pakvar and Jinshan on Abu Musa for years, right? Then how the hell does Gorji get him off there so easily?"

"I don't know." Chase realized that it did seem pretty odd.

Elliot said, "One possibility would be that Jinshan, or whoever is pulling the strings, wanted us to get Satoshi over here. In that scenario, either Gorji is one of them, or he is being played by them. Either way, Satoshi—or whoever you took home from Abu Musa—is not really here to help us debug the Dubai Financial Exchange."

Chase rolled his eyes. "Well, why send someone at all?"

"I don't know that either. Maybe their undersea cable connection isn't working out. Maybe they have other plans that we don't even know about with the bitcoin currency. But the bottom line is, this character who we've been calling Satoshi is not the real Satoshi."

"So we've been giving him access to—"

"No. We haven't. I've had the NSA clean up any malicious code in the bitcoin section of the Dubai Financial Exchange servers. Waleed helped me speak with the Emiratis and got us access. In exchange for our covert ability to monitor transactions, of course."

"How did they grant you that?"

"Because it would look pretty bad if the Dubai Financial Exchange collapsed in scandal. We allow them to save face, we ensure there is no funny business going on with manipulation of valuations, and we get to track transactional data. Without turning off the entire bitcoin-backed currency transition, it's about the best we could hope for. I've also had the NSA evaluate every upload Satoshi has asked us to make."

Chase nodded. "So you've been playing him for the last month?"

"Yes."

"And you've been playing me."

"Need to know. You know how it is, son."

"I understand. Find anything out?"

"He's not trying to help us, that's for sure."

"Why are you still having him work on it?"

"Espionage 201. Follow the rabbit hole. I want to see where it goes. That's how the game is played. I want Jinshan and Satoshi to think everything is just fine. Let them keep placing money in the pot until the last card. Until I have the upper hand."

"Why are you telling me this now?"

"A few days ago, we allowed Satoshi outside Internet access. He saved a draft of an email. It was just a friendly hello email to someone in his family. But he never sent it. Yesterday, we checked his email account. It had been read by him."

"I'm not following."

"We didn't allow him access to the Internet yesterday. That means someone else accessed his email and read his draft. He was using tradecraft, so that there would be no other source for us to look into."

"What was he trying to communicate?"

"I'm not sure, but I have a guess."

"What?"

"I'm guessing that he said something to the effect of: 'I've made my changes to the program, so it should be working now.'"

"What's the next step?"

"We're hoping that Jinshan will try something and it will reveal his participation. I don't—"

The phone rang. Elliot picked it up. "Jackson." He listened to the person on the other end speak. "Christ. I'll be right there." He hung up the phone.

Elliot said, "Come on. We're needed in the TOC. This is the second reason I needed to speak with you today."

"What happened?"

"I'll explain as we walk. I heard from Lisa Parker."

* * *

Chase looked around the Tactical Operations Center. He counted ten people. That was twice the usual number, and all of their eyes were glued to the same screen. Elliot was there, looking pissed off.

There were over a dozen flat-screens on the front wall. Some of them were tactical displays showing various contacts of interest in the operating area. Other screens showed rows of information concerning reconnaissance and other air missions that would be checking in and the times they were expected.

Several of the monitors were the actual video feeds from these surveillance aircraft. Drones and manned aircraft alike linked secure data down to the TOC. But today, people only cared about one of these screens.

Underneath this particular screen was a bright red digital display that said *SHORTSTOP 23*. That was the call sign of the US Air Force RQ-180 drone that was transmitting the video feed from several miles up.

The screen showed a truck blocking a highway. Three black cars were stopped in front of it. There were bodies strewn about the road, and a firefight was in progress.

"You see that?" Elliot said.

"See what?" Chase replied.

"Zoom out." He looked around for the person controlling the drone. "Zoom out!"

An Air Force first lieutenant sitting in front of a mass of computer screens and joysticks clicked a few buttons. The screen flashed and then showed a wider, more distant view of the scene.

Chase could see a beach to the south and a naval base with ships to the southeast. There was an airport over to the west. Bandar Abbas. Home to Iran's largest naval base, it was positioned just north of the Strait of Hormuz.

With the view zoomed out, everyone could see another truck —a troop transport by the look of it—barreling down the highway, toward the firefight.

"This is going to get worse. I counted three heat signatures still in that truck that started the shooting."

Chase leaned over to Elliot and whispered, "So what did Lisa's email say?"

Elliot kept clenching and unclenching his jaw. "Very little. Just that the 'operation' was on. And then she listed these GPS coordinates written down below with this time and date." He nodded up at the screen, implying that the coordinates were the same location the drone was observing. "I came over here to make sure that we had surveillance coverage of the location and told the duty officer to let me know if she saw anything suspicious. The thing is, Lisa sent that message to me over unclassified email. It was addressed to me and a few of the higher-ups in Langley. Like she wanted it to be picked up by outside sources."

Lisa hadn't been heard from in several weeks.

Until now.

Until the email that Elliot had just received. It implied that she was part of a CIA operation near Bandar Abbas. A few weeks ago, she had saved Chase and Waleed from getting shot by Pakvar and company in the Dubai Mall.

Days later, she had headed off to Langley for official business. At least, that was what Chase had been told. She was there when they debriefed the Dubai Mall incident with Elliot. She claimed that she was there to meet another asset when she heard the gunfire, that it was a coincidence that she was there at all. In the aftermath of that incident, with the amount of activity going on, this explanation had seemed reasonable to Chase. Now he felt like a fool.

Going over the events with Elliot, a different story became clear. When Chase arrived back from Abu Musa, he finally had time to sit down with Elliot and go over everything in detail. Lisa had not, in fact, been cleared by the counterespionage team, like she had told Chase. She was being sent back to Langley because the counterespionage team had recommended to Elliot that she be reassigned. Apparently, she'd had several inconclusive answers on her polygraph. She would perform administrative duty at Langley while the investigation proceeded.

But Lisa Parker had never shown up at Langley. Airport footage showed her getting off her flight at LAX, which seemed normal. The subsequent footage showing her as she walked out of the airport—and *not* onto her connecting flight—was decidedly abnormal. That was the last time anyone at the CIA had heard from Lisa Parker. Until yesterday, when Elliot received his cryptic email.

So why had she lied to Chase about being cleared by the counterespionage team? Was she the leak in Dubai Station? Chase didn't want to believe that. He had been close to her over the past few months. He didn't want to think that she was capable of this. Between his brother and her, he wasn't sure what to think anymore.

Chase had come clean to Elliot and let him know that he had talked to Lisa about David being on the list, not realizing that Lisa hadn't been cleared. Elliot had been disappointed, but he'd understood the conflict. Elliot had read Chase the riot act and told him to consider that his mulligan.

David, too, was still missing.

Elliot had reported David Manning's inclusion on the list up through the CIA's chain of command. But having come from an Iranian source, the information was deemed only somewhat reliable. Elliot was in the process of evaluating the claim with investigators near Washington, D.C.

Then came Victoria Manning's voicemail to Chase, letting him know that David had not called Lindsay. They contacted a representative at David's work, In-Q-Tel. The folks at In-Q-Tel sent back crossed signals. Some were sure that David's trip was sanctioned and official, per CIA instructions. But a quick check with the CIA and a few more phonecalls to In-Q-Tel uncovered several irregularities. Something about David Manning's "work trip" was very wrong. They discovered that David had gone missing over three weeks ago now. Elliot felt awful for not acting sooner, but was concerned about whether David was actually doing something illegal. Chase knew that couldn't be the case, and blamed himself for letting it come to this.

"Elliot?" the duty officer, phone to her ear, called over to him. "We've confirmed that the passengers in the car are Ahmad Gorji and his wife. They were attending a ceremony at the Bandar Abbas Naval Base."

Elliot shook his head. He whispered, "Son of a bitch. This is an assassination. She's making it look like the CIA is assassinating Gorji."

Chase watched the screen. The troop transport pulled up and as men started climbing out and opening fire, the screen zoomed in again.

Chase saw a white flash on the display and thought that the first lieutenant had zoomed back out, but that wasn't it.

One of the Air Force guys said, "Holy shit."

As the screen became clear again, Chase realized what he had seen. Someone had just set off a bomb.

12

Bandar Abbas, Iran
Several Hours Earlier

Lisa Parker lay hidden, nestled in the brush on top of a small ridgeline. From her position, she was able to observe Iran's largest naval base, the harbor, and the Shahid Rajaie Highway that ran parallel to the shoreline. About a mile to the west, the occasional multiengine turboprop airliner took off from Havadarya Airport.

Her body ached from being in the prone position so long. She had been baking in the desert heat for almost forty-eight hours, and her stomach grumbled from lack of food. She had a small stash of rations, but now was not the time to eat.

The ghillie suit made it all but impossible for someone to spot her, but it didn't give her good access to her pockets. If she had stood straight up, she would have looked like some type of dread-locked swamp monster, covered in desert plants and roots.

Her dedicated mind fed off of the arduous conditions. She relished the pain and enjoyed the hunt. The long wait for that one critical moment where she would strike her target. Lisa was only bothered by one thing—the stench of the large black plastic bag that lay next to her, cooking in the sun. The smell had started off bad and become progressively worse over the duration of her stay on this mountain perch. Soon enough she could get rid of the bag's contents and wash the horrid smell off her body in the salty waters of the Arabian Gulf. The Persian Gulf, she corrected herself. After all, she was in Iran.

Lisa looked through her rifle scope at the people who would soon die. A part of her felt bad about that, but she told herself that the innocent victims who perished today would serve a greater purpose. For this was the start of a tremendous war. A war that would catapult the entire globe into a new era of progress and prosperity. The great rebalancing, as Jinshan called it.

This part of the plan was not supposed to have happened for a few more months. But with the escape of the two Americans from the island in the Pacific, Jinshan had thought it wise to act soon. Moving up the timetable meant that they had to compromise in several areas. Her own participation was not ideal. A woman of her ethnic background would quite possibly attract undue attention. The original plan had been to contract this job out to local personnel—or perhaps employ Chinese special operations commandos.

Because the timeline had been moved up, however, Lisa became the best option. Jinshan had told her that he would make other arrangements to complete this mission. He'd said that it actually might not be such a good idea to send a woman into Iran to do this type of work. He informed her that one of her less-capable male counterparts would go instead.

She'd known Jinshan was manipulating her. This Iranian step —the staged war—was a crucial part of the macro-plan. There could be no mistakes made. It was sheer sexist stupidity to think that a man would be better suited to perform this task. Lisa was better than any man at this type of work. Jinshan knew that. And he knew that she knew it. In the end, she didn't care if Jinshan manipulating her. She had worked too long and hard to see someone of lesser ability fuck it up.

To compensate for the risk of being seen, Lisa had approached and would soon exit from the sea, and under the cloak of night. She'd had assistance from Chinese naval commandos, embarked on their Shang-class submarine, while she'd traversed the waters of the Arabian Gulf. Now on land, however, she was by herself.

Well, almost. There were a few hired gunmen that knew nothing of who was really pulling the strings. Still, strings could be traced—and Lisa was here to make sure that didn't happen.

She checked her watch. It was thirty minutes past sunset. Almost time. She took another look through her binoculars. She was just able to make out the Iranian Kilo-class diesel submarine that was docked in the base's small harbor. A brass band and several dozen ornately uniformed Iranian servicemen stood in formation next to it. In front of them, just beside the sub, was a small tent. The water in the cove had a rough chop. The winds were just a bit stronger than she would have liked.

Three sleek black cars with tinted windows pulled up to the tent. Each of the cars had two Iranian flags flapping from its hood. The ceremony was wrapping up. Iran's newest submarine was a source of national pride in a country that was often challenged by the mightiest militaries in the world. This was a good opportunity for national leaders to be seen. Hence, Ahmad Gorji and his beloved wife had attended the ceremony. Killing a prominent Iranian politician would make national news. Killing his wife, a relative of the Iranian Supreme Leader, would start a war.

Lisa looked at the tiny phone that lay in the dirt next to her. She had two spare batteries and a solar charger in case she ran out of power. She typed a text message in Farsi: *LEAVING NOW*. She squirmed in her position, trying to loosen up her muscles.

The real test would be after she fired her weapon and began her departure. By her estimate, she would have about twelve minutes to make it to the beach. There would be a lot of running. She had been through worse before, but that didn't make this any easier. She kept calculating the times and distances in her mind, going over the details of each step and evaluating options. She wondered what would go wrong. Something always did.

Adrenaline began pumping through her veins as the time for action drew near. Lisa reached for the large, narrow bag that lay next to her. Inside was an Israeli-made Galatz SR-99 sniper rifle. It was over forty-three inches long and weighed a moderate thirteen pounds. There was one 7.62mm round already in the chamber and a box of extra ammunition in the pack. Lisa unfastened the cover of the very large scope mounted on top of the rifle and looked through it, making sure that her earlier adjustments were still appropriate. She typed in a few buttons on her phone and got wind estimates. She then made a few adjustments on the scope to ensure her shots would be accurate.

It had been a long time since she had been to sniper school. Her instructors there had immediately noticed her natural talent. She was able to relax her body and control her breathing better than ninety-nine percent of the other sniper school students. Her body was limber and her eyes sharp. She also had an innate predictive ability. When faced with a human target, she seemed to know exactly how they would move and could adjust her aim appropriately. And more important than all of those qualities, she was patient.

She was an expert shot at the farthest of distances. At this range of only four hundred meters from her intended target, Lisa was lethal. She repositioned the stand that propped up the barrel and gave her stability, then looked through the scope towards the highway. The dusty black cars with flags streaming from their front had about a mile to drive before they reached the contact zone.

A large cargo truck was pulled over along the side of the road in between the base entrance and the airport entrance. Right where it should be. The driver was looking at the engine under the shade of its raised hood. Lisa observed him slam down the hood and get back into the rig. If all went according to plan, he would remove the truck to block the highway just as the black cars arrived.

The men hiding inside the back of that truck had all been chosen because they had two things in common: One, they knew how to fire a weapon. Two, they each had a loved one who had been killed by the Iranian regime. Before yesterday, many of them had never met. It didn't matter. They didn't have to perform well as a team. They didn't even need to win the firefight that would soon erupt. This was revenge, they were told. Revenge for what had been done to their wives, their brothers, and in some cases, their children.

When the black cars stopped, the would-be assassins were supposed to get out and fire their Israeli-made submachine guns into them until they ran out of ammunition. Several of the men carried armor-piercing rounds. They were told to fire at the drivers first, and then proceed to walk their fire through the rest of the targets. They were all to stand on the north side of the highway so they would not chance firing at each other.

In one of the cars, the men were told, was a prominent Iranian politician. The men in the truck knew what the future held after they pulled the trigger. Most of them probably suspected that they would not live through the night. But to them, a chance to take aim at the Iranian regime, to fire on the symbol of everything that they hated in their nation's corrupt government—and a chance for revenge—was well worth it.

The black cars turned out of the base security gate and headed west on the highway, moving fast. Their tinted windows made it impossible for the men to see the faces of those that they would be firing upon. They would likely never know that the politician's wife was also in one of the cars.

Lisa sucked water from a straw connected to a CamelBak pouch while looking through the scope. She moved her hands into firing position on the weapon. She took one glance into her pack, rechecking the location of the extra rounds. She could easily grab them if she needed to reload. But if all went as planned, she shouldn't need more than the six rounds that were already loaded in the magazine.

The cars were about one minute away from the target zone when Lisa sent another text: *START MOVING*.

Through the scope, Lisa observed the truck shake to life and begin to roll forward from the road shoulder and onto the highway. The cab swerved to the left and blocked the entire road with its large frame. One hundred yards away, the black cars began to rapidly slow down. The caravan of vehicles crept up to a point about fifty feet behind the truck and came to a halt.

The first car's doors flung open and two men in Iranian Republican National Guard uniforms hustled out, one holding an AK-47. The other man was waving his arms, clearly agitated.

Sweat dripped from her forehead and stung her eye. She wiped it away and looked back through the scope. Any second now the truck's back door should open. The men should jump out and open fire on the cars.

But it wasn't happening.

Lisa watched as one of the military men walked all the way up to the driver's side of the truck, looking like he was trying to get the attention of the driver.

What was going on? Why hadn't they begun their attack?

The rear door to the truck remained closed. The three cars were at idle, waiting behind the truck, which was sprawled across the highway. Lisa's hand muscles were getting tense, her finger digging into the metal ring that formed the trigger guard.

Out of the corner of her eye, she saw movement at the base entrance. She looked up in time to see a military troop transport, loaded with men, leave the front gate of the naval base and turn onto the highway, taking the same route as the cars. A whistle. It was very faint, but she could make it out in the background. Someone at the entrance to the base was blowing a whistle over and over, alerting members of their security team.

Then it began.

From her distance, the gunfire sounded like the far-off snapping of firecrackers. A few pops rang out, spaced a second or two apart. Then more cracks spaced closer together as the firing became more rapid. Looking through the scope, Lisa saw bright red blood splatter on the front windscreen of the truck as the guard with the AK-47 gunned down the driver.

The back doors of the truck finally slammed open and several of the men ran out. They fired wildly in front of them. The first one off the truck was accidentally shot in the back by someone from his own group. He dropped to the pavement, blood spewing onto the dusty black surface. The other men fired into the cars, walking their rounds throughout the first car, just like they'd been told.

The rear car's doors popped open and two Iranian security men stumbled out, taking cover behind their doors and firing their weapons at the men coming out of the truck. Sprays of bullets from AK-47s and Israeli submachine guns tore through metal, glass, and flesh.

The second car's driver put it in reverse and slammed on the gas. It went crashing into the rear car, which was parked behind it. Two of the men hiding behind the rear car's doors were knocked to the ground, dropping their weapons as they fell.

Lisa placed her crosshairs over the driver's-side window of the second car. She moved her sweaty finger over the metal trigger, relaxed her breathing, and pulled. The recoil reverberated through her, the stock of the weapon slamming back into her shoulder, but she had been ready for it. She had braced herself and immediately reloaded without taking her eyes away from the scene. The front windshield of the middle car exploded into a spiderweb of white and pink lines. The car's wheels stopped turning.

The primary targets were in the second car. Now that it was immobilized, the men in the truck would have a better chance of succeeding. She looked at the troop transport that had driven out of Bandar Abbas Naval Base and was now screaming down the highway toward the firefight. The assassins needed to hurry, or they would be outnumbered.

Lisa heard a near-constant stream of gunfire from her mountain perch. She watched as the three remaining assassins hobbled out of the rear of the cargo truck. These were the cautious ones. They had waited and watched. Now they approached the second car and fired into the shattered windshield.

The military transport skidded to a halt behind the rear car. A dozen uniformed men funneled out and began cutting down the remaining assassins. There were too many for Lisa to shoot with a sniper rifle.

She waited until all but one of her attackers was down. This lone survivor was crouched behind the first car. He had been hit in the leg by the look of it. She moved her scope view back over to the second car. It was riddled with bullet holes. There was a good chance that all of its occupants were dead. Still, the truck full of soldiers that had just arrived would try to take any survivors to get immediate medical attention.

That would not do.

Lisa reached for her phone and scrolled down to a contact marked XEXECUTE-FIREX. She typed in the five-digit code and sent it as a text message to that contact. She watched through her scope.

The US-manufactured directional fragmentation mines exploded in rapid succession, like a series of sideways-pointing cluster bombs going off one after another.

The carnage was instant. At that close range, the dozen or so men that remained standing were decimated. Lisa had never seen so many die so quickly. It was exhilarating.

The pressure-blast from the explosion had shattered all of the windows of the vehicles. Fragments of molten-hot metal shot through and ripped apart the limbs of everyone in the kill zone. The interior of the second car was now visible, and that was all Lisa needed.

She moved the crosshairs of her rifle over to the backseat of the second car and found her target: the wife. While she looked dead, Lisa needed to be sure. She pulled the trigger, reloaded, and fired again.

She then jumped up from her prone position and lifted up the Zero MMX electric dirt bike. Designed for use by American Special Forces, the bike gave her fifty-eight horsepower of near-silent propulsion, and enough stability to race down the mountainous desert terrain. She made sure that the body bag was attached to the rear and wouldn't drag on the ground, then flipped the On switch, twisted the handle, and accelerated downward, toward the bloody street below.

She rode standing, careful to keep her balance as the bike raced and bounced over sand and stone. She hoped that she had tied the body bag on tight enough the night before so that the corpse wouldn't fall off.

Fifteen seconds later, Lisa sped up to the second car and looked inside, confirming that all of the passengers were indeed dead. Satisfied, she looked down the darkening road, towards the gate. A second Iranian troop transport van, followed by a police vehicle with flashing lights, was now racing her way. She retrieved the H&K MP-5 from the side holster mounted to the bike and flipped the safety switch to the symbol with three red bullets. She took careful aim at the front windshield of the incoming vehicle.

It was a far shot for such a weapon. It was unlikely that she would be able to hit anyone from this distance. But her goal wasn't to kill, it was to ensure that they followed her. It was getting darker out. They would see the muzzle flash. With any luck, a round or two would hit the truck. She didn't want to get to the water without being noticed.

Lisa pulled the trigger. On full auto mode, the MP-5 emptied thirty rounds in the direction of the truck in three bursts. The weapon rattled, but had little recoil. Lisa could just make out the windshield cracking as one of her rounds hit its target. She dropped the weapon onto the sweltering pavement and rolled the accelerator of the bike. She sped down a sandy road, heading to the beach.

Almost there. Multiple sirens in the distance.

She glanced back. The truck turned off the main highway and onto the dirt road to follow her, but Lisa had already built up a sizeable lead. She was several hundred yards ahead when she skidded the dirt bike to a stop, careful not to fall off with the weight of the dead American body behind her. She pulled the pin on the incendiary device that was attached to the underside of her seat and hopped off, letting the bike fall on its side. She unzipped her ghillie suit and let it drop to the ground, her metamorphosis almost complete.

The bike began smoldering. Then thick black smoke erupted from intense blue flames as the incendiary charge went off. As the security truck raced up to the scene, the dead body became engulfed in flame, artificially intensified by chemical accelerants. The fire was supposed to confuse the Iranians into thinking that he had died trying to escape, and not several days ago as he actually had. Whether it worked or not wasn't important. It was enough to implicate the United States.

The dead man was named Tom Connolly. Once a CIA agent, then a private contractor, and then a traitor to his country. He had been working for Jinshan for a little over a year now. This was his final assignment. He would receive no payment.

Behind the smoke, Lisa trudged into the sea wearing a tight black wetsuit. Before submerging, she looked up at the sky. Up there, somewhere, was an American drone. Or perhaps a satellite. She wondered if their network link was still operational, or if the cyberattacks had rendered them useless.

She blew a kiss to the sky.

Then she pulled a scuba mask over her face and unlatched the fins from her belt. She threw them over her feet, twisted open the oxygen valve of the thirty-minute container that was strapped to her back, and dove into the warm waters of the Arabian Gulf.

13

Al Dhafra Air Base, UAE

Elliot and Chase stood looking at blank screens. The last thing anyone in the room had seen of the Bandar Abbas attack was the roadside bomb going off and destroying the troop transport.

"What in the hell is going on?" Elliot was fuming.

The screen was black. A small bit of text read: *Satellite Signal Error 33948.29.2*

Chase noticed that the other screens around the room all had similar error messages. Even the tactical displays seemed off. The main tactical display on the big screen, front and center of the room, was showing double the number of tracks it had a minute earlier. They weren't syncing up with the datalink.

One of the enlisted Air Force men at the console said, "Sir, the system's shit the bed."

Chase frowned. It seemed odd that the tactical display, which used a different datalink than the drone, would fail at the same time. He looked around the room and saw just about everyone was troubleshooting some type of error.

The commotion in the room was getting louder. Someone said, "Use the radios."

"Satcom radios are down, but we've got line-of-sight comms like VHF and UHF."

Elliot said, "Well, that's not going to get that video stream over Bandar Abbas back up, is it?"

"No, sir."

One of the women manning a tactical display screen said to no one in particular, "All the links are down. The instant messengers are down. What the hell is going on?"

Chase felt a chill. This reminded him of 9/11. He had only been in high school. But the way multiple problems were occurring all at the same time...this had to be a coordinated attack.

Elliot sounded exasperated. He held a red phone to his ear and shook his head, looking at Chase. "Nothing."

One of the men who had been talking on a radio headset called to the duty officer, "The next pass for surveillance in that area will be an EP-3, but they're troubleshooting on the ground. They're experiencing systems problems too."

Elliot walked over to the Air Force officer who had been controlling the drone over Bandar Abbas. "Does that thing record video to its own hard drive?"

"Yes, sir."

"Is it going to crash somewhere over there if it doesn't have a network link-up?"

"No, sir. It should automatically go back to its emergency landing field and make an instrument landing."

Elliot said, "Okay, let me ask a real easy question." He looked at the duty officer. "When this thing lands, how soon can you get me the video that it recorded on its hard drive?"

The duty officer said, "We'll look into it, sir. It will probably be at least twelve hours or so."

Elliot said, "Understand that this"—he motioned to the blank screens around the room—"and this"—he picked up the red phone without a dial tone—"is an attack. Someone has just attacked us."

The room was quiet as they all listened to Elliot's rant.

"Get me that freaking video as soon as possible. I need to know who was responsible for this attack."

"Yes, sir."

The room came alive as everyone scrambled to troubleshoot the communications and link problems they were having.

Chase noticed that the only screen still showing anything of value was the Fox News channel. The volume was off. It was on a small screen in the corner of the room, but to Chase, it may as well have been a billboard. He walked up underneath it.

His brother David's face was being broadcast to the world. Underneath it was the headline: *Manhunt in Australia Underway.* A subheadline read: *US men suspected of selling cybertechnology to Iran.*

Chase looked over at Elliot to see if he had seen it. He was looking right at him.

* * *

They went to an office around the corner from the Tactical Operations Center, where they had been talking before. The door was closed. A small TV in the room showed CNN. The news channel was flipping between coverage of the two Americans on the run in Australia and the Iranian attacks at Bandar Abbas. They had the volume on low.

"We can now provide you the names of the two American men that are considered armed and dangerous. David Manning and Henry Glickstein are believed to be somewhere in Australia or the Philippines. A global

police manhunt is underway. Authorities say they have recordings of the men claiming responsibility for stealing US military cybertech-nology secrets and selling them to Iran. They also participated in plan-ning attacks against the United States. No word yet on whether any of this is related to the other major news coming out of Iran today.

"And a breaking news update on that other major Iran story—the violent attack that has killed a top Iranian politician and his wife, who we have now learned is the niece of the Iranian Supreme Leader. The Iranian government has stated that they now have indisputable DNA evidence linking the American government to the attack. They have provided a name—Tom Connolly—a man who Iran claims was the CIA operative who was behind the gruesome attack that left over two dozen dead. The US State Department has condemned the attack but has yet to put out a formal statement regarding this new DNA evidence. Another report coming out of Tehran cites a second American CIA oper-ative by the name of Lisa Parker who was involved in the operation. Thus far the CIA has declined to comment."

Chase spoke in a quiet voice. "There's something you should know. I just checked my email and voicemail. David called me today." Chase was conflicted. He knew what he wanted to do and he needed Elliot's help, but he wasn't sure that he'd go for it.

Elliot raised an eyebrow. "Now, you listen very carefully, Chase. I know he is your brother. But if you have any idea about where he is, if you know his whereabouts, then you need to let me know. Let's hear the message."

"I understand. But listen for a minute. Let's think about this. You know my family. You've known my dad for years. Do you really think someone in my family would do something like this?"

Elliot breathed in through his nose and closed his eyes. When he opened them, he said, "No, I do not. But I've seen enough screwed-up things lately that I can't tell up from down."

Chase put his phone on speaker and played the voicemail.

"Chase, it's David. I...I'm okay. Please tell Lindsay that I love her. I couldn't get in touch with her and...I'm not sure what's going to happen to me yet, so just please let her know that you heard from me and that I'm okay and that I love her. Listen, I'm in trouble. Some pretty bad things are going on. Some people may be after me and I...I'll call you soon."

Elliot said, "Play it again."

He did.

Chase looked him in the eye. "Does that sound like someone who's voluntarily betraying his country?"

Elliot raised his voice. "How the hell should I know?"

"I think that this is connected to what we've been working on. Yes, David was on that list. But maybe this list isn't of volunteers. Maybe it's something else."

"What are you getting at?"

"Have you seen anything through official channels about my brother? Any official policy on what we're supposed to do with him?"

"No. Just this stuff on the news. And what Langley said a few weeks back about Gorji's list not being a good enough source to go on."

"Then you probably have some license to solve the problem your own way, right?"

Elliot's eyes narrowed. "What do you mean by that?"

"I mean, what if my brother was taken into custody by the CIA? Since he may have information that's relevant to our work, could Dubai Station take hold of him?"

"Now, how are we going to do that? They don't even know

where he is and there's supposed to be some doggone international manhunt out for that boy."

"Not anymore." Chase pointed at the TV screen. *Manhunt ends in Darwin, Australia, as two US men taken into custody by Interpol*, it read.

Elliot scoffed. "What are you asking, Chase? You can't really be suggesting what I think you are."

"Hear me out. Let me bring him here. We'll ask them some questions and find out what's really going on. You know as well as I do that this could be related to Abu Musa and to Lisa Parker's exploits."

"How are you going to bring him here? He's in custody. You want me to ask Interpol to give him to us?"

Chase said, "I don't want to ask anyone. Where there is confusion, there is opportunity. Let's create a little confusion."

"Are you out of your goddamn mind? Even if I was going to authorize it, which I am *not*, how would you do it?"

Chase smiled. In his experience, very few people wanted to know how to do something that they were not interested in doing.

14

Darwin, Australia

Henry Glickstein sat on his cot, biting his fingernails. The two young Australian military police guards sat outside his jail cell watching TV.

The rotating groups of MPs had watched the twenty-four-hour news channel all night long. They were excited. The news reports kept referring to David and Henry being captured in Darwin.

Henry was pissed. Since the TV had been on all night, he couldn't get a lick of sleep. This place sucked. It reminded him of a jail cell in a John Wayne Western. Half the room was where they sat, behind bars. The other half of the room was the area where the Australian military police sat.

Supposedly they were going to be moved soon. The MPs said that they would get a shower at the next place. They had only been here for twelve hours, they were told. Just be patient. Right. Patience. That was what Henry needed.

Several weeks ago, David and Henry, along with another eighteen Americans, had been taken to a remote island under the pretense of participating in some top-secret CIA project. There

were experts from a variety of fields that were with them. Some
people were experts in defense, others in information technology,
and others in military tactics. A lot of them were in the government or military. Each of them had been sent there by a trusted
superior at their place of work.

Once on the island, they were told why they were there. China
was planning to attack the United States. Everyone on the island
was part of an American Red Cell: a team of experts that would
plan out how China could best attack the US. The idea was that
this would then help America to prepare its defense. They were
told that Chinese spies had already infiltrated many of the US
defense and intelligence agencies, so this carefully vetted team
had to do their work on the island—a secret compound where no
one would find out what was going on.

One minor problem—the entire operation was a ruse. The
head woman there, Lena Chou, claimed to be a member of the
CIA. Everything had seemed legitimate until David Manning
discovered that the other half of the island was filled with Chinese
military. Lena was working for them.

David had led the group in a revolt, but Lena and her mole,
that no-good Indian bastard Natesh, had foiled that plan. As a
storm pummeled the island, three Chinese helicopters landed and
began to take over the buildings where the Americans waited.

Henry and David had escaped. David swam halfway around
the island and commandeered one of the Chinese motorized
rafts. The two of them had barely survived that night in the
deadly storm. But luck was on their side. A day later, they had
been picked up by an Australian fishing trawler and taken to
Darwin.

Already paranoid about the Chinese coming after them, David
and Henry didn't tell the people on the trawler what was really
going on. They also decided not to make any communications that
might allow the Chinese to catch up with them while they were

vulnerable and at sea. They needed to speak with the right people, and make that first communication count.

During the week or so that it took the trawler to reach Darwin, however, Lena's spy network had apparently been hard at work. When David and Henry had called one of David's trusted friends at his work, they had been too late. A bulletin had been put out by Interpol that David and Henry were wanted for selling cybertechnology to Iran. So when the two men thought they were being picked up by the Australian government and taken to safety, they were actually being taken to jail. Even the good guys were against them now.

David held on to one of the cold bars and asked the guards, "Can you at least tell us when we'll be able to speak with an American representative?"

Henry knew what the answer would be.

The skinny guard looked like he'd just hit puberty a few weeks ago. Thick Australian accent. "Afraid we can't help you. Interpol is in charge. We're just doing them a favor, keeping you here until they can move you."

Henry checked the spot on his arm that normally housed his Rolex. It must have been the tenth time he'd done so. Habit. A pale patch of skin told him nothing of what time it might be. He had traded his watch to a pawnshop the day before and used the funds to buy phones and pay for hotels. Their grand plan to get word out about the Lena and the Red Cell and the island. Lot of good it had done them.

The wall clock said six fifteen. About ten minutes had gone by since the last time he'd checked. Henry kept telling himself that this would all get sorted out. That any minute now a lawyer would come through that door and demand that his clients get fair treatment. But the TV had been tuned to the news channel, so Henry knew that no lawyer would be coming.

They were being called international terrorists. The TV was

saying that US authorities had audio evidence that David Manning and Henry Glickstein had conspired in an Iranian cyber-attack on allied nations. This was total horseshit.

Yesterday, soon after they had arrived in Darwin, they had called David's office. Gotten hold of someone he knew and thought he could trust. Told him and a group of people on the phone everything. But Lena's crew had already put plans into motion. They had put out information that David and Henry had given classified information to Iran. Which was a complete lie. But in the information age, perception was reality. Neither David nor Henry knew whether the people on that phone call were really American loyalists who had been tricked, or Chinese agents posing as Americans.

However they had done it, the Chinese had convinced enough people that David and Henry were international terrorists. Interpol had captured them in Darwin. David hadn't even been able to contact his wife.

Just as bad as being captured was what they learned from watching the news.

The Red Cell's plan for a Chinese attack on America began with a staged war. The plans called for attacks on Iran that would frame the United States as the aggressor. This would trigger retributive attacks from Iran against the United States, further fanning the flames. Covertly, the Chinese would actually execute some of the attacks. If the fire of an Iran-US war burned bright enough, the American military would be forced to overallocate its global military assets to the Middle East. The Chinese would launch a cyberattack and make it look like Iran was the culprit. This cyberattack would disrupt global communications, especially the ones that the US military relied upon. The effect of these initial plans was to leave the best American military assets stuck in the Middle East, fighting a war with Iran, and unable to quickly react to a Chinese attack.

As David and Henry first sat down behind bars, the news channel had rattled off three frightening stories. First, David and Henry were wanted for selling a cyberweapon to Iran. Second, the CIA had assassinated a prominent Iranian politician and his wife, who was related to the Iranian Supreme Leader. Third, global satellite and communications outages were occurring. Lena's Chinese team had implemented the Red Cell's war plans.

It would have sounded preposterous if anyone had told Henry this stuff a few weeks ago. But now that he had seen what was on that island with his own eyes, he was a believer. David had seen even more. On the other side of the island from where the American Red Cell was held, David had seen a second Chinese encampment. A man-made cave had been created out of one of the island's mountains. David surmised that it was some type of bunker, possibly for Chinese Navy ships or submarines. Henry had overheard another part of the Red Cell plans which suggested the use of electromagnetic pulse devices in the Pacific. For years, the Chinese had been building large military bunkers into their coastal mountain bases to protect their assets from EMP attacks. If they proceeded with that plan, it would leave any remaining US Pacific Navy vessels paralyzed and unable to respond to a Chinese assault.

"What a crock of shit," Henry said when he heard the newscast. The Australian guards glared back at him. "What? Do I look like a friggin' terrorist? I like beer and hamburgers. I'm not a friggin' terrorist!"

David said, "Give it a rest."

David was lying on his back on the other cot. He hadn't said much since last night. Henry figured he was worried sick about what this meant for his chances to be reunited with his family.

The door burst open and an ogre in a military uniform walked in.

The man filled the frame of the door. He had to duck his head down so as not to hit it. A second, shorter man in a different uniform walked in after him. They stood there at the entrance to the small brig, taking everything in.

David looked at the man and sat up, wide-eyed. *Hmm.* Henry saw something in David's eyes that he hadn't seen since they'd been arrested. *Hope?*

Henry looked at the large man and then back at David. Whatever David was seeing, Henry was missing it. Two more big mean military guys had just come in. From Henry's perspective, the situation didn't look like it had gotten any better.

The ogre was six foot six and easily 250 pounds. His face was red from the sun, and his eyes bulged out of their sockets like he was in the middle of bench-pressing a bulldozer. Those crazy-looking eyes searched around like they were deciding what to scream at. The veins in his neck were thick and purple, sticking out like the muscles in his shoulders and back were demanding more room.

"Who the *fuck* is in charge here?" The ogre spoke in an American accent. Interesting.

Henry noticed that his uniform had an American flag patch on the shoulder. The man next to the ogre had a uniform like the ones worn by the two guards. There was more shiny stuff on his chest and shoulders, but it was the same type.

The guards were standing at attention, looking back and forth between the two arrivals. The skinny guard said, "Uh, sir...the Interpol officer is—"

"*Wrong answer!*" bellowed the ogre. "Try the fuck again."

"Sir, we were told to—"

The ogre said, "These men are American citizens. I am Major Josh Brundle. And you will relinquish custody of these men to me immediately. Captain Sirek here is our Australian liaison and can back me up that this has been fully approved by Australian authorities. No paperwork is needed, gentlemen. Open the cell now, and I'll see that your names aren't mentioned in this colossal clusterfuck."

The guards looked at each other. "Sir, should we call base operations?"

The Australian captain shook his head. He said, "Won't be necessary, boys. I've just spoken with base ops. We need to get these men moving riiiaght noww. Let's go." The accent sounded a bit funny. Exaggerated, even. Like he had just gotten done watching *Crocodile Dundee* before he came and had been practicing.

The skinny guard grabbed the key to the cell and opened it up. "Do you need cuffs?"

The major said, "Not necessary."

Henry and David were marched outside to a beige Humvee. The major and the Australian captain thanked the guards, and then the Humvee drove away in a cloud of dust. No one said a word.

The man in the Australian uniform said, "That went well." He no longer had an Australian accent.

Major Brundle looked at them through the rearview mirror. "David, your brother says hello."

"My brother knows where I am?"

Brundle laughed. "David, everyone knows where you are." He looked back at him through the rearview mirror every few seconds. "Do you remember me from the Academy? I was in Chase's company."

The Humvee was moving fast. Ninety miles per hour, easy. The big SUVs drove on the left side of the two-lane road, weaving around the slower civilian traffic.

"Yes, I remember you. Did...did Chase send you?"

"Officially? I have no idea what you're talking about. Off the record? You bet your ass. I served with your brother several times over the past few years. And I remember you from school. I don't care what the news says, I know it's bogus. Your brother called. He told me what was going on and asked for a favor. Now I might get in a lot of trouble for this, but the way I see it, the rules are a little unclear. You see, if someone tells me that the CIA wants to establish immediate custody of two US citizens, then I'm pretty sure that I'm supposed to go do it. Now, the fact that the person representing the CIA is a family member of one of the men in custody, and a former friend of mine in college, is irrelevant."

David and Henry looked at each other.

"Shit. We got flashing lights in back of us," the guy in the Australian uniform said.

Major Brundle said, "We're five minutes from base, let's just keep going. They aren't going to shoot us. We'll probably end up having a conversation at the gate. I'll take care of it."

David said, "Where are we going?"

The big man, looking in the rearview mirror at both David and the flashing lights of the car behind them, said, "Ever ridden on an Osprey?"

Henry said, "The bird? Well, if I'm being honest there was this one time in Tijuana. I did have a lot to drink and—"

David said, "It's a tilt-rotor aircraft. Marine Corps. It replaced the CH-46 for transport and logistics missions." He looked up at the men, curious. "But it won't be able to cross the ocean. Where is the Osprey taking us?"

The guy in the Australian uniform watched the car behind them and said quickly, "It'll take you to Bathurst Island. About fifty miles north of here. It was where we thought we'd have the least explaining to do as far as flying you out. If we'd done it at the Darwin Airport, we might get stopped by the authorities. There's already a small passenger jet there waiting for you. No passenger manifests, no flight plans. Small airstrip."

Henry said, "So we're once again getting flown to an island. And the CIA is involved. Look, I hate to be a spoilsport, but we tried this a few weeks ago and we ended up getting dropped off at a secret Chinese military base."

The two men in the front seat looked at each other and then back at Henry like he was crazy.

Henry stared back and blinked.

The Humvees stopped at a large military base gate. There were sandbags stacked up into bunkers on either side of the road. Machine guns pointed at the cars as they approached. A gate guard in the same uniform as Major Brundle walked toward the convoy of two Humvees and one Australian police car, complete with flashing light. The gate guard looked confused. Brundle got out of the driver's seat and held up his ID to the gate guard.

He said to the gate guard, "Sergeant, I've got high-priority passengers that need to get over to the pads for immediate transport. I don't know what this idiot in the police car is doing, but I might need your help. Whatever he tells you, he has absolutely no authority here on our base."

Henry watched as the Interpol man who had arrested them the night before got out of the car, holding up a badge. The driver remained in the police car. The Interpol officer's face was red as he looked at David and Henry in the back of the Humvee.

"I demand that you turn over my prisoners to me immediately!" He had a French accent.

Major Brundle looked at the gate guard, who looked uneasy. Then he looked back at the Interpol man. "These are US citizens. We are US Marines. I have been ordered to turn them over to the proper US authorities immediately."

"Under whose authority? What is your name?"

"My name?" the big man said. "You don't know my name? Do you have any idea who you're speaking to?"

The Interpol man said, "No." He was perplexed at the question.

"You really don't know my name? You're sure?"

The French-accented man was red-faced. "No, I assure you that I do not!"

"Good." Brundle had been covering his name tag, which was stitched on his chest. He kept his hand covering his name and walked back into the Humvee. He told the gate guard, "Don't let them in, Sergeant."

"Yes, sir."

The sergeant took hold of the M-16 that was slung over his shoulder, keeping it pointed at the ground. The Interpol man began swearing in French, but remained where he was.

They drove around a set of hangars. Henry heard the engines of the large grey aircraft starting up as they approached a wide-open area that was apparently an airport for these strange-looking aircraft. They had wings like a plane, but two small rotors like a helicopter on each side.

Henry said, "Do these things really fly?"

The Humvees stopped fifty yards behind the aircraft.

"Okay, listen up, gents. You're going to get IDs and a phone on the plane. If they check you when you land in Dubai—"

"Dubai?"

"—just say you're tourists. They'll have someone pick you up at the airport and Chase will take it from there."

David shook hands with the two men in the front seat. "Thanks, guys. Listen...before we go, I need to tell you something. It's going to sound crazy, but it's the truth."

David gave them the two-minute version of everything that had happened to them on the island.

When he was finished, Brundle said, "Is that what this is all about? The Chinese?"

David and Henry both nodded. Then David thanked them again and he and Henry walked up the rear ramp entrance of the Osprey. An enlisted air crewman helped them to put on a vest and helmet, then strapped them into the passenger seats. The twin engines grew enormously loud, and then they slowly came to a hover. Henry watched the base behind them grow smaller as they moved forward and began to climb. The blue lights of the Interpol car were still flashing at the entrance.

A few moments later, they were flying north over the ocean.

15

12 Hours Later

Chase and David embraced in the lobby of the Burj Al Arab hotel.

David's voice broke as he hugged his brother. "Hey, bro. It's good to see you."

Chase gave him three hard pats on the back while they hugged. "Hey, man." He held his shoulder and looked him over. "Let's get you upstairs. Come on."

Following Chase, David said, "Chase, this is Henry. Henry, my brother Chase." Chase shook the short man's hand as they walked.

They took the elevator up to the twenty-first floor and walked into a room fit for a king. Deep violet decorative bedcovers and pillows. Gold trim on all the furniture. The room's expansive window overlooked the beach to the north, and David could just make out the large towering skyscraper in the distance.

Three men sat in the room. David thought they looked a lot like the SEALs Chase used to work with. Two had beards. They were all young and fit and looked like they knew how to fight. All three wore button-down shirts and shoulder holsters. Suit jackets were draped behind their chairs. They nodded at Chase as he came in.

Chase said to the group of men, "How's our friend?"

"Typing away."

"Any word from the boss?"

"He's on his way."

"Thanks."

Chase didn't introduce David and Henry. The men didn't ask any questions. Chase led David and Henry to a sitting area beyond the men.

David said to his brother, "This is some hotel. Why are we here?"

Chase said, "We were in need of a secure location for another project. This hotel is on its own island, connected by a single short road to the mainland. It's the only road in or out. Doesn't get much more secure than that. The room is courtesy of a friend in UAE intelligence. We figured that it would be the best place to stash you until we decide on our next steps."

David looked at his brother. He wasn't dressed like his usual rugged self. David was used to seeing him in casual clothes or his fatigues that he wore with the SEALs. Today, Chase had on shiny leather wingtips and a tailored suit. "Chase, what exactly do you do here?"

Chase gave him a sheepish look. "Just have a seat. We'll get into all that." David had the feeling that he was about to learn a lot about his brother.

A knock at the door. One of the three men opened it and a man entered. He was a black man in his mid- to late fifties, with close-cropped greying hair.

"Gents, this is Elliot Jackson. He is head of the CIA station here in Dubai, and my boss. David, Elliot's also a friend of Dad's. You can trust him." They made eye contact.

Surprised by several of the things Chase had just said, David managed to simply say, "Nice to meet you, sir."

"Same."

Elliot didn't look very happy, but they shook hands.

David saw an older Asian man in the adjoining room. A glass window separated them. Three computer monitors stood on a table in front of the man. He stopped typing for a moment and looked up at David. He looked worn down. He turned back to the computer and continued.

Chase saw David's expression. "That's the person who we originally set this room up for. He's working on another project, and he also needs to keep a low profile."

Henry said, "What's he working on?"

Chase said, "You don't need to worry about it."

"You guys do a lot of this?"

Elliot said, "Come on, let's have a seat over here."

They walked over to the kitchen area and took a seat at the table. Elliot took out a small black device that looked like an iPod. He pressed a red button on it and said, "David Manning and Henry Glickstein debrief."

Chase said, "Alright, fellas, here's the deal. I went out on a limb to get you here. You have Elliot and my friend in the UAE intelligence service to thank as well. David, I know that the news reports can't be accurate. But I don't have proof. I should let you know that we're bending the rules a lot by bringing you out here, and we've yet to hear back from Langley or Washington through official channels on what your status is. Communications problems. I tried calling Brundle after getting word that you'd left Australia, but the phone lines have been shit for the past day or so. So...we need to know: what the hell happened to you guys?"

David said, "It all started about three weeks ago now. I was on retainer with the CIA as a Red Cell participant. I got activated on very short notice, but I had no reason to doubt that it was real.

They put me in a private jet with three people on board. One was a director at In-Q-Tel. I knew him. But it turns out he was really working for the Chinese, although I didn't know that at the time. His name was Tom Connolly."

"Say that name again?"

"Tom Connolly."

Elliot whispered to Chase, "That's the body that the Iranians found on their beach near Bandar Abbas. Tom Connolly. He was ex-CIA. Hasn't been in the Agency in years. But the Iranians and the press wouldn't believe that at this point, even if we showed them proof."

Chase said, "Keep going."

David said, "They briefed me on that initial plane ride across the country and explained that China was going to attack the US."

Elliot and Chase looked at each other. Elliot said, "Who is 'they'? Who briefed you?"

"Tom Connolly, on the plane. He said that he was CIA, but that the Red Cell we were to be a part of was being organized by a group of people from the military and other government agencies. We were supposed to come up with how the Chinese would do it. How they would attack the US..."

Chase and Elliot were incredulous.

Elliot said, "Excuse this question, David. But how did they get Americans to do this for China? Why would anyone believe them?"

"We were all on DoD and CIA Red Cell rosters. The CIA normally schedules these things out months in advance. The only difference here was how abrupt the activation was. But we still all got the right phone calls, proper codewords, all that stuff. Our respective bosses were informed that we were participating in an important national security project for a few weeks, because that's something the government has to do – notify your place of work so you don't get in trouble. Then they took us across the country on a small jet, and then we met up with others. Then we got on more jets and they didn't tell us where we were headed. They had about twenty people in all. Experts in various fields. I was the expert on Project ARES. It was something that I was working on at In-Q-Tel. A new type of cyberweapon that has the ability to take out satellite and data networks."

Elliot leaned forward and said in a deep voice, "It can do what now?"

David sighed. "It can shut down satellite and data networks. I know what you're thinking. And, yes, I believe they've used it. That's probably what all this GPS and communications difficulty is about."

Elliot placed his hands on his face. Chase looked at him, worried. Elliot moaned, "Continue."

David said, "The second flight was about nine hours. Henry and I now know that the island was somewhere in the South China Sea. We aren't sure where exactly, but we did enough studying of maps on our boat ride last week that we've got a few ideas. We believe that the island they took us to is located in between the Spratly Islands and the Philippines."

Chase said, "We'll need to narrow down the location, but we can do that later. So what happened on the island?"

"It was a small tropical island. A single volcanic-looking mountain, covered in jungle. It was probably about three miles across. It's a Chinese military base. I'm sure of that now. A woman named Lena Chou...well, that's what she called herself anyway... was running the show. She had some Silicon Valley consultant helping her out. An Indian guy named Natesh. Young—probably still in his twenties."

Chase said, "Hold on. Say that name again."

"Natesh."

Chase looked disturbed.

David said, "What, do you know him?"

Chase was looking at the ground, his eyes darting back and forth as he thought through something. He leaned over to Elliot and said, "That's the name of the guy on Abu Musa that showed Ahmad Gorji the list. They weren't talking about a list of people that would supply information to Abu Musa. Natesh showed Gorji the list of names on the Red Cell several months ago."

Elliot didn't react. He turned to David and said, "Please, continue."

"We spent a week or so doing brainstorming sessions, coming up with ways to defeat the US military and national infrastructure —utilities, communications, everything. A lot of us had top-secret clearances. People talked about specific frequency ranges and tactics. I mean...Chase, it was bad...I feel like shit about it all. I feel like such an idiot. But I'm telling you, the setup was very elaborate. We really, truly didn't know. I swear to God. And there was, I don't know...kind of a weird groupthink thing going on at first. Everyone fed off each other. We thought we were going to help our country." David hung his head. "That feeling didn't last."

Henry said, "David was the one who broke the spell for the rest of us. He saw something in the first couple days. One of the guys got sent off the island in the middle of the night. They carried him away and threw him in a helicopter. He was unconscious. This guy—Bill—went to see this Lena chick about getting off the island to go take care of his wife, who had cancer. And that was what we thought happened. But David saw him that night being carried away, unconscious. None of us knew that part. So David got suspicious and a few days later, he swam around the island. He saw the guy that was supposed to have been flown home to his wife on the other side of the island. But he was a prisoner of the Chinese soldiers."

Elliot said, "You saw Chinese soldiers? How'd you know they were Chinese?"

David said, "We know. It only makes sense. Who else would

want the information that they took from us? We suspected as much once. But we're definitely sure now. Hell, we saw the red star painted on their troop transport helicopters on the last day, when the jig was up. We took a motorized raft and escaped. A storm helped us evade capture. Then we got picked up by an Australian fishing boat and taken to Darwin. I have no idea how they found us, but this whole international terrorism thing has to be a Chinese setup. We called home and tried to warn people, but it didn't work."

Elliot said, "What happened?"

"I called a guy at my work. We told him everything—the quick version—and asked him to set up a call in an hour so we could spread the word to all the different agencies about what was going on. After that, we tried calling other people—Lindsay, you—but we never got through. Then we called back the guy at my work and he claimed to have reps from a bunch of military and government agencies. We were trying to warn everyone before an attack came."

Chase said, "It's alright, man. We know you were just trying to do the right thing. Do you remember any of the names?"

"I don't think it matters. I have no idea who was really on the phone. Hell, it may not have even been Lundy."

Elliot nodded. "If they knew the numbers that you were going to call, they could have had trained operatives and a preplanned response. That's what I would have done."

Chase said, "It's alright. You're gonna be alright. Give us another day and we'll get you back to the States. We need to figure some stuff out here."

Elliot said, "Chase, I think I'm going to want you to personally escort them back home. We need to get a warning to the right people. And based on what I'm hearing, I don't trust our normal method of communications. Shit, those methods might not be available anyway."

"Understood."

A buzz went off and Chase picked his phone up out of his jacket's inner breast pocket. He looked at the phone and said, "Waleed says he's a few minutes out. I'm going to need to head upstairs."

Elliot looked over to the other room where the Asian man was typing. He wasn't paying attention. Elliot then said in a quiet tone, "He doesn't want to meet here?"

David shook his head slowly. "No. But he said to make sure that our friend stays here until we have our chat."

Elliot nodded.

David looked worried. "What for? Why do you need to leave?"

"Nothing. It's something else. Another issue. I'll be back soon. Elliot will continue this."

Elliot was looking at his phone.

He said, "Chase, before you go, you might want to see this. They sent me the video feed from the drone over Bandar Abbas. It's two minutes long. They sent me the highlights."

Elliot held up his phone. All four of them watched as a roadside bomb destroyed two trucks and three cars on a highway. Then a dirt bike drove down the adjacent mountainside and through the wreckage. The rider fired a small machine gun at another military truck that was heading towards it. Then the bike raced about a mile to the shore, the truck in pursuit. Just before reaching the water, the rider slammed to a halt. A large sack was thrown onto the beach and set on fire. Then the rider threw off what looked like a ghillie suit and walked into the beach. It was a woman. A long-haired Asian woman. She looked up at the sky and placed her hand to her face just before diving into the water.

"What was she just doing?"

"It looked like she blew us a kiss."

Chase said, "Well, that's definitely Lisa Parker."

David said, "Mr. Jackson, would you mind pausing the video so I can see her face?"

He gave David a strange look, no doubt wondering whether someone that had unwittingly just provided the Chinese with classified secrets should be shown anything this sensitive. Still, he did as David asked.

Elliot changed the angle of his phone in his hand and David caught a glimpse of the screen. It held an image of a pretty Asian woman blowing them a kiss from several miles below the drone's camera.

Henry said, "Hey, that's *her*."

David said, "Brother, I don't know any Lisa Parker. But I one hundred percent know that face."

Elliot and Chase looked at each other, confused, and then back at David.

"That's the Chinese woman that was running the Red Cell. That's Lena Chou."

Shang-Class Submarine
15 Nautical Miles off the Coast of Dubai

Lena stared at the email on the computer screen in disbelief. The submarine had just gone up to periscope depth, downloaded a good deal of data from Chinese military satellites, and then plunged back to a depth of 250 feet.

The email was from Jinshan himself.

Hello, Lena,

I hope this finds you well. I am extremely impressed with your most recent accomplishments. My congratulations on a job well done.

Unfortunately, the Abu Musa operation was not successful. Not only has the physical link to the submarine cables proven faulty, but also our backup plan using our "faux" Satoshi plant seems to have been detected by the Americans. I received word from him recently that all of his uploads are complete, yet we still have no ability to artificially control the bitcoin valuation. I surmise that US intelligence is respon-

sible for this. Alas, we knew that this operation was high-risk, and this outcome is not completely unexpected.

As I stated to you when we last spoke, the rapid execution of our plans is my primary concern. If one option fails, we shall move to the next. With the unfortunate failure of the Abu Musa operation, and the apparent success of your excursion to the north, I have decided that a change of direction is now prudent.

I have ordered an accelerated timeline for our Dubai operation. It has been brought to my attention, however, that there is a window of opportunity to recover certain assets prior to the commencement of the Dubai operation. Your mission is as follows. I leave it to your expert judgment to determine what, if anything on this list, can be accomplished. Your air transportation will be at rendezvous point #4 within one hour of your scheduled communications window.

She read the details of the mission outline, shaking her head. She looked at her watch. If she was to do this, she needed to move now.

She stormed out of the room, squeezing through the long, narrow corridor of the submarine until she reached the bridge. The captain saw her and immediately rose from his seat. Normally the captain of a submarine was like a god on earth. But when the highest-ranking official in the Chinese Navy had spoken to him personally about this secret assignment, he'd had but one warning: do not anger Lena Chou.

"Miss Chou, how can I help you?" The sailors and officers in the bridge were all looking at her. There were no women on board Chinese submarines. One as attractive as Lena caused a lot of commotion. One enlisted man had made the mistake of groping her in a dark passageway. He'd made it seem like an accident. Perhaps it had been a dare from his friends. Lena had put him in the infirmary. Word had spread quickly after that.

Everyone on board had now heard the same warning that the captain had.

Lena addressed the captain. "We need to surface immediately."

He looked like someone had just struck him. "Excuse me?" Submarines were covert. Surfacing this close to Dubai was heresy. "I'm sorry, but that's not possible. We can't surface. The American Navy has ships and aircraft throughout this region. If we surfaced, they might—"

"Captain, I understand the risk. But this is not a request. I am needed in Dubai. I expect that you will be getting your official orders any moment now. Also—I recommend that you make preparations for combat."

A yellow light began blinking near one of the computers.

One of the young officers called out, "Sir, we're receiving an urgent message from PLAN Submarine Force."

The captain looked at Lena with a mix of apprehension and frustration. He said, "With respect, you are untrained in the art of submarine warfare. You cannot expect me to surface my boat in broad daylight when we are barely outside of the territorial waters of the United Arab Emirates, and very close to one of the busiest ports in the world. An American aircraft carrier just pulled in to that port. It would be extremely unwise to surface here."

Lena didn't want to risk having this go awry. She decided to take a soft approach. "Captain, surely there is a reason that a man of your skill was assigned to this mission." She looked at her watch. "In a few moments, there will be a helicopter not far from our current location. It will be sent to pick me up and take me back to Dubai. You only need surface for a brief moment. Leave me in a raft if you must. But I need to be on that aircraft. This must be accomplished or our nation's security will suffer greatly."

The young officer near the communications station ripped off a printout of the urgent message and brought it over to the captain. The captain read the message. His eyes grew wide, and then fearful. He turned to his first officer. "Please find us a good place to come up." He then continued reading the message.

Lena said, "Thank you, Captain. I'll be at the main sail hatch in one minute."

She turned and headed back to her room. She needed to find something more appropriate to wear. She hurried to the room and dug through her bags. There it was. A bit wrinkly, but it would do nicely. She quickly put her new outfit on.

Her mood improved as she thought of what she was going to do. She smiled to herself as she ran through China's newest attack submarine wearing a tight black dress and flats. Her jet-black hair flowed over her shoulders. She reached the main sail and climbed up the ladder. The captain was there, wide-eyed, a crumpled message in his hand.

He said, "Do you know what this says? Do you know what they are having me do?"

"Yes, Captain."

"If I fire my missiles at these targets, we will be destroyed."

She stopped climbing up the ladder and gave him a stern look. Two sailors stood next to him, looking nervous. She said, "Captain, are you going to carry out your orders?"

Red-faced, he replied, "Yes. Yes, of course."

"Very well, Captain. Good luck."

He muttered under his breath. "But this is lunacy."

Still looking at him, she replied, "No, Captain, it is war."

She turned and lifted herself up the iron ladder and through the hatch. She stepped into the oven of the Persian Gulf air. Sure enough, three enlisted men held a raft in the water, waiting for her. The sailors wore masks over their faces, but she could still tell that they had open mouths as she slid down the main sail ladder and onto the hull wearing her dress, a long slit up the side of her skirt.

Within two minutes, the submarine had resubmerged and she floated by herself in the raft.

Lena had enjoyed "the game" that she had played for over a decade. Pretending to be an American spy, all the while working for her Chinese master. She also enjoyed using the skill that Jinshan had trained her for—killing. She wouldn't lie to herself and say that she didn't like it. It was an unexpected feeling, the first time she had taken a life, so many years ago. But now...she looked forward to it each and every time. The rush that she got was unlike anything else in life.

She was good at it. And everyone liked to do things that they were good at. Athletes loved to play their sports. Workaholics loved their work. Lena loved to kill. If there was a God, which Lena doubted, then why would he have made her so good at killing if he didn't want her to do it? It was her calling.

A twinge of worry—an emotion her psyche rarely lent itself to —crept in. As fortunate as it had been that Chase and David had been brothers, she wondered if she would feel any regret in disappointing Chase. Their relationship had begun as pure lust. Most of Lena's relationships were like that. A way for her to satisfy her physical needs without creating an emotional vulnerability that could be exploited by her many potential enemies. It frustrated her that she felt a connection with Chase, now. When she had found out that David Manning worked for In-Q-Tel, and on the ARES project, she had pulled strings to get him onto the Red Cell list.

Getting that list in front of Gorji had been a bit harder, but Natesh had done well there. She had used Chase, in more ways than one. She had used him to satisfy her sexual cravings. She had used him to find out what Elliot Jackson knew. And she had used him to identify someone who turned out to be a key member of the Red Cell. While David Manning's Red Cell performance had turned out to be less than productive, that could change with the proper motivation.

The effects of the ARES cyberweapon had been strong, but not as strong as Natesh had predicted. Further expert consultation was needed.

If she was honest with herself, she did not wish to hurt Chase. She had enjoyed their time together, even if most of what she had told him was lies. She was very attracted to him, and not just physically. They were alike, in many ways. They were both heroes. Warriors who fought for what was right. The fact that they were on opposing sides was a shame, in a way.

As she looked to the east, she could see the tallest of Dubai's skyscrapers peeking up over the horizon. The setting sun was behind her. The sound of a helicopter's rotors grew louder. She closed her eyes and breathed in the salt air, stretching. It was a good day. She was getting ready to do what she was meant to do. Something she loved to do. Kill. She just hoped that she wouldn't have to do it to him.

17

A crimson sunset flooded the monstrous panoramic glass walls of the Skyview Bar. The bar sat atop the famed Burj Al Arab hotel, five hundred feet above the warm waters of the Arabian Gulf. The Burj Al Arab was built to look like a magnificent white sail cast upward and surrounded by water. The fourth-tallest hotel in the world, it was built on an artificial island and was advertised as the world's only "seven-star" hotel. Movie stars, royalty, and heads of state regularly stayed in the lavish resort with rooms that could exceed one hundred thousand dollars per night. VIPs sometimes arrived by helicopter to a landing pad that was suspended in air on the twenty-fifth floor. When they landed, fireworks and drums greeted them.

Directly below, multimillion-dollar yachts cruised past. Fading daylight, sea, and the Arabian Desert collided with Dubai's sleek and modern skyline. Through the haze, Chase could just make out the ethereal tower that dwarfed the rest of the city, the Burj Khalifa. It rose up to the heavens, reflecting the sun like a gleaming fiery sword.

He sipped ice water as he turned his gaze back inside. From his corner table for two, he held the perfect field of view as he waited for Waleed. He had called Chase, frantic, just as they picked up David and Henry from the airport.

Waleed wouldn't go into details on the phone, but he said that he had heard from Gorji, and that it was imperative that Satoshi remain in his room at the Burj Al Arab.

It was one more crisis that Elliot had to deal with. Iran was still spewing threats of war. US forces in the area were on high alert. Moments ago, Chase had watched as his father's former aircraft carrier had sailed into the Dubai port of Jebel Ali. He wondered if they would even let the crew off the ship for liberty, or if they would just resupply and go back out to sea. He also wondered how their communication lines were doing.

In the past thirty-six hours since Lisa...or Lena...had executed her attack in Iran, global Internet and GPS networks had been spotty at best. The news said that it had mainly affected US-based assets. TV and phones in Dubai still worked. They could send emails, although most of the ones that went to the US bounced back. Phone calls to the US weren't getting through.

The global stock markets had plummeted in panic. The markets were still functional, but businesses were starting to suffer from network interruptions.

The classified networks were all down. Datalink, Satcom. David's revelation of this ARES cyberweapon was scary. Scarier was the thought that China was responsible. Why would they do that? If Lena was acting on behalf of the Chinese, why would they have wanted Gorji dead? Chase needed to get back downstairs so that he could finish hearing David and Henry's story. Elliot and he needed to finish connecting the dots.

Chase scanned the spacious room. It was a work of art. The ceiling was adorned with colossal turquoise half-ovals that gave the impression of crashing waves. The richly carpeted floors and luxurious booth cushions were similarly patterned.

He looked at his watch. Where was Waleed?

The sound of a helicopter landing on the elevated pad caused a stir of commotion in the room. It lasted for about thirty seconds, and then faded away. From Chase's seat, he couldn't see that side of the hotel. Perhaps Waleed had been flown in?

A waiter brought over a silver plate of green olives, hummus, and warm pita bread, still puffed and steaming. Compliments of the house, he said. Chase was hungry. He nodded in thanks and popped an olive into his mouth.

He stopped mid-chew when he saw who walked in.

Strolling in from the entrance to the Skyview Bar was Lisa Parker. She looked stunningly attractive. Her long waves of black hair hung over her smooth bare shoulders. She wore a tight black dress that outlined her curvy yet athletic body. Chase went through a dozen responses in his mind as Lisa walked towards him, smiling.

He thought of reaching for his gun, but he didn't. She looked unarmed. And there was something else...he didn't know if he was capable of shooting her. Whoever she really was, whatever her motives, Chase still felt something for her.

In the intimate moments that they had shared, wrapped in sheets and each other's embrace, there had been an emotion in her eyes. Fire, longing, desire, yes...but something else, too. Something like affection or adoration. Chase wanted to believe that those were true feelings behind those eyes.

Even now, knowing what he knew about what she had been a part of, he had feelings for her. And he hated himself for it.

Chase finished his olive, took another sip of his cool drink, and placed the glass down on the white tablecloth.

As she arrived at his table, Chase remained seated and expressionless.

An Indian waiter quickly came over to their table and pulled out her chair. She sat, thanked the waiter and looked at him carefully. She then asked for a glass of ice water in what sounded like

Hindi. The look on the waiter's face was that of delight. He nodded happily, smiling and quickly filling her glass from a chilled bottle of Italian sparkling water.

"You're quite the talented linguist," Chase said.

"I knew the right words."

A moment of silence passed before she snapped up some of the still-warm pita bread and dipped it in the hummus. She chewed and stared at him. The look again. Like she was glad to see him.

She said, "So much of our world's history is shaped by the hands of so few. Back channels and smoke-filled rooms. That's where the real decisions get made. It just takes someone in the right position, saying the right words at the right time. For instance, if I was to say the right words to you, you might take me somewhere and get to see what's under this dress."

"Would I find a gun?"

She cocked her head. "Wouldn't you like to know?"

"I've heard some disturbing things about you recently."

She didn't reply.

He said, "I had hoped that you would at least deny them."

She looked out the window at the fiery sunset. She looked lost in thought. Then she said, "I read a book about the Pacific theater during World War Two recently. It got me thinking. Who do you think was responsible for the plan to bomb Pearl Harbor? I mean...who was really responsible? The one who thought: *this* is how it should be done. Was there a meeting of midlevel managers and military tacticians who brought the idea to their leader and appealed to his ego and quest for national power?"

"What the hell are you talking about?"

"Just humor me."

"Yamamoto was in charge of the attack." Chase couldn't understand where this was coming from.

Lena looked disappointed. "Yamamoto was in charge of the

attack, that is true. But my point is that history is filled with small groups of unknown thinkers and planners. Although, in that particular example, they made a large mistake."

"And what mistake is that?"

"The only way to ensure that the will of the attacking country is carried out, is to—as they say in financial circles—buy and hold. The same holds true for invasions. Conquer and hold. Bring the dominant policies and progress that made the attacking nation great to this new country. Don't half-ass it…"

Chase said, "What's your real name?"

She smiled. "So I see you've been reunited with David. You can call me Lena. That's a butchered pronunciation of my birth name. But it was the American name that I took as a teenager. And it suits me better than Lisa, which I've been calling myself since I joined the Agency. The CIA has given me several cover names over the years, but it's mostly been Lisa Parker. I'm tired of those fake names. I'm tired of pretending to be someone who I'm not. Lena will do just fine."

"Whose side are you on, Lena?"

She took a sip of water. "The winning side."

"Why are you here today?"

She bowed her head and pointed at him. "Now there is a good question. I am here to start a war. The greatest war the world has ever seen."

Chase just looked at her. Her attitude was getting to him. This was a different person than the woman he had been with. He wasn't sure how this conversation would end, but she was giving him information, so he would keep asking questions.

"How will the war start?"

She looked out over the skyline. "Truly, it already has." She sighed and looked sad. She spoke softly. "I know you are disappointed and probably upset with me. I do not wish to fight with you. I didn't have to come see you. I *wanted* to. I wanted to tell you something."

"What?"

She looked into his eyes. "If you live past the next few days…if you live past the next few years, someday you may ask yourself, was it real? Between us, I mean. And I wanted to tell you that it was. I see, in you, much of myself. There aren't too many of us, Chase. The people that prop the world up on their backs. The ones that can change the world, if they try. That's what attracts me to you. And I don't want to see you hurt."

He narrowed his eyes, slightly alarmed. "Just what do you think is going to happen?"

"I think that you, like so many people, have been conditioned to believe certain things. I want you to know that what I've done is to make the world a better place. And it will be, eventually. I hope that you see that someday."

His face flushed. "How could you think like this? How could you betray the country that you served?"

"It's not my country, Chase. And honestly, America will be better off for my actions."

"You said you lived there since you were a teenager. I assume that before that, you lived in China."

"I did."

"And you came to the United States knowing that you would betray it?"

She tilted her head. "Yes."

"If you lived in America as long as you did, you know that the United States stands for principles of freedom and morality. How could you betray it after living there? I don't care where you were born."

"Now listen—"

"You want to turn America into China?"

She whispered, "I told you that I admired you because I recognize greatness in you."

"So what?" He tried not to sound too angry. His emotional ties to her were interfering with his ability to think clearly.

"Well, there is another person who I also admire greatly. He is a great leader. Cheng Jinshan. You would be impressed with him, Chase. He is an amazing man. His vision of what this world can become...Chase, it's the only future that our world can have. One globally unified government that makes the right decisions for its people. Yes, I've lived in America since I was a teenager. But you know what? America isn't so great. It has faults just like everywhere else."

Chase shook his head, disgusted. "It's better than the rest. Trust me, I've been to most."

"So have I. Nowhere is perfect. People aren't capable of that. But Jinshan will get us closer. You know what the problem with democracy is? Freedom. People don't know what is best for them. It's not a popular sentiment, but you know in your heart that it's true."

Chase said, "You're naïve if you think that a dictator is the answer."

"Democracies around the world let voters choose politicians that create unsupportable entitlement programs. Their politicians know better, but they promise their constituents the moon because it gets them elected. By the time the programs fail or bury the nation in debt, the politicians that put us there are long gone. The proper period of performance measurement does not fit within the same timeframe as the voting cycle. And even if it did—most people aren't like you and me. They have not lived lives filled with sweat, and stained with blood. They don't have the wisdom to make the right choices."

"You're advocating for a global government where the people don't have a say?"

"Important decisions must be made by the wise, not the popular. So, yes, I believe that a global government under proper leadership, with real power and good decision makers, is the best thing that could happen. I will also tell you that the only way it will happen is through force. Again, not a popular opinion. Again, truth. When the sick, the weak, the sucking leeches and self-interested pigs have taken over the thrones, the strong and brave must stand up for what is right. We will not let our children be trampled by a corrupt and ignorant world." Her chest heaved as she spoke.

"You mean your one child, right? Because you can only have one child under Chinese law. Maybe it's two now? Either way, I don't want to live in a world where a dictator tells me how many kids I can have."

Her face reddened and she glared at him. "Well, there's a good chance you won't live in that world. But trust me, that world is coming."

She sat and remained silent for a while, cooling off. Then she whispered to him, her beautiful eyes looking directly into his, "This will likely be the last time we speak."

"I'm sorry to hear that."

She flipped back a lock of her black hair that had fallen over her shoulder. The steady noise of the Skyview Bar remained in the background. Aside from them, it was a jovial atmosphere. Chase saw a large silver platter of lobster wheeled past their table.

A glance at his watch. Waleed should have been here by now.

Lena stood and regained her composure. She spoke in her confident tone. "Well, Chase, it was a nice time that we shared."

She looked like she was contemplating whether to say something else.

He wasn't sure what to do next. He said, "Lena, you know that I can't let you leave."

She cackled. "I thought you would say as much. Could you

double-check the time?" He showed her his watch. "Thanks." She looked back over her shoulder. Chase followed her gaze.

A very large man with a black beard stood at the entrance of the Skyview Bar. He had his hand hidden under his coat. Chase's blood chilled as he realized that it was Pakvar.

Chase looked at Lena. "Is he here for me?"

"Only if you try to stop me. I was very specific about that. I told you that you meant something to me."

"That's touching. Didn't you shoot one of his men? Isn't he pissed at you for that?"

She frowned. "You let me worry about that. Listen, Chase, I'm sure you doubt my honesty at this point, and I don't blame you. I can't quite reconcile why, but I would prefer that you were unharmed in what comes next. My gift to you now is a chance at living. But once I walk out this door, all bets are off."

She stood.

Chase looked at Pakvar. He glared back at Chase. "What do you mean when you say, 'what comes next?' What do you think is coming?"

She leaned over to whisper in his ear. Her low-cut dress hung open in front of him. She said, "Whether you think that I am crazy or not, know this—your world is about to be turned upside down. Be safe. I hope that we can meet again sometime long from now, in a different place." She kissed him on the lips, slid her thumb down his cheek. He didn't kiss back. "Now don't move, or Pakvar will shoot you right in the chest."

A woman across the restaurant let out a yell of alarm and Chase's eyes reflexively glanced in that direction. Lena didn't turn.

She said, "Sounds like my time is about up." Chase couldn't see what the woman in the restaurant had yelled about, but others were starting to raise their voices as well.

Lena turned and walked away, leaving Chase at the table. He

gritted his teeth and stared at Pakvar, who smiled back at him. He was clearly holding a weapon, daring him to move.

Another yell from across the restaurant. Now people stood, looking out the windows. Lena made her way through the crowd, ducking in between people and starting to run.

The restaurant came alive as people started getting up from their tables and heading over to the large panoramic windows. When Lena passed Pakvar, he walked backwards to trail her, careful to keep his eyes on Chase. A moment later, they were gone.

Someone else screamed. Chase was frazzled by Lena's departure. It took a second for him to realize that something drastically out of the ordinary was going on outside the building. The patrons of the Skyview Bar began jockeying for space to look out the windows.

There was a blaze of reddish orange on the horizon that Chase had thought was the remnant of the setting sun. But that didn't quite fit. It seemed to be in the wrong place.

He looked back out the window and finally he saw it, in the direction of the Port of Jebel Ali. It wasn't a fiery sunset at all. It was fire. A giant, blazing fire with plumes of thick black smoke spiraling up into the sky.

There came several flashes in the same vicinity, with more smoke plumes following them shortly after. Chase knew that pattern of light and smoke from his time in battlefields in various war zones. The restaurant crowd let out shocked gasps as Chase realized what he was witnessing. Multiple conversations in different languages were all saying the same thing: *Dubai is being attacked*. But it wasn't Dubai. It was the port. Jebel Ali. That's where the US Navy ships were, and where the aircraft carrier *Truman* had just sailed into port.

Chase got up and darted toward the elevator. A crowd was gathering there now, many of them frantic to get to safety. Some people were running down the stairs.

In the chaos, someone gripped his arm.

It was Waleed.

"Chase, you must come with me immediately. I need to speak to you now."

Chase said, "Those explosions were coming from Jebel Ali."

"My sources tell me that they were Iranian cruise missiles. Our air defense radars picked up Iranian surface missile radar signatures in the last hour. We have been on high alert, but the cyberattack has hampered all defensive efforts. Other US Navy ships in the Gulf have reported similar attacks within the last hour."

Chase couldn't believe what he was hearing.

He listened to Waleed as they ran down the stairs. Chase was hopping three steps at a time. The Arab man was out of breath as he struggled to keep up. They had to weave through the crowd of frightened people that had decided to head down the stairs instead of wait for the elevator.

Waleed said, "I received a message from Gorji. That is why I needed to see you."

"Gorji's dead. I thought he was killed at Bandar Abbas. How did he send a message?"

"He sent the message two days ago. But in this mess with the communications, I only today received it. He said Jinshan knows. He knows about Satoshi."

"What do you mean?"

"In the message, Gorji apologized that he wasn't able to have Satoshi meet us in Abu Musa. He stated that Satoshi was dead. That he had been killed almost two years ago, not long after Gorji had met him. His contact on Abu Musa discovered that Jinshan had sent someone else in his place. This man that you and Elliot have been supporting...he is working for *Jinshan*."

Chase said, "Waleed, we know."

Waleed's eyes were wide. "What do you mean?"

Chase stopped. They stood on a platform, a turn in the stairway. Chase filled him in on what Elliot had told him about Satoshi.

Waleed said, "So you *knew*?"

"I just found out a day ago."

"Well, Gorji's attempt to get information out of Abu Musa turned up something else—Jinshan is upset, he said. Apparently, he feels that the Abu Musa operation has been unsuccessful. Gorji warned of a violent response, but he did not expand on that."

"Do you think this was it? The attack that is going on now? Do you think Jinshan had something to do with this?"

Waleed said, "I honestly do not know."

Chase said in a low tone, "I just met Lisa Parker. She's working for Jinshan. She and Pakvar are here in the hotel."

"What?"

They opened the stairway door to the floor that Elliot, David, Henry, and the others' rooms were on. Chase needed to speak to Elliot. He would know what do to.

Waleed said, "Why would she be at the hotel?"

Chase had been thinking about that the entire way to the room. What he saw confirmed his worst fears. When they got to the hotel room, the door was open. Chase's pulse raced. He drew his weapon and bolted in.

The three security men, and Elliot, lay dead on the floor. Each of them had suffered multiple gunshot wounds. Chase swept his weapon from side to side, clearing each room of the hotel suite. Waleed followed behind him. He also had a weapon drawn.

Once he was sure, Chase said, "No one's here." A panic filled him as he became sure why Lena must have come. She had come to reclaim his brother. Chase couldn't let her take him again.

A moment later, Chase stood in the doorway, looking into the hall, his gun pointed at the floor.

Waleed was on the phone, calling for an ambulance and additional security.

The TV was on. Sky News. There were videos from different angles of the USS *Harry S. Truman* in flames. One video looked like it must have been taken from someone's phone. The footage was taken from the Dubai beach, and incredibly, it showed a missile streaking across the sky towards the carrier before the explosions began. The news kept showing the freeze-frames of the missile. Just a bunch of whitish pixels, going from right to left. Then a few moments later, the black smoke. *A lot of jet fuel on that carrier*, Chase thought to himself. He prayed for the people on board.

Chase paced back and forth. He said to Waleed, "Where would they go?"

Waleed tried to sound reassuring. "There is only one way out of here. And I have already deployed my men. There are over a dozen Dubai police behind a concrete barrier. If she is here, she won't be driving away."

Chase thought about that. He shook his head. That wouldn't be his exit choice. He bet that it wouldn't be hers either. "No. She would know that." He looked up. "We need to get to the helipad."

18

Chase sprinted up the fire stairs, leaving Waleed behind. He had fourteen rounds available, but he didn't know how many people Lena might have brought with her. She was deadly, he knew that. So was Pakvar. He had to respect them as opponents. He must be deliberate in his actions. Chase couldn't afford to move too quick and get picked off by a pop shot. He had to save his brother.

Chase tried to push away any feelings he might have had for Lena. She had placed his brother in danger. That warranted deadly force. But as he strode up the steps, weapon pointed out in front, he kept seeing flashes of her in his mind. Chase was torn between fear for his brother's safety and disappointment in Lena's betrayal.

Arriving on the twenty-eighth floor, he opened the grey fire door and walked into a palace. The room he was in was the waiting room next to the hotel's helipad. It reminded him of a church or temple, with its ultra-high arched ceilings and vast size. Extravagant carpets, tropical plants, and exquisite stained glass windows decorated the room. There were richly upholstered thick-cushioned couches, and a granite wet bar near the door.

A row of lit candles lined the bar. No one stood behind it.

There were stacks of liquor and wine bottles. A white cloth curtain half-covered them.

Chase opened the door next to the bar area and slowly stepped out onto the hot white surface of the hotel rooftop. The wind was strong this high up. Hot air whipped in his face. One hundred feet above his head, the two white arcs that formed the framework of the hotel met with another vertical white structure. Together they formed the shape of the sail. About one hundred feet in front of Chase, and elevated thirty feet, was the circular white helicopter landing pad. It stretched out over the ocean below.

Chase couldn't see what was on the helipad from his viewpoint. He needed to traverse the long open walkway, complete with red carpet, to get there. He began walking. No one in sight. It was quiet.

He started to doubt his theory that Lena had taken David and Henry up here. Perhaps they had intended to depart the hotel another way?

The sound of gunfire changed his mind.

David and Henry sat next to each other on the edge of the helipad. Lena and the giant Arabic-looking guy were in the prone position near the entrance of the helipad. Pakvar, David had heard her call him. Pakvar was shooting a small rectangular machine gun wildly at something down below. David hoped it wasn't Chase.

Grimacing at the screams of close-proximity gunfire, David prayed that if it was his brother down there, he was taking cover. He was worried about Chase, but felt something else as well. A strange eagerness. His secret weapon had just arrived on the field. Chase was trained as a US Navy SEAL. He was the toughest bastard David had ever met. Lena and this big Arabic guy were armed, and he knew that they were dangerous. But David relished the thought that those two, no matter how good they might be, were now in for a world of hurt.

Henry leaned over to David to try and speak. He looked shaken.

David and Henry hadn't seen Elliot and the others get killed in the hotel room. Lena had restrained and removed them by the time Pakvar had opened fire. But they had heard the gunshots. They were both upset.

When Henry was distressed, he tended to joke.

Henry said, "Hey, David. I gotta say, I'm really happy to get to see all these great places with you. I always wanted to go to Australia. Loved it. This hotel in Dubai. Amazing. But would it be possible for you to stop getting us kidnapped?" He winced involuntarily as another gunshot went off.

David said, "It'll be alright. Just hang tight. My brother is down there. He knows what he's doing."

While their hands were bound, both of them could get up. But every few seconds, Lena kept looking back at them to make sure they were still there. David tried to think about why she had come back for them. Or more to the point, why she had spared their lives. On their way up the stairs, she had made clear that it wasn't mandatory for her to do so. She announced that she would not hesitate to execute them if they tried to escape. David wasn't so sure. She must need something from them still.

The Asian guy sat next to them, unarmed and unrestrained.

David said to him, "So what's your deal?"

He didn't reply.

Henry said, "Not a talker, huh?"

David saw Lena come to a crouching position and fire several shots with her pistol. Echoes of stone bursting below. Soon after Lena fired, Pakvar ran down the stairs of the helicopter pad and out of sight.

Here he comes. Come on, Chase.

* * *

Chase had not been in many firefights like this. Normally, he was much better equipped and had a support team to work with. Here, he had only a handgun. There was a multinational team of spies and Special Forces advancing on his position, using precision covering fire to pin him down. One of whom he had slept with a few weeks earlier. That was a definite first.

The stairway door opened behind him, and he saw Waleed walk out.

"Waleed, get down!" he screamed, then he rolled around the wall edge that he had been using for cover and fired two shots toward the stairs.

It was instinct, really. In the split second that he had looked down the long walkway that led to the helicopter platform, he had seen a target, characterized him as an enemy, and aimed for center mass. At this distance, aiming there made sense. Any variation in his breathing, aim, grip, or the wind would throw off his shot. But Chase was a pretty damn good shot. Pakvar took two rounds in the chest and crumpled down the stairs. His small semiautomatic weapon clanged down the steps after him.

Chase smiled. Not because he had taken a life, but because he could practically hear Lena cursing.

"Chase?" Waleed was hunkered down behind the other corner wall that served as the entrance to the long walkway.

"Stay down. Lena's up there. Can you call for help?"

"Yes. Hold on."

Chase crouched down behind the small barrier that formed the corner to the long helipad walkway. One hundred feet away, Pakvar's corpse lay sprawled on the ground. And up the stairway, a hidden Lena watched his every move.

The steady noise of a helicopter rotor blade beating through the air could be heard in the distance. It changed pitch ever so slightly. It was getting closer. *Shit.*

Chase had been waiting for that. It would force his hand. Now he had to act soon. If he had to charge down that long open walkway toward the helipad, Lena would have a clear shot at him. But if he didn't do that, she would take his brother away again. Since Chase had been on the rooftop, he hadn't yet gotten a clear view of Lena. She had a very small cross-section and was smart enough to keep down. Not good for him.

He wanted to see if she would still honor her promise to let him live if he stood up right now, but that was a big risk. They had grown apart in the past few minutes, he decided.

He yelled, "Lena!"

No answer.

"Lena, I need to speak to you." He didn't know what the hell he was going to say, but he was desperate.

A burst of white in the plaster wall next to him. Apparently she wasn't interested in rebuilding their relationship either.

Chase glanced over his shoulder, trying to stay low. He could see the helicopter now. About a mile away. It looked like a Huey. Funky blue camouflage paint. Probably Iranian. Could Waleed and he take that thing out with small-arms fire? Probably not. They would need a lot more than a few 9mm rounds. He would need something explosive.

He bolted up and ran back into the hotel.

* * *

Lena watched Pakvar fall down dead on the stairs. That was most frustrating. She hadn't been particularly fond of him, and could care less that he was dead.

An hour ago, she had been looking at Pakvar in the back of an

Iranian helicopter as they flew to the hotel. He had glared at her the entire trip. Lena took that to mean that Pakvar knew it had been her that had stridden into the Dubai Mall and shot one of his men in the head. She hadn't had a choice. Pakvar had overstepped his bounds in trying to ambush Chase and Waleed. His assignment had been to keep an eye on them during their meeting with Gorji. She was pretty sure that he hadn't listened to her because she was a woman. That was a common problem for her in this part of the world. But she couldn't have allowed Pakvar's shortsighted attack on Chase to disrupt her plan to send "Satoshi" to the Americans. It may have been a long shot, but it had been their only remaining opportunity to upload their program that would manipulate the value of bitcoin.

As usual, nothing had gone according to plan. The bitcoin-backed currency might still be adopted, but it would not be manipulated by China, as Jinshan had intended. The damage from the ARES cyberattacks was reported to be at fifty percent of what had been expected. David and Henry, experts on ARES and US communications networks respectively, were needed at the Red Cell. Whether they wanted to participate or not, Lena and her minions would extract any remaining relevant information that could boost the effectiveness of the cyberattacks.

But first, Lena would need to get them away from this damned hotel. Pakvar's death tilted the tactical advantage away from her. She still held the high ground, but there were now two weapons versus her own.

She looked back at David, Henry, and the man everyone had been calling Satoshi, and gave them a mocking smile. She waved for "Satoshi" to join her. She couldn't remember his real name. He was one of Jinshan's expert hackers. Someone who had worked closely with the real Satoshi until they had needed to dispose of him several years ago. This man had failed them. The Americans had discovered his true intentions and had been trying to use him to gain more information on Jinshan. Still, he could possibly fire a weapon. But she only had one. If she had known that Pakvar wasn't going to bring an extra weapon for Jinshan's man, she would have brought one herself. But she wasn't about to give up her only gun.

She said, "That helicopter will be here in another minute. When it arrives, I'll need you to get them on board. I'll provide covering fire. Is that understood?"

"Yes, Lena."

Lena heard Chase call her name from his position on the other side of the walkway. She smiled to herself. She was going to miss him. She hoped that taking his brother away again wouldn't irreparably harm their relationship. She decided to let him know that she was still interested. She took aim at a spot near the wall he was hiding behind and fired.

The helicopter was making its final approach into the wind. It wouldn't be much longer now. Soon she would be on Abu Musa, and then on one of Jinshan's personal jets. In twelve hours, they would all be back on the Red Cell island. She would personally extract the required information about ARES and the communications networks needed to increase the effectiveness of the initial cyberattack. Then she could be done with these two Americans. They had caused her much grief.

Lena looked back at David and Henry, obediently sitting on their haunches, looking pissed off. When she turned back towards the walkway, she saw Chase running back into the hotel. Where the hell was he going?

She thought about running down the steps and grabbing Pakvar's weapon, but she wasn't sure how good a shot that UAE intelligence man was. She decided that she didn't want to risk it. The helicopter was almost here anyway.

* * *

Chase hoped that he wouldn't burn the hell out of his brother and
Henry. Once inside the building, he placed his gun down on top of
the bar and hopped over. His hand quickly crept over the bottles
until he found ones suitable for his needs. He looked for high-
proof alcohol, and bottles with long necks. He lined four of them
on the bar and opened them. Then he ripped the white curtain
that had been half-covering the liquor selection into long pieces
and stuffed eighteen-inch strips of the torn cloth into each of the
four bottles. Each strip of cloth became soaked in the alcohol.

He used his strong arms to hurdle the bar again, careful not to
knock over any of the makeshift bombs. Then he grabbed the first
bottle and walked over to one of the lit candles near the entrance.
The cloth flashed in blue flame, then settled into a steady yellow
burn.

Chase leaned into the door with his shoulder, took a jumping
step back outside and threw, all in one motion. It was like a Hail
Mary pass, except that the bottle wasn't traveling in a spiral, but
flipping end over end, arcing towards the elevated helicopter
landing platform.

Chase shouted at Waleed, "*Take a few shots at her on my next
throw.*"

Waleed was sitting on the ground, holding his pistol with both
hands, looking like a scared deer illuminated by the headlights of
an eighteen-wheeler. He stammered in response, "Alright."

Chase heard the crack of gunfire in the distance, and the wall
next to him burst into a sprinkle of white dust. Chase threw
himself back inside and lit another Molotov cocktail.

He opened the door and saw that his first one had landed just
in front of the stairs, which had erupted in flames. That should
impair Lena's aim. He targeted his throw a touch farther this time.
Again, he didn't wait to see where it landed. He just went back in
and lit the next bottle. After throwing all four of them, Chase was

rewarded with a series of alcohol-fueled fires on and near the landing pad.

Smoke from the first bottle's flame had reduced the visibility down the walkway. Chase could no longer see the stairs. The helicopter grew closer. Time to move. He tapped Waleed as he sprinted by him. "Come on."

Chase ran with his Sig Sauer in his right hand. He covered the distance to the stairs in about ten seconds. The noise of the rotors grew loud enough that he could no longer hear the sound of his dress shoes echoing on the ground.

Even with the flames, the helo was still trying to land. Chase had hoped that the fire would cause it to wave off. The helicopter was close enough that he could make out the two pilots. Tinted visors covered their faces. A long-barreled automatic weapon hung out the side of the Huey. The door gunner didn't yet have enough angle that Chase was in his field of fire. But he would soon.

Chase slowed to a jog as he came closer to the platform stairs, where Lena had last lain. Fifteen feet from the landing pad, he saw her.

She was on fire.

* * *

David and Henry had jumped into one of the nets that surrounded the large circular helicopter pad. Having seen the first two Molotov cocktails explode on the stairs and in the center of the platform, David had been waiting for the next one. If they hadn't moved, it would have landed right on top of them, so David had acted fast.

He nudged Henry toward the net, hoping that it would hold their combined weight. Thank God it had. Now they were stuck, hands still bound, looking through the safety net at the rocks and ocean twenty-eight floors below. David looked up at Lena and the Asian guy just in time to see the last of the flaming bottles land a bull's-eye. It hit right next to Lena and exploded, covering her black dress with burning alcohol.

David watched, incredulous, as the Asian man started rolling her around on the deck, trying to extinguish the flames. The high-velocity winds of the rotorcraft were hitting them now. David looked up and saw the blue-camouflaged Huey yaw to the left. The door gunner began firing tracer rounds toward the entrance area, where Chase had thrown the bottles. Then the tracers stopped, and David saw the door gunner fall from the helicopter onto the flaming landing pad below. Chase must have gotten him, David realized. He must be close.

The violent winds of the rotor wash helped extinguish the flames on the pad. The Huey set down hard on its skids. The Asian guy dragged Lena's limp body onto the aircraft and was going back for the door gunner when Chase came walking up the stairway of the helipad.

* * *

Chase ran up the stairs. He tried to remember how many rounds he had left, but in the melee, he'd lost count. He thought of firing at the pilots but didn't want to risk the spinning helicopter crash killing everyone, including his brother and Henry.

He looked through the sights of his weapon, aimed at the rear passenger compartment of the helicopter. Satoshi had just rolled a limp Lena into the aircraft. The pilots were turning their heads back and forth, looking like they wanted to lift back off.

Downrange, Chase had a choice. He could take out Satoshi, Lena, or both. He fired once and dropped Satoshi. Lena sat up. Her arm, as well as one side of her neck and face, were black and red from burns.

She looked right at him as he kept his gun aimed at her. Chase clenched his jaw, knowing what he should do, but not wanting to do it. He should kill her, he thought. She had betrayed and attacked their country. She'd taken his brother prisoner, and lied to him. His arm muscles flexed.

He fired. And missed.

* * *

David saw Chase fire once and Satoshi fell to the ground, limp. At the same time, the Huey surged up into the air and Chase hunkered down as the rotor wash tried to force him down the steps.

Chase climbed up the stairs and fired again.

Then the helicopter's nose dipped down and to the left and it accelerated away, out to sea.

"David!"

"Over here," he called back to his brother.

"Are you guys alright?"

Henry's face was pressed up against the net, looking down at the water hundreds of feet below. Due to the awkward position he had fallen into, he was completely unable to move. He answered, "Oh, yeah, we're great. Hey, they weren't kidding about the great view you get at this hotel. Would it be possible for you to help us up?"

Chase clutched his brother's arm and pulled him up and back onto the helipad, then he did the same with Henry. He looked up at Waleed as he approached.

Waleed said, "Well done, my friend."

Chase looked over David. "Are you sure you're okay?"

"Yeah, I'll be fine. Thanks, Chase."

Waleed said, "What happened to Lisa Parker?"

"He means Lena."

David said, "I saw her get put on the helo. She wasn't in good shape. Burns all over her body. If she lives, she's not going to be happy."

Emirati police officers and emergency personnel began coming up through the entrance.

Chase turned to Waleed and said, "Hey, Waleed, do you think you could arrange another jet for us?"

"Of course. Where to?"

He looked at David. "Home."

19

Langley, Virginia

Chase sat with his brother in a corner office at the CIA headquarters. A balding man in his upper fifties entered and closed the door behind him. He sat behind the cherry desk and looked at the Manning brothers. A gold nameplate on the desk said Assistant Director, Clandestine Operations.

"Gentlemen, thank you for meeting with me. I realize that you've had quite a few debriefings over the past few weeks, and that likely won't end soon."

David said, "We understand."

"I was a close friend of Elliot Jackson. He was a damn fine man, and one of the best spies I knew."

The brothers didn't respond.

"You're likely wondering why you're here. Or maybe you've been to see so many people by now that you don't really care. Chase, Elliot told me about you as he was updating me on the Abu Musa operation. You should know that he thought very highly of you and the work you did under him."

"That's good to hear, sir. Thank you."

"And if Elliot thought highly of you and trusted you as he did, then that's good enough for me. I think this nation owes you two boys something. I think it owes you gratitude and praise. And instead, you're getting second-guessed by a bunch of politicians. I abhor this Washington nonsense. But I didn't get to be in this seat by not learning to play the game."

Chase turned to look at his brother and then back at the Assistant Director. He now understood why they were here. This man was going to give them the biggest gift anyone in the CIA could provide: information.

"Since the Blackout occurred, it's been hard to get good intelligence. Emails and instant messaging have been spotty at best. Texts and phone calls can't be trusted, because since our satellites were hit, we've been forced to route them through compromised networks."

He threw up his hands. "Frankly, we've been spoiled. We got used to getting information at the snap of a finger. And now, the fog of war has descended upon us. So let's look at the events of the past few weeks from the perspective of the Washington decision makers. Here's what they saw: One of our US Navy destroyers in the Gulf sinks one of their patrol craft when the two vessels inexplicably start firing at each other. The jury is still out on what really happened. Then a rogue CIA agent and an ex-CIA agent participate in the murder of an Iranian politician and his wife on Iranian soil. Iran believes it was a US-Israeli operation. Iran attacks US military assets near Dubai and in the Persian Gulf. Right around this time, the Blackout Attack occurs."

David nearly leapt out of his seat. "*But that's not what happened. We've been telling everyone from the members of the Senate Intelligence Committee to the White House chief of staff to the Pentagon: Cheng Jinshan and Lena Chou and God knows how many other Chinese military and intelligence operatives staged this attack. Iran could never pull all that off. It was China. And for

God's sake, Henry Glickstein and I were pretty much prisoners of the Chinese. We were almost killed—"

Chase grabbed his shoulder. "David, it's alright. I suspect that you may be preaching to the converted." He looked across the desk.

The assistant director for clandestine operations nodded back at Chase. He looked at David. "Son, I just want you to try and understand what they've seen, so you can better understand the decisions they're making. You aren't going to like all of them. But I don't want you doing anything self-destructive to change it. Please, listen to me speak, and then I'll let you ask questions. Trust me, I'm one of the few people in a position of power inside the Beltway who believes everything you've said."

David crossed his arms. "I just don't understand why that is. Why doesn't everyone believe us? We have Lisa Parker, or Lena Chou, on video in Iran. Hell, there are still people missing. I've given names, and those missing persons are verifiable. These are Americans we're talking about. They're still probably on that island in the South Pacific. Are we just going to leave them there? I mean—"

The Assistant Director held up his hand. "Think about it this way. Let's say that Pearl Harbor or September eleventh just happened. Every bit of evidence points to a specific culprit. Then you've got two guys that come along and say that it's all a conspiracy. That September eleventh was really the Russians, and they just made it look like it was Al Qaeda. But meanwhile, ninety-nine percent of the news coverage is of Osama bin Laden. Troops and planes are being sent to Afghanistan. The world gets its message from the news cycle. Now fast forward to today. The news cycle has told us that Iran is now public enemy number one. Iran is the reason that no one can get on Facebook for the past three weeks. Iran is the reason that the stock market has crashed. Iran has killed thousands of US sailors with a cruise missile attack. And you know what? There is good evidence that they really did that. Our military air defense commanders picked up Iranian surface-to-surface radar signatures just before the attacks. David, I'm sorry. But you and Henry Glickstein are just two tiny voices in a choir of TV media that is in wartime coverage mode. To be honest, you should be happy that they've dropped the idea that you and Henry sold secrets to Iran."

David said, "They never had any evidence of that. It was just part of Lena's attempt to get us locked down long enough to recapture us."

Chase said, "Sir, I'm guessing that you've got something you want to share with us?"

The man nodded. "I thought you should know that you have a cadre of believers in your story. A few of us have seen enough truth in your story that we want to take some precautions. Yes, I want to share a few things. Can I have both of your word that it won't leave this office?"

The two men answered yes.

"A week ago, we sent an Air Force reconnaissance plane over the area where your Red Cell island is likely to be."

David leaned forward in his chair. This was the first positive action that the US government had admitted to. "What did it find?"

"It found a very full Chinese military base. There were two dozen helicopters and another dozen light-attack fighters. Heat signatures indicated over two thousand personnel on the small island. And what's more, our imagery experts from the National Reconnaissance Office believe you to be correct—there is, in fact, a submarine pen built into the coastal mountain."

"Any sign of the Americans?"

"No. But without getting personnel or some very small drones ashore, that would be hard to detect."

"So...what, then?"

"That's one of the things I wanted to let you know, David. I know you've been very vocal about this. And it's come to my attention that you even want to go to the press, if you don't see results soon."

David's face flushed. Chase felt bad for him, but he needed to hear this.

The Assistant Director said, "Please do not do that. If you do, you will not only hurt yourself, but you will risk reducing the effectiveness of an active operation to locate and rescue those other missing American personnel. Is that clear?"

David nodded. Chase was relieved.

"Now, I can't provide any more information on that specific operation. And I shouldn't mention this either, but again...I feel you two gentlemen deserve to know. There are those in Washington that are taking your warning about the Red Cell very seriously. This goes back to what Chase and Elliot were originally working on with Jinshan's Abu Musa operation. We feel that we have a strong case showing that Jinshan, if not more in the Chinese government, was involved in an attempt to take down the US dollar. The US State Department has made formal complaints against Jinshan's bitcoin tampering. China has politely acknowledged this, and told us that he will be reprimanded. But as you both know, Jinshan is a powerful man there, and fills many roles. With our intelligence communications network hampered, it is hard for us to ascertain what Jinshan's real status is. But I believe the Chinese threat to be real. And so do many good men in the military and intelligence community here. There *are* people that want to heed your warnings."

David said, "Then why are we sending three carrier battle groups to the Persian Gulf? Why is the news saying that our military buildup in the Middle East is larger than Desert Storm? It looks very much like we're preparing for an all-out war with Iran.

You understand what that means, right? We're playing right into Jinshan's plans."

He nodded. "I appreciate how you feel. But the Iranian threat *is* real. And the Chinese threat may just be the plans of a lone wolf —Jinshan."

"A lone wolf that can deploy his military and order attacks on the United States? This wasn't just one man."

"There aren't enough of us yet that believe Jinshan was really responsible...that Chinese assets were really responsible...for those attacks."

"So they think Iran has the ability to launch this cyberattack that still has our Internet down? You know better."

"Yes, I do. But fighting the bureaucracy of Washington is a delicate task. I can't call them a bunch of idiots and change their minds. I need to give them solid proof. Trust me, I'm trying, David. My friends in the Pentagon and Congress have assured me that Washington and Beijing are having very high-level talks on a regular basis now."

"About what?"

"About keeping the peace. The Chinese ambassador was summoned to the White House about this, did you know that?"

"Well, I would goddamn hope so. They have eighteen Americans hostage. What did they say to that?"

He looked uncomfortable.

"You didn't ask the Chinese about the Americans being held prisoner on the island?"

He shook his head.

Chase said, "Why not?"

The Assistant Director sighed. "Because we don't have enough agreement on that issue."

"Unbelievable. That's what this all comes down to. They don't believe me or Henry. Unbelievable."

"The president and the secretary of state don't want us to

broach that subject until we have concrete proof. They appreciate the warning of a possible Chinese war plan, but they feel that since a warning has been given, even if the Chinese were planning to attack the United States, they would be crazy to do so after we already know about it. And since there are no Chinese military assets storming across the Pacific, it appears that you've accomplished your mission anyway. Look, David, I wanted to speak with you men to let you know that I *do* believe you. We are working on ways to prove that those men and women in the Red Cell are or were on that island. And once we get that proof, we'll work to free them. But understand that I agree with the Washington leadership that China no longer has plans to attack. You brought us the warning and the information in time. You have *saved* us, David."

20

Chase sipped from his bottle of Sam Adams lager. He wore a woolen sweater and jeans and sat comfortably in a wicker chair on his brother's patio. David sat in the chair next to him, feeding his baby girl from a bottle. The two men watched David's three-year-old play fetch with their Jack Russell terrier in the backyard. Lindsay, David's wife, was making a spaghetti dinner inside in the kitchen. Every so often she would look through the window at them, smiling at David.

Lindsay was still worried about someone coming after them. Chase didn't think that was likely. Not at this stage. David had already spilled the beans on everything he knew about Lena and the Red Cell. Chase had done the same. They were no longer a threat to Jinshan's plan. Besides, there were two armed FBI agents standing watch in an unmarked car down the street.

Chase took another swig of beer. It was almost December and the air had a chill to it. He said to his brother, "Have you heard anything from Dad?"

David said, "No. You think we will?"

"Probably not much. He'll be busy as hell again with the *Ford*

Strike Group. Just the way he likes it. We'll hear from him when he's back in port, I guess."

"I just worry about where they're sending him is all."

Chase said, "He'll be fine. The *Ford* is just doing training exercises off of Norfolk. He won't be in the Pacific..."

David nodded and shut his mouth. The two brothers were both glad for that.

The United States was a different place since they had arrived home. It reminded Chase of the way things were in the months after 9/11. People were nicer, but more afraid. There was a sense that something big was on the horizon. A sense that the world had changed, and was changing still.

The Blackout, as it was being called, had created chaos in more ways than one. The US Internet, for all intents and purposes, was a shell of what it once was. In the first few days of the Blackout, nothing worked. People would just get error messages on every webpage they went to. Air travel was grounded. Store shelves dwindled down to scraps. The stock market, down for the first day, plummeted enough that trading had to be stopped on the second day. Three weeks after the attack, things were getting better—but major damage had been done.

When David and Henry had given their testimony, they had informed the many government agencies that would listen of the Red Cell plans, which called for simultaneous attacks on US communications, utilities, and defense networks.

This had not occurred, however. Either the plans had changed, or they'd been disrupted. A cyberweapon *had* taken down GPS networks and data centers. The US-based Internet had been greatly harmed, but the damage was being repaired. The US government was taking David and Henry's word seriously, but their reaction was slow. And not everyone believed their allegation that China as a country would attack the United States. It was a large pill to swallow. Many of the government executives really thought that it was Iran who had attacked the US, that the cyberattack was their doing. David and Henry explained that this was part of the plans. That it was a staged war —a ploy.

The skeptical politicians and government executives balked. Cruise missiles had destroyed several American military assets in the Persian Gulf, and inflicted catastrophic damage to the aircraft carrier *Harry S. Truman* while it was docked in Dubai. US military air defense crews in the region had picked up Iranian missile radars just before the attack. This was clear evidence that it was Iran who had launched the attacks.

Chase thought the answer was obvious, and consistent with David's statement. Every step of this plan had been a deception. Whether Jinshan had acted with the authority of the Chinese government or not, he had succeeded in sending the US into an economic recession, and perhaps worse. The value of the dollar had collapsed. Despite the cries of foul play from the US, the Iranian-UAE bitcoin-backed currency was being adopted by more nations as a substitute for the ailing dollar.

Many American politicians were hesitant to outright accuse China of an act of war. After the Persian Gulf attacks, American military assets were immediately moved to reinforce the Middle East. Shortly after, the network blackout had set military communications back to the World War II era. When David and Henry's story finally convinced enough of the American national security circuit to be wary of China, they saw the risk of leaving the Pacific theater underdefended. With the military communications networks in disarray, however, correcting that error was proving to be a slow process.

Several units in training and maintenance cycles were being made ready for deployment. This included the newest American carrier, the *Ford*, commanded by Admiral Arthur Louis Manning IV. While the *Ford* was technically not yet ready for deployment, hordes of contract maintenance personnel were working around the clock to finish what needed to be done.

The decision had been made to confront China through diplomatic channels. China officially denied any and all of the accusations. They refused to grant US investigators access to Cheng Jinshan. And they claimed to have no knowledge of any person by the name of Lena Chou.

Henry Glickstein opened up the slider door and came out on the porch with a beer in his hand. "You got a bottle opener?"

Lindsay called from the kitchen. "There's one next to the sink." She had instantly liked Glickstein, finding him quite funny.

The FBI had suggested that both David and Henry go to a safe house for a few weeks until they were sure that no one was coming after them. David had insisted on remaining at his home with his family. Glickstein was staying at the safe house with a rental car. Lindsay invited him over for dinner frequently.

Through the sliding glass door, Chase glanced at the TV screen inside. He couldn't hear it, but he saw the ticker tape of the news on the bottom of the screen. It was all about the effects of the network blackout. Some people hadn't been able to work in three weeks because their jobs were so dependent on the Internet. Smartphones were much less smart, so people were forced into the ancient practice of social interaction. TV and radio had seen record audiences.

The economic impact of it all scared Chase a little, but David's stories of the Red Cell invasion plans scared him more. It had been weeks since the Blackout Attacks, though. David and Henry had gotten word to the authorities. Aside from the cyberattack and the purported Iranian missile attacks in the Gulf, there had been no other evidence that the Red Cell war plans were being executed.

Chase held up his bottle and David and Henry clinked theirs together. "Cheers. To saving the country. Good job, you two…"

* * *

Victoria Manning stood on the flight deck of the USS *Farragut*, watching the sun set over the Eastern Pacific. Several of her enlisted men climbed on top of the MH-60R Seahawk helicopter, turning wrenches and checking oil levels.

"Hey, ma'am, you got a minute?"

"Sure, Plug, what's up?" Plug was her maintenance officer. A twenty-nine-year-old from Michigan who loved college football, flying, and beer. He was also pissed off that their ship wasn't being sent to Middle East like just about every other US Navy ship.

"Just wondering if you heard any rumors about when we might turn this ship to the west and cross the pond."

She snorted. "You know something I don't?"

"No, ma'am. It's just that everybody else is headed that way. The *Vicksburg* and Det Six are headed there now."

"Are they? When did that happen?"

"I just got an email on the secure email exchange."

"Is that working now?"

"It's still sporadic. They're so backed up from the satellites going down, I think about five percent of all communications are getting through. The communications officer is running around with his hair on fire."

Victoria could hear the water lap the sides of the hull. Their ship was at all stop. The ship guys were doing engineering drills.

She said, "Plug, I'll tell you the same thing I told the chief two hours ago. We're staying put. We'll be the last ones to go anywhere. And that's a fact."

"You've got to be shitting me. Everyone else is getting sent to Fifth Fleet. Guys are saying that the Iran stuff is heating up. Chief was on deployment during Iraq Two. He said this is just like that. One day Iraq had the fourth-largest army in the world. The next they had the second-largest army in their own country.

If Iran shoots again, I think this thing is going to blow up. And I just—"

"I know, Plug. You don't want to miss out."

He had a sheepish look on his face. "I feel bad saying that."

"You didn't say it. And don't let your men hear you say it, for God's sake. Being in the military is like playing a sport. We practice and practice and everyone wants to see what it's like to play a real game."

"Well...yeah, kind of. I guess. I mean, what the hell are we doing all this for if we don't get to protect our country when it's in danger?"

Victoria said, "I know. But, Plug, listen...if Iran and the US really do start a shooting war, and the US Navy sees fit to keep us here, two hundred miles west of Panama, then everyone on this ship, including our air detachment, is going to be burning to get over there. No one wants to get left out of the big game. But you, as a leader, need to set the example. You need to keep your focus on making sure everyone does their job here. We need to ensure that people keep focus on procedures and safety. Because if we're stuck here, Iran isn't a threat to us. But there are still a hell of a lot of ways that people can get hurt out here. And if those guys up there are thinking about how pissed off they are that we aren't fighting Iran, they might not tighten the Jesus nut on the main rotor. And then what happens?"

Plug smiled. "The rotor falls off?"

"No. I catch it in preflight because I'm a shit-hot pilot, then I kick your ass and make one of your junior pilots my new maintenance officer."

Plug laughed. "Yes, ma'am."

"Hey. I know this sucks. We're going to be doing exercises while everyone else in our squadron gets to do the real thing. I'll tell you what. I've never been shot, but I don't really want to be, either. Running to war for glory and adventure is something ignorant little boys do. I'll defend my country with my life if I ever get the chance. But I have a healthy respect for my profession. Combat isn't a game, and it isn't a sport. We're going to focus on training to keep our men sharp, and prepare them in case we're ever called up for the real test. Understood?"

He nodded. Serious eyes. Chin up slightly higher than before. "Yes, ma'am. I'll talk to the chief. He was saying something similar about making sure everyone doesn't get distracted."

"Well, he's a chief. So he knows a thing or two."

Plug gave her a half salute and walked over to the helicopter. He began joking with his enlisted men. He was a good kid. Victoria hoped that everyone's morale remained high. It really did suck to be the only US Navy ship that got left in this part of the world.

Two miles to the west, hidden in the bright orange rays of the setting sun, a periscope broke the surface of the ocean and rose just high enough for its digital cameras to see the USS *Farragut*. It was China's newest nuclear fast-attack submarine. The captain was quite disciplined. He did one sweep with the periscope, recording a 360-degree image that he would later review with several members of the crew.

The executive officer approached him and handed him a paper copy of the high-priority message they had just received. The transmission had come from the Chinese Naval High Command. It stated that there were only a few naval vessels in the area, and only one US Navy ship. In a few days there was to be an exercise where all these Navy ships would be positioned together. It would be the perfect time to strike.

PAWNS OF THE PACIFIC:
The War Planners #3

A CIA operative joins a Marine special operations team to infiltrate a secret Chinese base in the jungles of South America.

A female navy helicopter pilot is thrown in charge of her destroyer when an unthinkable catastrophe strikes.

And the Admiral of America's newest aircraft carrier strike group must save his daughter from a Chinese naval attack.

Filled with pulse-pounding action, well-rounded characters, and unpredictable twists, Pawns of the Pacific delivers a satisfying third chapter to The War Planners series.

Get your copy today at AndrewWattsAuthor.com

ALSO BY ANDREW WATTS

The War Planners Series

The War Planners

The War Stage

Pawns of the Pacific

The Elephant Game

Overwhelming Force

Global Strike

Max Fend Series

Glidepath

The Oshkosh Connection

Books available for Kindle, print, and audiobook.

Join former navy pilot and USA Today bestselling author Andrew Watts'
Reader Group and be the first to know about new releases and special offers.

AndrewWattsAuthor.com

ABOUT THE AUTHOR

Andrew Watts graduated from the US Naval Academy in 2003 and served as a naval officer and helicopter pilot until 2013. During that time, he flew counter-narcotic missions in the Eastern Pacific and counter-piracy missions off the Horn of Africa. He was a flight instructor in Pensacola, FL, and helped to run ship and flight operations while embarked on a nuclear aircraft carrier deployed in the Middle East.

Today, he lives with his family in Ohio.

SIGN UP FOR NEW BOOK ALERTS AT
ANDREWWATTSAUTHOR.COM

From Andrew: Thanks so much for reading my books. Be sure to join my Reader List. You'll be the first to know when I release a new book.

You can follow me or find out more here:
AndrewWattsAuthor.com

Made in the USA
Columbia, SC
21 June 2020